SHAUN HUTSON

Assassin

WARNER BOOKS

A *Warner* Book

First published in Great Britain in 1989
by Star Books, a Division of W H Allen & Co Plc
Published in 1990 by Sphere Books Ltd
Reprinted by Warner Books 1992
Reprinted 1993, 1994, 1996, 1997, 1998, 1999, 2001

ISBN 0 7515 0197 2

Printed in England by Clays Ltd, St Ives plc

Warner Books
A Division of
Little, Brown and Company (UK)
Brettenham House
Lancaster Place
London WC2E 7EN

Acknowledgments

I would like to thank the following people for their help before, during and beyond the writing of this novel.

Thank you to Bob Tanner (I said I could save it, Bob . . .). To Ray 'kill 'em all' Mudie (The Angus Young of WH Allen). To Peter 'technical director' Williams. To my editor, Bill 'PG Tips' Massey (Next time it's a kneecap, right?). Extra special thanks to 'The Wild Bunch' (WH Allen's Sales Force): we came, we saw, we nicked everyone else's shelf space. In fact, to everyone at WH Allen, thanks from your resident slob.

Thanks to Dennis Poole and all at Tiptree (I *shall* return). Many thanks also to Mick Wall (not so much a 'Market Square Hero' more a 'small screen superstar'. I still owe you one, mate). To Doc Doom and 'Krusher' (the only men I know who've achieved immortality through death . . . and Mescal). To Stella Clifford at *Monsters of Rock* (for allowing me to periodically intrude). Thanks also to *Kerrang*.

To Bruce, Steve, Dave, Adrian and Nicko (Not just any old 'Iron' but the best metal. Cheers.). To everyone at Smallwood Taylor, especially Terri N Berg (Now you've got no excuse, you've got to read it!). Many thanks also to Wally Grove (Pass the Players Number Six).

To Allan 'Is' Trotter (shelf arranger extraordinaire. Don't leave *this* one on the bonnet of your car. Show your mates first). To Gareth 'overworked' James, John Gullidge, Phil 'Silver Screen' Nutman, Brian '*next* time you're dead'

Baker, John Hellings, Ray 'Harpist Again' Pocock, Bill Young and Andy Wint (I don't expect to have to *think* in interviews, you sadists!). Thanks also to Ian 'Mad Max' Austin.

Indirect thanks to Guns 'n Roses, Ronnie James Dio and Sword. Also many thanks to Liverpool FC.

And finally, as ever, extra special thanks to my Mum and Dad, for everything and, of course, to Belinda who was there when I needed her, just like she always is.

This novel was written on a Silverette Typewriter using Croxley Typing Paper (and if that isn't enough to get me a new typewriter and a couple of free sheets, I don't know what is . . .)

Many thanks to all those who've supported me. You'll never know how grateful I am.

Shaun Hutson

He heard a sound that was all too familiar.

The swish-click of a flick knife.

Then he felt it against his cheek, the point gouging into his flesh, digging deeper until blood began to run from the wound. And yet the knife was wielded with immaculate skill, drawn in light quick movements through the skin of Weller's face to expose the network of muscles beneath his forehead then down the other side of his face.

When it reached his neck he *did* pass out.

The figure with the knife cut the last piece of flesh free then slid two fingers beneath the skin as if it were some kind of mask.

Pulling carefully, the figure pulled the skin free, coaxing it away from the eyes with the aid of the blade.

It came away in one piece.

One dripping piece of skin.

The figure turned to those watching and held the mask of living flesh aloft like some kind of bizarre trophy.

Two of the others stepped forward and began removing Weller's clothes, tossing them aside until he was naked.

Then they set to work.

Also by Shaun Hutson:

Better to burn out
than fade away

'. . . Look like the innocent flower.
But be the serpent under't . . .'

Macbeth

Catalyst

The priest was mad.

The men who forced him into the back of the ambulance had seen the face of insanity before and they recognised it now in those haggard features.

He screamed, he cursed, he threatened.

All to no avail.

He warned them that they were committing heresy. A word none of them had heard spoken before. A word better suited to distant years. To superstition.

And, as he fought to escape their grasp and return to his derelict church they found that superstition was a word which circulated with greater intensity inside their minds.

He told them they were making a mistake, told them they were desecrating Holy Ground, destroying something of untold value but they didn't listen. The old priest was insane. Who else but a madman would have lived in a derelict church in London's East End for the past eight months with only damp, mildew and rats for company? The windows had been broken, the holes boarded over in places but the priest had not left. He could not leave he had told them as they hauled him from his haven and into the waiting vehicle. They must not enter the church, must not disturb its contents.

When they told him that the remains of the church were to be demolished, that a block of flats was to be erected on the site he had

11

grown even more uncontrollable, flying into a paroxysm of rage which the uniformed men found difficult to cope with. He had run back towards the church screaming words which made no sense to them.

Someone had suggested sedating him but one of the men had feared the effect which a calming drug might have on a man of such advanced years and such precarious health. So, they had let him scream.

Scream that he had something valuable in his possession.

Scream that he guarded a secret.

That he and he alone knew that secret.

That he, in that stinking, vermin infested shell which had once been a place of worship, had kept the thigh bone of a Saint hidden.

One of the ambulancemen had chuckled quietly to himself as he'd listened to the aimless rantings.

To the priest's exhortations that the bone could bring life to the dead. That these men, these builders who were coming to destroy his home, were also eradicating a power which came from God himself.

The power to raise the dead.

He must have the bone.

He had to have it. Had to retain the power. The secret.

They strapped him to the stretcher inside the ambulance to prevent him damaging himself, then they drove off, one of them seated in the back of the vehicle still listening to the madman's insane ramblings.

The church must not be destroyed.

Must not be . . .

Must not . . .

Must . . .

He had lapsed into unconsciousness within a few minutes, his eyes bulging wide for a split second then his chest falling as if all the air had been drawn from him by a powerful suction pump.

Despite the efforts of the man in the rear of the ambulance, the priest had died before reaching hospital.

A day later the builders moved in.

Within a week, the church, and all it contained, was rubble.

Tuesday, 3 September

Prologue

It looked like a battlefield.

Thick clouds of dust and smoke rolled like banks of noxious fog across a landscape of devastation. The thunderous roar of collapsing buildings was punctuated occasionally by the sound of explosions and the ever present rattling of catterpillar tracks.

But this was no war. It was organised destruction. Not the hectic random obliteration which comes with conflict but a carefully contrived scheme, plotted and planned by experts and now executed not by an army of uniformed men but of civilians.

There had been three tower blocks on the East End development originally known as Langley Towers. Three blocks designed to house up to a thousand people – they had intruded onto London's skyline like so many before them, jabbing towards the heavens like accusatory fingers. Around them shops had been built, even a youth club, but the residents of the blocks had been more concerned with the structural faults in the buildings than with how to occupy their leisure time. Countless complaints of cracks appearing in walls had flooded into the local council offices, some within less than a month of the blocks being occupied but, as is their way, the civil servants had seen fit to ignore the complaints.

When the stairwell in the second of the blocks had finally collapsed, five people had died.

No one knew how it happened. The builders didn't know. The architects were baffled. The complaints which had been filed were relocated to avoid embarrassment.

The decision had been made there and then to rehouse the residents and demolish the blocks. Besides, those who owned the land had seen the sense of selling off the acreage for development.

Hence the arrival of the demolition men.

JCB's and other vehicles battled over and through the tons of fallen concrete and steel, like vast metal dinosaurs over some surreal new world. Men in yellow overalls swarmed over the ruins like termites – only their business was destruction not construction. Others watched from a distance as the tower blocks were brought down, men in white overalls untouched by the dirt and grime of this devastation they had engineered.

The ball of the crane swung into the side of one of the buildings smashing through the stone as if it had been balsa wood. As the metal ball swung back it carried fragments of the tower's interior, pieces of girder which hung from it like metallic intestines.

There was a loud explosion as one of the men clad in a white overall pressed a button on the console he held. Bricks were sent flying by the force of the blast and the third of the blocks fell like a house of cards, several hundred tons of concrete and steel crashing to the ground, adding to the piles of debris which already rose into the air like eroded cliffs.

The smaller buildings such as the youth club, the supermarket and one or two of the other shops which had once served the residents of these vertical housing estates were still intact as yet. Their windows were smashed, their insides gutted, but their exteriors remained untouched by the ferocious attentions of the men and machines whose only function was to eradicate these final testaments to the stupidity of modern architecture. It had cost more than fifty million pounds to erect the trio of blocks two years earlier. More than one man on the site thought that it would have made as much sense to merely shovel the money into a furnace. The blocks had been built too quickly, too many corners had been cut but it had taken the loss of five lives to demonstrate such niceties as architectural inadequacies. Still, five lives were small change in the world of property speculation.

And how grand were the replacement buildings to be? Fine new houses, fit for anyone to live in. Provided they had an income in excess of half a million a year. The East End was being cut up, split down the middle between the poor and the rich, the 'haves' and the 'haven't got a hopes'. The rich got richer, the poor got poorer.

And more resentful.

A bulldozer moved effortlessly across the uneven terrain, pushing a huge mound of debris ahead of it, its tracks scraping the very foundations of the first block.

The foundations had been laid deep but even they had been laid bare by the strategically placed explosives planted by the men in white.

Smoke and dust mingled with the clouds of bluish fumes which belched from the exhaust of the bulldozer as it rumbled past.

Half a dozen mechanical diggers drove their buckets into the shattered remains of the buildings, lifting tons of brick into the backs of waiting lorries.

The massive iron ball on the crane continued to swing back and forth.

The destruction continued.

No one saw the hand.

It protruded from the cracked concrete foundations of the first block, mottled green in places, caked in dust and dirt. And as the ground shook the concrete cracked open even more widely.

The arm attached to the hand appeared. Slowly at first.

No one noticed.

Just as no one noticed when the fingers on that hand flexed once then balled into a fist.

PART ONE

'Where Lie your greatest dangers? – In pity.'

Nietzsche

'All hell's breaking loose,
In the streets there's a brand new way . . .'

Kiss

One

The gavel banged down hard, the sound reverberating around the panelled walls of the Old Bailey's Number One court.

There was only a brief pause in the frantic babblings – so Lord Justice Valentine gripped the wooden mallet more tightly and brought it crashing down repeatedly, continuing even after the murmurings had finally died away.

The judge glared reproachfully around him, his eyes flicking from the witness box to the public gallery then to the barristers and clerks who were gathered before him like bewigged undertakers.

During his thirty-three years as a High Court judge, Valentine had presided over many trials but none that he could remember had generated public and media interest to match that over which he now presided. Members of the public had been warned beforehand by the media that the facts of the case were particularly repellant. That simple statement alone had been enough to ensure that the public gallery was full every day and, so far, the trial had reached its third day. Valentine flicked at his plaited wig and exhaled deeply, anticipating another outburst shortly. The evidence which had sparked the last bout of indignant chattering was to be repeated.

'If there are any more disturbances I will have no choice

but to clear the court,' said the judge before looking towards the tall, thin-faced QC before him and nodding. 'You may continue Mr Briggs.'

Thomas Briggs nodded curtly and stepped towards the witness box, his robes flowing behind him like the black wings of a huge carrion crow.

The occupant of the box regarded him impassively through eyes which resembled chips of sapphire, unblinking and quite relentless in their appraisal of him.

The counsel for the prosecution glanced down at his notes then looked directly at the defendant.

'Did you know that Mrs Donaldson was still alive when you cut off her breasts?'

The words came out flatly with no inflection, and were all the more chilling because of that.

Again a babble of conversation began to grow but the judge silenced it with three sharp blows of the gavel.

'Did you know?' Briggs repeated, leaning on the edge of the witness box.

'I knew,' said Jonathan Crawford, indifferently. 'She started screaming when I cut her.'

'And yet you continued until you had severed both breasts?' said Briggs, now turning away from Crawford for a moment.

'Yes.'

Again the beginnings of a murmur.

Again the sharp report of the gavel.

Silence descended once more like a heavy blanket, with only the voices of the prosecutor and the defendant cutting through the oppressive stillness.

'Why did you choose this particular form of mutilation? Mrs Donaldson had already been stabbed,' he hesitated, consulting his notes again. 'She'd already been stabbed sixteen times to be exact. Wasn't that enough?'

'She had children,' Crawford began. 'Rich brats to suck at rich tits.' He chuckled.

'But you had already killed the children too,' rasped Briggs, his face darkening. He was finding it increasingly difficult to apply his usual detached professionalism to this case. Crawford was almost intolerably arrogant and that attitude was beginning to unsettle even the QC.

'We killed the kids first to shut them up,' Crawford told him. 'You know how noisy kids can be.'

There was a note of condescension in his voice which the prosecutor wasn't slow to pick up.

'You entered the bedroom of the Donaldson children,' Briggs began, raising his voice, walking towards the jury. 'Where Melissa and Felicity, aged four and two respectively, were sleeping.' The QC pulled a number of black and white photos from a manilla file and handed them to the foreman of the jury. 'What did you do then?'

'We killed them.'

'You killed them,' Briggs repeated, the knot of muscles at the side of his jaw pulsing. 'But first you cut out Melissa's tongue and removed Felicity's eyes with a kitchen knife, correct?'

'Oh Jesus,' the groan came from somewhere at the back of the court.

'Correct?' snarled Briggs, rounding on the defendant.

'See no evil, speak no evil,' said Crawford, smiling.

'Answer the question,' Justice Valentine said, scribbling something in his notes.

'Yes, we killed them,' said Crawford, brushing his long hair from his collar. 'Just like we killed the other fucking parasites.'

'By parasites I gather you refer to the other people who you stand accused of murdering?'

'The rich bastards, yes. How many do you think have died to make them *their* millions?'

'The Donaldson family were scarcely millionaires. Mr Donaldson owned a small factory complex in Woolwich.'

'From little acorns,' hissed Crawford, softly.

'So, that was sufficient reason to butcher Mrs Donaldson and her two children? I suppose we should be thankful that *Mr* Donaldson escaped this bloodbath.' The QC turned to the judge. 'The prosecution will not be calling Mr Donaldson as a witness M'Lord. He is under sedation at the moment.'

Valentine nodded.

'Why did you pick out the Donaldson family?' Briggs continued, turning his attention back to Crawford.

'They had money,' the younger man replied. 'We had to start somewhere.' Again that smile hovered on his lips.

'By "We" I gather you refer to the others who helped you in these murders?'

'There are others apart from me, yes.'

'But you chose to appoint yourself leader to fight this . . . "class war" as you call it?' Again the QC raised his voice. 'You declared war on the rich, on, as you call them, "the enemies of the state". Is that correct?'

'We are fighting a class war, yes, but I didn't appoint myself as leader. I was chosen.'

'Because of your natural charisma and organisational abilities presumably?' hissed Briggs, unable to control the sarcasm in his voice.

'Very possibly,' Crawford said, smiling.

'And this . . . war against the rich, it was to consist of a series of brutal murders of men, women *and* children whose only crime, in your eyes, was that they were fortunate enough to have enough money to live comfortably. Perhaps how you would secretly like to live yourself, Mr Crawford?'

'They were killed because they were parasites. They made their money by exploiting ordinary people. People who had no way of striking back at them.'

26

'Oh I see,' Briggs exclaimed, tapping his forehead. 'You undertook the role of avenging angel, you and your followers decided to act as executioners on behalf of all those not as fortunate as Mrs Donaldson. Mrs Donaldson who had begged for the lives of her children. Who had begged that her own life be spared but who ended up like this.' Briggs roared the last sentence and slammed a black and white photo of the dead woman down on the witness box in front of Crawford.

The younger man took the photo and glanced at it, raising his eyebrows.

'It's not a very good likeness of her,' he said, pushing the photo back towards the QC. It fell from the side of the witness box and lay on the floor.

The silence was broken by that insistent burbling of voices which was again stilled by the gavel.

At the back of the room Detective Inspector Peter Thorpe nudged his companion and nodded in the direction of the door which led out of the court.

Detective Sergeant Vic Riley got to his feet and the two men slipped out of the court.

In the corridor outside, Thorpe pulled a packet of Rothmans from his jacket pocket and offered one to Riley who accepted, fumbling for his matches when Thorpe's lighter refused to work.

The two men sucked hard on their cigarettes, Riley leaning against the wall. At thirty-seven, the DS was three years younger than his superior although it was he who had smudges of grey in his hair.

'Class war my arse,' said Thorpe. 'The bloke's a fucking headcase.'

'Yeah, him and his followers. Whoever the hell *they* are,' murmured Riley.

'Probably more like the two we've already got locked up,' said Thorpe, taking another hard drag on the cigarette.

'Christ, this bastard Crawford is going to take some cracking.'

'There's no doubt that he'll be sent down, guv,' Riley said.

'Yeah, maybe. But if we get *him* out of the way we still have to find his followers.' He dropped the cigarette and crushed it beneath his shoe. 'Before anyone else ends up like Mrs Donaldson and her kids.'

Two

'You sure it's safe in here?'

Danny Weller pulled the blanket around his neck and glanced up at the roof of the building. Through one of the holes he could see the night sky, dotted with stars as if someone had hurled sequins at black velvet.

'What do you mean, safe?' Sean Robson wanted to know. 'If you're worried about the coppers finding us . . .'

'No, not the coppers. I mean, the bloody place isn't going to fall down around our ears is it?'

Robson shook his head and wiped his nose with the back of his hand, studying the mucoid smear for a moment before scraping it off on his trousers.

'They're knocking down the tower blocks,' he reassured his companion. 'They ain't interested in this place. It'll do for one night anyway. At least it's better than sleeping in the street.'

He peered through the gloom at the interior of the super-market. The floor was covered by a thick layer of dust and dirt, parts of the roof were missing and most of the windows had been smashed but at least they wouldn't be disturbed. Robson regarded the empty shelves and felt his stomach rumble. He imagined the shelves full of food as they once had been but the gnawing pains in his belly convinced him that that was one fantasy best left alone. He concentrated on the bottle of Haig which he held in his hand. Robson took a long swallow then offered it to his companion, who drank deeply. Rather too deeply. Robson shot out a hand to take the bottle from him.

'Take it easy,' he snapped. 'That's got to last.'

Weller regarded the older man warily for a moment then licked his lips and nodded. At twenty-nine he was three years younger than Robson. Both had been jobless for more than five years, alcoholic for a little longer. Homeless for perhaps three years. They had eked out their living by, at various times, begging, stealing and, very occasionally, working in menial jobs where the promise of a meal had seemed more attractive than the prospect of wages. But what money they did come by was hastily spent on drink.

Robson in particular would do anything for the taste of whisky. He knew it was destroying him, eroding his brain cells, eating away at his liver, but he didn't care. It was only a matter of time for him now. Lung cancer had been killing him slowly over the past eight months, it was merely a question of which killed him first. The booze or the disease. It didn't matter either way to him.

He'd met Weller in Wormwood Scrubs two years earlier. He himself had been given seven days for disturbing the peace while the younger man was serving a two month sentence for aggravated assault. He'd used a Stanley knife on the owner of an off licence who had refused to serve him.

The relationship between the two men was a curious one. There was nothing sexual about it, although, in the beginning, Robson had wondered if his companion was a little dodgy. There was no other word to describe him. He looked dodgy. His face was very smooth, to the point where Robson doubted it had ever felt, or needed to feel, a razor. And his features were soft, almost feminine. But Weller had never made any attempt to get close to his older companion and for that Robson was grateful. Mind you, let him try it. Just once. He gripped the bottle more tightly and took another swig.

Weller knew little about the older man except that he had once been married, the marriage had floundered and Robson had been evicted from the house after repeatedly beating his wife. Weller had always been aware of Robson's capacity for violence and, on more than one occasion, had seen it put to use. He feared rather than respected his companion but was willing to put up with the older man's volatile nature. Weller had suffered enough loneliness to last him a lifetime and even the company of someone like Robson was preferable to the solitude which he had known before they met. He knew that Robson was dying but he did not dare to imagine life alone once the older man was gone. Only now, as Robson coughed and spat blood, did Weller consider him with something approaching pity. When the bottle was offered to him again he wiped the blood flecked sputum from the rim before drinking, the sound of his companion's choking coughs ringing in his ears.

Robson held his chest, gritting his teeth until the pain subsided slightly. He drew breath but even that simple act sent fresh waves of pain through him and he held out his hand for the bottle which Weller reluctantly passed back.

'Fuck,' muttered Robson, rubbing his chest.

He hawked again but this time the thick mucus merely

dribbled over his chin, hanging like obscene streamers from his beard.

'You all right?' Weller wanted to know.

'No, of course I'm not,' snapped Robson. 'But there's not much I can do about it is there?' He wiped the crimson saliva away.

Weller could only shrug.

The scream made them both look round.

'What the fuck was that?' murmured Robson, his pain momentarily forgotten.

The sound had barely died away when another split the night. Like the first. A scream yet something more. A howl. A roar of pain. Or rage?

Silence descended for a few seconds and then the sound came again. Louder this time, it seemed to fill the men's heads and Weller felt the hairs at the back of his neck stiffen and rise.

An uncomfortable silence descended and both men remained still, as if fearing that their own movements might trigger a repetition of the sound.

For interminable seconds they sat as if frozen. Then Weller got slowly to his feet and moved towards one of the windows on his right. It had been boarded up but there were gaps between the planks which enabled him to see into the darkness beyond. A watery moon illuminated the rubble of the site and cast thick shadows.

Weller cupped his hands around his eyes and peered out into the darkness, eyes flicking back and forth for the source of the sound.

Something moved.

A swift almost imperceptible deviation in the mounds of rubble drew his attention.

Before he could focus properly on it, the shape had gone, swallowed by the shadows.

31

'Probably kids pissing about,' said Robson, appearing at his companion's side.

'It didn't sound like kids,' the younger man noted, still scanning the gloom.

When the sound came again it seemed to reverberate inside the shell of the supermarket itself, so strident and loud did it seem.

But, this time the roar did not die away swiftly, it seemed to build slowly, from a low rumble to a deafening bellow which caused the men to shudder.

It finished with startling suddenness.

'Kids my arse,' hissed Robson. 'What the fuck *is* that?' His breath was coming in short gasps and, even in the gloom, Weller could see how pale his face was, as if all the colour had drained from it.

It was then that the doors at the far end of the building began to shake.

Both men spun round, squinting through the darkness towards what had once been the main entrance to the supermarket. The doors were padlocked and boarded up, but the pressure from outside was such that they continued to rattle. It sounded as if heavy blows were being rained upon them.

'Come on,' snapped Robson, tugging on the younger man's sleeve.

Weller needed no second prompting. He turned and followed him towards the back of the building where they had first gained entry. Through what had been a store room, on into an area which still held fridges the size of cars, once used to store meat. They finally reached the back entrance and Robson pulled it open.

Had he succeeded he would have screamed.

As it was, the sight which met him seemed to freeze not only the blood in his veins but also the muscles of his throat.

They seemed to lock tight, catching the cry of terror before it had time to escape.

He was rooted to the spot, only his eyes moving, flicking back and forth, up and down, rivetted to the shape which blocked his way. He tried to take a step backwards but there was no strength in his legs. He felt the bile clawing its way up from his stomach but even that seemed to clog in his throat as he finally managed to shake his head in disbelief. A final gesture.

The hand shot forward and fastened itself around his throat, lifting him bodily from the ground.

Weller began sobbing hysterically as he saw Robson lifted off the ground, legs kicking madly. Then, finally, the younger man turned and ran back into the supermarket itself.

By the time he stumbled into the enveloping darkness the front doors had been forced open and he saw dark shapes moving along the dust-filled aisles towards him.

Three of them.

Moving swiftly. Purposefully.

Behind him he heard a loud gurgling sound which he guessed had come from Robson but the noise was rapidly forgotten as he realized his own fate.

They were almost upon him, filling his nostrils with a stench unlike anything he'd ever encountered before, reaching for him.

The moon passed overhead like some kind of massive searchlight, its dull radiance searching through one of the holes in the roof and momentarily lighting the supermarket interior.

Illuminating the faces of the figures.

Weller dropped to his knees, hands clasped before him as if in prayer. As if some gesture to the Almighty would remove the sight before him. Tears of fear and terror coursed down

33

his cheeks and he wailed like a lost child until finally, as they drew closer, that wail turned into a caterwaul of desperation.

Then they were upon him.

Three

The radio hissed and spluttered as Ray Carter twisted the tuning dial. Music and voices filled the interior of the Jag as he passed different frequencies, finally tiring of the convoluted sounds. He switched the set off and sat in silence.

The wind was getting up, bringing with it the first drops of rain. Carter flicked on the windscreen wipers, allowing them to clear the glass. All around him a collage of neon signs above pubs, clubs and restaurants lit the night. Beneath the artificial twilight he could see figures moving. Two men were arguing loudly outside a pub just down the street. close by he saw a tall black woman tugging at the sleeve of a man who seemed intent on getting away from her. He eventually shook loose and scuttled off, pursued by the woman.

A powerfully built man in a suit much too small for him stood in the doorway of a club, a short cigar jammed in one corner of his mouth. He was tapping his foot in time to the music which was roaring from the interior of the club. The doorway was lit by a couple of red bulbs which made the doorman look as if someone had doused him in blood.

The wind whipped some discarded hamburger cartons across the street. They reminded Carter of bizarre tumbleweed in a strange Western. He chuckled to himself. This was no Western town. He doubted if the Wild West had ever been anything like Soho at eleven p.m.

A couple of youths passed the car, shouting. One of them banged the roof and they both looked in, grinning at Carter. Their smiles faded rapidly as they caught the expression on his face. If looks could have killed, the two youths would have been ready for wooden boxes!

Carter continued to glare at them and they moved away quickly, breaking into a run as they reached the end of the road, glancing back, perhaps to make sure they weren't being followed. Carter smiled and sat back in his seat, catching sight of his reflection in the rear view mirror.

He saw the dark shadow across his cheeks and chin and drew a hand across the bristles. He needed a shave.

Harrison was bound to comment eventually. He liked his men to look smart. It reflected badly on *him* if they didn't.

Carter glanced out of the Jag and found that he could see into the restaurant where his boss sat, gazing enraptured at the blonde girl opposite him.

Carter watched them for a moment longer and then began fiddling with the radio again.

The tap on the window made him jump and his right hand went instinctively to the 9mm Smith and Wesson automatic which nestled in its shoulder holster beneath his left armpit.

He twisted in his seat and saw the face of his brother grinning through the glass at him.

Carter pushed open the door and clambered out.

'Day-dreaming?' said James Carter, pinching his brother's cheek.

The younger man raised his fist as if to strike the newcomer – then they both laughed.

They were of similar build. Both about five eleven. Ray, if anything, slightly more heavily muscled. He was a year younger than James but they had often been mistaken for twins. Both had the same dark brown hair and both surveyed the world through steel grey eyes. But James carried a deep scar on his left cheek which ran from his ear to the edge of his nostril. A few inches lower and the cut of the Stanley knife would have severed his jugular vein. He'd been lucky to escape with only fifty stitches.

'I thought you might want a drink,' said James. 'Nip inside.' He motioned to the restaurant. 'I'll watch the car.'

'What about Harrison?' Ray enquired, indicating their boss.

'Don't worry about him, he's too busy with Tina.'

'I know, he's like a kid who's just figured out how his dick works.'

'Perhaps he has.'

'They've been in there for three hours already.'

'That's true love for you, my son,' chuckled James, sliding behind the wheel of the Jag.

Ray pulled up the collar of his jacket, dug his hands into his pockets and walked across the street to the restaurant, kicking at an empty Coke can.

He pushed open the door and walked in, the small bell over the entrance announcing his arrival.

Frank Harrison looked round momentarily and raised a hand in acknowledgement before turning his attention back to the girl who sat across the table from him.

At twenty-three, Tina Richardson was almost half Harrison's age. Carter had heard several stories about her life before she'd moved into a flat in Kensington which Harrison paid for. Some said she'd been a model, others an actress. Someone had even told him she'd been on the game. Maybe there was a little truth in all the stories. She certainly had the looks to make her a success in any one of those professions. Even the oldest one in the world. Her hair was almost silver –

but the colour was nature's handiwork not that of a peroxide bottle. It cascaded down her back as far as her shoulder blades like a shining waterfall. She wore little make-up, except on her eyes. Those blue eyes into which Harrison was gazing so raptly.

Carter watched as she lifted her wine glass, the sound of crystal on crystal drifting through the stillness as Harrison touched his own glass to hers. They both drank.

One of the waiters approached Carter, smiling his practised smile.

'Can I get you something, sir?' he asked in a heavy accent.

'Just a beer, please,' Carter said, glancing first at Tina and then at Harrison.

He didn't look his age. The beginnings of a paunch pushed against the waistcoat of his suit but his face was relatively unlined, his hair still thick and lustrous. In the dull glow cast by the candles his eyes looked sunken but Carter knew that was just a trick of the light.

From where he stood, Carter could not hear their conversation so he contented himself with snatching appreciative glances at Tina and sipping the beer which the waiter had just brought.

Apart from Harrison and Tina, the restaurant was empty. No one to disturb the carefully nurtured atmosphere. Carter reached across and pulled a menu towards him, scanning the prices. No wonder the bloody place was empty he thought, and glanced out of the window at the Jag. James was picking his teeth with a broken match, apparently unperturbed by the amount of time they'd been sitting around waiting for Harrison. But then, thought Carter, his brother had always been more patient. Ray was impetuous, sometimes dangerously impatient but James liked life to move at a slower pace. He never rushed.

Carter finished his drink and waved the waiter over to fetch him another. He pulled his cigarettes from his jacket pocket and lit one, glancing again at his watch. How much longer was Harrison going to be?

He was still pondering when he saw the black Datsun pull up alongside the Jag.

Probably some bloody tourist wanting directions, he thought.

It was difficult to see into the vehicle from where he sat so he got to his feet and moved closer to the front window, peering past the pot plants which filled the windowsill like an indoor jungle.

James Carter heard the car pull up alongside him and glanced across to see the driver pointing at him, motioning for him to lower his window. He hesitated a moment, squinting through the gloom to get a better look at the driver.

Squat, bull-necked. There was something vaguely familiar about him.

James saw the window of the other car being rolled down. Saw the driver leaning across towards him. Saw his hand move towards the parcel shelf.

Saw the barrel of the .357 Magnum pointing at him.

James actually had his mouth open in surprise when the gun was fired.

The bullet exploded from the barrel, shattering the side window of the Jag, hurtling into James' mouth.

The heavy grain shell blasted three of his front teeth backwards into his mouth, ripping away a portion of his upper jaw before smashing through the back of his neck just below the base of his skull. He fell across the front seat, blood spurting from the exit wound, spilling across the leather.

'NO,' roared Ray Carter as the back doors of the Datsun were flung open.

Two men came running towards the restaurant, one of them clutching a dark, bulky object in one hand. The other held what Carter knew to be an Ingram M-10 sub-machine gun.

The two men were within ten yards now and Carter spun round to shout a warning to Harrison who was already on his feet, alerted by the sound of the gunshot from outside.

The restaurant staff threw themselves down, two of them struggling to squeeze through a window in the kitchen at the rear of the building.

'Get out,' bellowed Carter, himself dropping to his knees. 'Use the back door. Now.'

The last word was lost as the Ingram opened up.

A hail of bullets struck the front window of the restaurant exploding the glass and sending huge lumps crashing into the dining area. The second burst blew in what was left of the window, bullets ricocheting off stonework and drilling into the ceiling. Two lamps were blasted to atoms by the fusillade. Plaster flew from the walls, mingling with brick dust to form a fine mist.

Harrison was on all fours, crawling towards the back of the restaurant, trying to cover Tina with his own body as they attempted to reach the sanctuary of the kitchen.

Carter followed, turning in time to see the second of the two men hurl the bulky package into the restaurant where it landed close to the bullet-shattered window.

The explosion came seconds later.

What was left of the window was blown outwards by the blast and Carter rolled over as he felt the searing heat. A piece of stone the size of a fist dropped from the ceiling and hit him in the side, momentarily knocking the wind from him but he rolled over, pushing Harrison and Tina ahead of him towards the rear entrance.

Flames rose in a yellow wall, fire sending out enveloping tendrils which fastened eagerly on tables and chairs, devouring them hungrily. But, through the fire, Carter saw that the two men had turned and were running back towards the Datsun. He scrambled to his feet and, shielding his face with one arm, dashed through the wall of fire and out into the street.

The sudden coolness washed over him and he tugged the automatic from its shoulder holster as the rear wheels of the Datsun spun on the wet road, screaming loudly as they tried to get a grip.

Carter fired three times, the gun jerking in his grip, the recoil slamming it back against the heel of his hand.

The first bullet blasted off one of the wing mirrors. The other two missed their target as the Datsun finally shot forward.

Carter ran into the street, aware that the back window of the escaping car was open.

He saw a muzzle flash and then felt a searing pain in his left shoulder.

The impact of the bullet sent him crashing back against the side of the Jag, blood running freely from the wound. It was as if someone had struck him with a red hot hammer and he felt his stomach contract. Felt consciousness slipping away from him.

Behind him the restaurant continued to burn.

People all along the street were spilling from the clubs, the pubs, some emerging from shop doorways to see what was happening.

Someone screamed.

Carter thought he heard the wail of sirens.

Then, as the pain in his shoulder became unbearable, he slipped sideways and lay on the wet tarmac.

He heard nothing.

Four

'Carter.'

He tried to open his eyes but it seemed as if they'd been sealed.

'Carter.'

He heard his name again and wondered if he was dreaming.

The hand on his shoulder told him that he wasn't.

He rubbed his face and managed to open his eyes, aware of the sharp pain in his left shoulder.

The figures who stood beside the bed were blurred and he shook his head as if that simple gesture would clear his vision.

It helped a little. He blinked hard and refocussed.

'Wakey, wakey,' said the voice and he found himself looking into the face of a man in his early forties. At least that's what he thought. As he struggled to sit up Carter also became aware of the smell in the room. The antiseptic. The smell of fresh sheets. But he had no idea which hospital he was in.

And now he recognised the figure which stood above him, dressed in a crumpled blue suit.

Detective Sergeant Vic Riley looked down at him.

'How's your shoulder?' asked the policeman. 'You were lucky. The bullet went straight through.'

'I don't feel very lucky,' said Carter, his throat dry. He reached for the jug of water on the bedside table but Riley reached it first and poured him a beaker of the clear liquid. The DS seated himself on the end of the bed, watching Carter as he drank.

The other man whom he'd seen, a uniformed officer, had stepped back towards the door of the room.

'Your brother's dead,' said Riley, quietly. 'They're scraping what's left of his head off the inside of Harrison's car.'

'I don't need the details,' rasped Carter, taking another sip of water.

'Who shot you, Ray?' asked Riley, pulling a handkerchief from his pocket and blowing his nose.

'I didn't see them,' said Carter.

'They killed your brother too.'

'I know that and I still didn't see them,' snarled Carter.

Riley nodded slowly.

'The automatic we found lying in the road *was* yours wasn't it?' the policeman asked.

'I haven't got a gun.'

'Oh come on, Ray. This isn't the time to pull the dumb routine. You could have been killed tonight. Not that it would have bothered me that much,' the DS added as an afterthought. 'Now tell me who shot you. What the hell was going on there tonight?'

'I told you, I didn't see anyone. Why aren't you out arresting tarts and nicking kerb crawlers, that's your usual business isn't it?'

'When restaurants get ·bombed and people get killed, *that's* my business. I don't like fuss, Carter, and right now you and your bloody boss are causing me more grief than I need so stop pissing about and tell me what happened or I'll have you inside for obstruction.'

'Because you can't pin anything else on me,' Carter observed, a satisfied smile touching his lips.

'Who might have wanted to have a go at Harrison?' asked the policeman.

'I told you, I don't know. And I don't know who shot me either. Satisfied?'

'Not really but I don't suppose there's much I can do

about it is there?' He got to his feet. 'I just thought you might have wanted us to catch the blokes who killed your brother. Next time it could be you who gets your skull ventilated.'

The policeman wandered across to the window and looked out onto the car park below. Another ambulance, its blue lights spinning silently in the darkness, had just pulled up.

'Do you think that Harrison would have given a damn if you'd been killed tonight?' said Riley. 'Do you think he'll shed any tears over your brother?'

Carter didn't answer, he was looking down at the beaker of water which he held, his face set in deep lines.

'You're protecting Harrison too by keeping quiet you know,' Riley continued. 'What have you got to gain by that?'

'Staying alive for one thing,' Carter said.

'If you decided to give evidence against Harrison, you'd be protected.'

Carter laughed humourlessly.

'Evidence about what?' he asked, innocently.

'About all the pies he's got his grubby little fingers in. We heard that he's just moved into child porn.'

'I'm only a driver. I don't know what he does. I don't care.'

'Maybe if you'd cared enough your brother would still have been alive.'

'Fuck you,' rasped Carter. 'It's not my fault Jim's dead. Do you think that's what I wanted?' His voice was a mixture of anger and sorrow.

Riley shrugged and turned towards the door.

'If you change your mind, you know where to reach me,' he said, turning the handle. 'By the way, Carter. We'll get you all one day. If you don't kill each other first.' He winked then closed the door behind him, leaving Carter alone in the room.

'Bastard,' muttered the younger man. He sighed and lay back, closing his eyes. The pain in his shoulder had subsided to a dull ache and he gently touched the heavily padded wound, wincing as he moved the shoulder.

He had been lucky, Riley had been right. Lucky not just because the bullet had passed through him without creating too much internal havoc but also because he hadn't been killed.

He'd been luckier than Jim.

The tears came suddenly, unexpectedly, and Carter cursed under his breath as if angry with himself for the private display of emotion. Not that he should be ashamed. Jim had been the only family he'd had. Their mother had died of cancer twenty years ago. As a ten year old, Carter could remember coming home from school and seeing her hunched in the chair in front of the fire, each day looking a little more shrunken until finally he'd arrived one Tuesday afternoon and found the ambulance waiting outside and seen two men carrying her out of the house. It had hardly seemed necessary to get two of them to carry her. In the final stages of her illness she'd withered to a mere six stone from her usual ten. It had eaten her away from the inside, slowly, painfully over eighteen months. But she'd never stopped fighting it, never surrendered to the pain.

Carter wept for his mother too, fresh tears that he didn't bother to wipe away.

The two boys had remained in the small house in Bermondsey with their father for another three years until a massive stroke had taken the old man. It hadn't killed him, just robbed him of his faculties, turning him into a helpless invalid who couldn't even feed himself. Ray and Jim would take turns looking after him, feeding him, cleaning him up when he messed himself. It was like having a sixty-eight year old child in the house and the strain eventually told on both boys.

When his father finally died, Jim decided he'd had enough. He joined the army.

Ray was left alone and, in the first few months, he felt resentment building up inside him. *He* needed to escape as well, not so much from the environment but from the memories.

Since the age of nine he had boxed at a club in Islington and now he turned his frustration towards the sport. He trained harder than ever, he fought with a ferocity that even he had not realized he possessed. it was like a purging, a cleansing of his soul and if part of that catharsis meant he was sometimes on the receiving end of beatings then so be it. He channelled his fury into boxing and it paid off. He reached the finals of the ABA Lightweight Division when he was nineteen and turned professional the year after that.

Jim returned from the army after his three year spell, his own demons exorcised and, for a time, the two of them saw little of one another. Ray's professional career brought in a steady wage but then came the setback which was to finish him in the ring.

He could still remember the fight. The other lad was overweight, ponderous in his movements. It seemed to Ray that he had no heart for the right. Carter had caught him with a powerful uppercut while the lad had been flat-footed. He'd dropped like a stone, his eyes glazed, almost opaque even as he hit the canvas. A doctor had leapt into the ring and Carter could remember being pulled away while efforts were made to revive his opponent.

He'd died in the ring. A massive brain haemorrhage.

Carter had never been back in a ring since.

Jim was out of the army. Ray had left the ring.

Then came Frank Harrison.

At the time he only owned a pub in Camden Town and two strip joints in the West End but he was expanding. He needed people. 'People with know-how and ambition' as he liked to put it, although Carter, having seen some of the men who worked for Harrison, was under the impression that sadism and psychosis were also useful qualifications.

So, in just eight years, Carter had risen from the post of nightclub bouncer to that of personal bodyguard.

He and his brother together. Just as it had been in the past.

It would no longer be so and that realization brought more tears.

He gritted his teeth and closed his eyes as if shutting out the light would shut out the pain.

It didn't.

Five

Frank Harrison dug his hand in the ice bucket and brought out three or four dripping cubes. He dropped them into the crystal tumbler then half-filled it with Jack Daniels, swallowing a large measure of the fiery liquid.

'I tell you,' he rasped, turning to face his guest. 'This is well out of order. I go out for a quiet meal and some mad sod tries to kill me. Fuck knows how much it's going to cost me to get my restaurant repaired and redecorated.' He downed more of the amber fluid and began pacing back and forth across the spacious lounge of the flat. Every now and then he would pause and look out of the large double windows that opened out onto a balcony which gave him a view of Holland Park.

46

'Who the hell would do it?' he rasped, not really expecting an answer. 'And why? For years there's been peace and now this. Somebody getting too fucking ambitious no doubt. So, one of my best men is killed, another one wounded. Thank God Tina wasn't hurt.' He turned to face the person who sat on the leather sofa. 'I'm telling you, some bastard is going to pay for this. If I let it pass then anyone will think they can walk over me and I'm not having that.'

He turned back to the window, gazing out over the darkened park. Trees swayed in the wind, spectral fingers that had lost many of their leaves rattled beneath the balcony.

'I'd just like to know why,' Harrison continued. 'I haven't stepped on anybody's toes, none of my interests conflict with any of the other organisations in London. Unless it's one I don't know about.' He finished what was left in his glass and poured himself another, his anger boiling up again as he rounded on the solitary figure who cradled a glass of brandy in his lap.

'Put the word out on the street,' Harrison rasped. 'I want to know who was behind that attack. I'll pay for the information if necessary and, before you say anything, I'll take care of who's behind it my own way, right?'

The figure shrugged.

'It's more than two years since there was any trouble like this. I should know, it was me who started it last time,' said Harrison. He pulled off his tie and threw it into one of the leather armchairs then, holding his drink in one hand, he began unbuttoning his waistcoat.

'Well I'm not having it. And it happened on my manor too. That makes it worse. What a fucking nerve.' He downed more of the whisky. Then he turned to face his visitor who sat quietly, allowing the gang boss to vent his fury, knowing that no words could calm him.

'You tell me if you hear anything, anything at all. I want to

47

know, got it?' Harrison snarled. 'Where do they think they are, fucking Belfast? Bombs, machine guns.' He shook his head, drained his glass and hurled the empty receptacle across the large lounge where it shattered against the wall.

'Fuckers,' shouted Harrison, furiously. 'You find out,' he growled, stepping closer to the other occupant of the room. 'And you do it quick, right? I don't pay you twenty thousand a year for nothing. Find out who wants me dead.'

Detective Inspector Peter Thorpe nodded slowly.

Six

He awoke suddenly, as if propelled from a nightmare, eyes jerking open, mouth forming soundless words.

As he was dragged to his feet Danny Weller shook his head as if trying to clear his senses. A vile stench filled his nostrils, a stench so rank that he thought he was going to vomit. He felt strong hands gripping his wrists, dragging him backwards towards the wall of the supermarket storeroom and, suddenly, the circumstances of his predicament came flooding back with a clarity which forced a moan from his throat.

The figures were standing in front of him.

Three of them.

Two others held him against the wall as he struggled in their grip, aware of the numbing coldness which seemed to radiate from them. It was as if the chill ran from their own hands into his veins causing him to shudder as they slammed him back against the wall and held him there.

The first of the watching trio stepped forward and gripped Weller's chin in one powerful hand, running his fingers over the flesh, enjoying the smoothness, stroking the skin as a man might stroke the face of his lover. But there was no emotion in this gesture.

Weller felt the pressure on his chin increase and he let out a grunt of pain. By now, the stench was almost overpowering and it was all he could do to keep a grip on consciousness. The moon had retreated behind a thick bank of cloud so the supermarket was once again in almost total darkness. But, even so, Weller knew that his captors were close.

Exactly who, or what they were he *didn't* know.

The one that held his face took a step back and glanced across at the two who held Weller's arms. He nodded slowly and the younger man felt his hands being forced back against the wall. He tried to struggle free but the pressure on his wrists only increased.

'Who are you?' he wailed, tears of fear once more running freely down his cheeks.

He heard a metallic rattle and looked to his left.

One of the figures had taken a handful of flat-headed nails from his jacket pocket.

He pressed one into the palm of Weller's left hand.

The movement was so swift he barely had time to scream.

The figure gripping his wrist dropped down and retrieved a piece of broken concrete; then with one powerful blow he struck the head of the nail.

Weller shrieked in pain as the metal spike was driven through his hand, each successive stroke sending it deeper into the flesh of his hand then beyond into the wall.

Blood burst from the punctured palm, spurting on to the jacket of the one who stood before him but the figure did not move, merely continued to stare into Weller's face as he tried one last time to escape.

His right hand was pressed against the wall and, quick as a flash, he felt another of the metal spikes being pounded through that palm until he was supported not by the freezing hands but by the thick steel nails that transfixed his palms. Blood dripped to the floor where it soaked into the dust like ink into blotting paper.

Weller sagged forward, his own weight threatening to pull him free of the wall but a cold hand was fastened once more beneath his chin. He fought to retain his senses, pain stabbing up both his arms now. It felt as if his hands were on fire. Yet still he was denied the mercy of unconsciousness. Still he found that he was looking into a face which could have been plucked from a nightmare.

The skin of the man's features was stretched so tight over the bones of his face it seemed that it would tear, like plastic which has been pulled beyond its breaking point. Weller expected to see the skin burst. Instead, he saw it begin to heave, as if there was something beneath that dry skin.

The flesh began to undulate, slowly at first but then with greater speed until a bulge appeared beneath the left cheekbones, rising like a boil, swelling like some obscene tumour, growing before his eyes until finally it burst.

The boil was filled with maggots. Dozens of the writhing white forms twisted and turned in the festering hole until they spilled forth, dropping to the ground, some of them dropping into the puddles of Weller's blood.

He screamed loudly.

'Who are you?'

The leader moved closer and Weller recoiled as the stench threatened to choke him.

Then the others joined their leader, staring at the young man nailed to the wall with something akin to fascination.

He felt his stomach contract, felt it trying to expel its contents.

He heard a sound that was all too familiar.

The swish-click of a flick knife.

Then he felt it against his cheek, the point gouging into his flesh, digging deeper until blood began to run from the wound. And yet the knife was wielded with immaculate skill, drawn in light quick movements through the skin of Weller's face to expose the network of muscles beneath. He screamed again as he felt the blade moving beneath his right eye, scraping against his cheekbone up and across his forehead then down the other side of his face.

When it reached his neck he *did* pass out.

The figure with the knife cut the last piece of flesh free then slid two fingers beneath the skin as if it were some kind of mask.

Pulling carefully, the figure pulled the skin free, coaxing it away from the eyes with the aid of the blade.

It came away in one piece.

One dripping piece of skin.

The figure turned to those watching and held the mask of living flesh aloft like some kind of bizarre trophy.

Two of the others stepped forward and began removing Weller's clothes, tossing them aside until he was naked.

Then they set to work.

Seven

The footsteps outside his door woke him.

Carter sat bolt upright, awake in an instant, ignoring the slight ache from his injured shoulder. He heard the footsteps and peered towards the door, watching the shadows beneath.

There was someone out there.

Listening.

Waiting.

He glanced across at the emergency button beside his bed, his finger poised over it.

The door handle turned slowly.

Carter swung himself out of bed, his eyes never leaving the slowly-turning handle. To hell with the emergency button, he thought. He'd deal with this himself.

The door opened a fraction, light from the corridor beyond spilling across the floor.

He saw a figure illuminated in the light.

The door opened further, the figure took a step inside.

Carter sat on the end of the bed and waited.

Tina Richardson closed the door behind her and smiled at him.

'You'd never make a hitman,' said Carter, quietly, a smile spreading across his lips. He stood up and she walked towards him, throwing her arms around his neck, drawing his face to hers. Their lips pressed together, her tongue pushing against his, seeking entry to the warm moistness inside his mouth. He pulled her hard against him, aware of the growing warmth spreading around his groin, the heady scent of her perfume and her hands now gliding across his chest and back as he responded fiercely to his kiss.

When they finally parted, Tina was breathing heavily.

'I thought you'd been killed too,' she told him, gripping his right hand tightly.

She sat down on the bed beside him, shrugging off her coat.

Carter saw that she was wearing only a thin sweater and a leather skirt. Her hair was freshly washed. She smelled as if she'd just stepped out of a shower. He touched her cheek with his free hand and she kissed his fingers as he traced a pattern over her lips.

'How did you get in?' he asked, glancing at the clock. 'It's nearly three in the morning.'

'I sat in the car outside the main entrance,' she told him. 'There was only one porter on duty. It was just a matter of waiting.'

He smiled.

'For what?'

'Everyone has to pee eventually,' she informed him. 'I sneaked in then. I knew you'd be in this room, Frank always uses the best facilities for his men if they're injured.'

'Where is he now?' asked Carter, anxiously.

'He went back to his own place about midnight. I told him I'd be OK on my own.' She leant forward and kissed him again, quickly. 'I was so worried about you. I had to see you. I'm sorry, Ray.'

'We'll both be sorry if Frank finds out. We'll end up propping up a flyover somewhere,' Carter told her sardonically.

'I'll go if you want me to,' she said, getting to her feet.

Carter held her hand and pulled her back down beside him, pulling her close, feeling her breasts pressing against his chest as they kissed. He allowed one hand to slide beneath her sweater, reaching higher until it closed over one unfettered mound. He rubbed gently, feeling the hardness of her nipple against his palm. She sighed and reached for his

53

growing erection, encircling it in her hand, coaxing his stiffness. She pushed him back on the bed, slipping free of his hands to lay beside him. She kissed his chest, nipping the flesh between her teeth, sliding lower until her tongue flicked at the bulbous head of his penis.

'No,' gasped Carter, somewhat reluctantly. He sat up. 'Not here. Not now.'

She didn't speak but merely sat on the edge of the bed with her back to him.

'How much longer have we got to go on like this?' she asked. When she turned to face him he saw tears in her eyes. One solitary, salty droplet ran down her cheek. Carter leant forward and kissed it away.

'Meeting in secret, both of us frightened of what we say in case we give ourselves away,' she persisted. 'It's been like this for six months now. The odd night together if we're lucky but always looking over our shoulders. Looking for Frank.'

'That's the way it's got to be, Tina,' said Carter quietly. 'We have to be careful, both of us.'

'I hate the way things are,' she said wearily, clutching at his hand. 'But I know you're right. To a certain extent we both *need* Frank. Without him I'd have nothing . . .'

Carter interrupted her.

'That's bullshit,' he snapped. 'We don't need him. He doesn't own us.'

'But we can't just walk out on him can we?' she said challengingly. 'He'd kill us.'

'Then we'll take that chance,' he said and pulled her to him, gripping her by the back of the neck, feeling her hair on his powerful hand. She responded fiercely, her hands once more drawn to his erection. This time he didn't stop her; instead he allowed her to rub his shaft gently while he lifted her sweater and bent forward. His lips fastened around one of her hardened nipples and she lay back, across the bed. Her own hands now left his penis as she undid the zip of her skirt and wriggled out of it, pushing the expensive leather to the floor.

Carter slipped off his pyjama bottoms and stood naked before her for a second before dropping slowly to his knees. He gripped each of her ankles and parted her legs further, nuzzling the silky gusset of her panties, his tongue lapping at the edges of the material before squirming inside the loose elastic.

She lifted her legs and snaked them around his shoulders, drawing him closer, allowing him to pull her panties aside, urging him on as he began to probe her liquescent cleft with his tongue. She stroked his hair, her breathing becoming more laboured as he began flicking at the hardened bud of her clitoris. Tina felt that familiar warmth spreading across her thighs and stomach and she moaned aloud.

There was movement outside the door.

They both froze, as if turned to stone. A moment of passion preserved for interminable seconds.

Footsteps.

Carter backed away from her slowly, his eyes on the door.

Tina lowered her legs, trying to control her breathing.

'Mr Carter.'

They shot each other anxious glances.

'Mr Carter.'

He recognised the voice of the night nurse and crossed to the door.

The handle turned but he gripped it, easing the door open himself.

He peered round the door and saw the nurse standing there.

'Are you all right?' she asked. 'I thought I heard a noise.'

'I couldn't sleep,' Carter told her.

'Would you like something to help you sleep?'

'No thanks.'

'You should try to rest.'

He nodded then gently closed the door, listening as her footsteps echoed down the corridor.

When he turned back towards the bed, Tina was pulling on her skirt.

'I told you it was useless, Ray,' she said dispiritedly.

He returned to her side and kissed her forehead.

'I'll have to go,' she told him, her cheeks still flushed from the excitement she felt.

'I hope you can get out as easily as you got in,' he told her, smiling.

She nodded.

'We can't go on like this forever,' she said. 'We have to get away.'

Carter didn't answer, he merely crossed to the door and looked out. The corridor was empty so he ushered her out, pausing to kiss her.

Then he closed the door, listening as her footsteps receded.

Carter stood with his back to the door, head bowed.

She was right. They had to get away.

But there was still Harrison.

Eight

The house had been empty for over a year.

The last paying tenants had moved out and other occupants had made the building their own. Rats, mice, spiders the size of a baby's fist – all moved freely within the derelict shell. Damp had crept up the walls like a malignant black shroud, stripping paper from crumbling brickwork. It hung in reeking tatters like putrescent flesh.

In the kitchen woodlice and silverfish scuttled over the cracked worktops, prey to the spiders that had spun their webs in the sink.

The sitting room was large, with an open fireplace which, at one time, must have been a welcoming sight. Now, instead of a glowing fire the black hole contained only a mound of dust and some rotting excrement.

The windows, smashed long ago, had been boarded over. Upstairs the three bedrooms were in a similar state of decay. In one lay a grime encrusted blanket, stiff with stale vomit. The legacy of the last human visitor to the place. A drunk who had used it as a place of shelter during a storm. But even squatters had steered clear of the house, unable to tolerate the vermin and the stench. The building and those that flanked it had been marked for demolition by the Whitechapel authorities over six months ago. The cost of making them habitable again had proved to be prohibitive and a developer was rumoured to be interested in the land. It seemed that the derelict buildings might yet prove to be worth some money but, as yet, none had been forthcoming.

The three houses stood empty and unwanted; grass and weeds in their small front gardens had grown as high as the boarded front windows. Other residents of the area stayed clear of the empty buildings. No children played near them for fear of what might lurk inside. The minds of children are capable of imagining far worse horrors than catching tetanus from a rusty nail or getting a rat bite. As far as the children were concerned, the houses were home to all manner of vile monsters and demons – which was fine by their parents as long as it kept them out of the filthy dwellings.

But there were others who found the darkness and the solitude welcoming. Others who lived happily amidst the filth with the other vermin.

Those who moved as quietly and stealthily as the creatures of darkness with whom they shared the crumbling abode.

The houses had human occupants and had done so for the last two weeks.

They paid little attention to the stench and the decay. They had known worse. Much worse.

No one had seen them arrive. No one ever saw them leave. They chose their times carefully.

They had searched for just such a building, somewhere untended, a place shunned by those who lived close to it. Somewhere isolated and yet still close to the centre of London.

Close to their prey.

The light from the hurricane lamp cast thick shadows over the room in which the figures sat. As each one moved, its silhouette looked as if it were about to detach itself. Find a life of its own and leave the room. The room was quiet apart from the clanking of cutlery on tin cans. The assembled group didn't need plates, they ate straight from the tins, huddled around the hurricane lamp like vultures waiting for someone to die. They ate in silence.

In one corner a rat scuttled along a rotting skirting board. One of the men in the room twisted round and flung his empty can at the rodent, smiling as it scurried out of sight.

Phillip Walton chuckled to himself and then belched loudly.

He glanced round at his companions. They were all roughly the same age as him. Early to middle twenties. All were dressed similarly, too. Jeans, T-shirts or sweatshirts, boots or trainers. One of the girls was barefoot, the soles of her feet as black as pitch. Walton succeeded in catching her eye and he smiled.

Maria Chalfont returned the gesture, finished what she was eating and then wiped her mouth with the back of her hand.

Mark Paxton was picking at the head of a large spot which swelled on his chin. He eventually succeeded in bursting it between his thumb and forefinger, sniffing at the yellowish pus before wiping it on his jeans.

Paul Gardner licked the inside of the tin of meat, careful not to cut his tongue on the ragged edge. Then he too tossed it aside.

In the next room, Jennifer Thomas was defecating into a bucket already full to the brim with urine and faeces. When she'd finished she wiped herself clean with a piece of cloth then draped it over the slop bucket and wandered back to join her companions.

Michael Grant waited until she had seated herself, then turned to the wall beside him, a long-bladed machete gripped in one powerful fist.

The wall was covered by photos, some from newspapers and magazines, others taken with a camera. Some poster size, others little larger than passport photos.

Film stars. Pop performers. TV personalities. Sportsmen and women. Politicians. Businessmen.

The wall resembled a collage of the rich and famous, assembled by some insane fan.

Grant leaned close to one of the photos, an actress in a well-known soap opera and spat at it, watching as the sputum rolled down the wrinkled paper.

'Rich scum,' he said. 'All of them.' He smiled, running the tip of the machete very slowly across the pictures.

Over one of a pop star.

'Parasite,' he whispered.

Over a poster of a model.

'Whore.'

And a politician.

'Liar.'

'There's so many of them,' said Jennifer Thomas.

'We've got time,' Grant said.

'The papers have called Jonathan a madman,' Mark Paxton said, prodding his face for more spots, finding a larger one and rubbing it.

'Anyone who doesn't conform to their ideas is a madman, so they tell us,' replied Grant running his eyes over the photos once more. 'But who is to say what's mad and what's normal? Is this normal?' He gestured angrily at the photos. 'Are the lives these bastards and whores lead normal? No. What do ordinary people know of the kind of wealth that *they* have. Ordinary people, people like us, we'll never know what it's like to have that kind of money to abuse.'

'You grew up in a rich family,' said Phillip Walton, brushing his long hair back over his shoulders. 'So did Jonathan. You know what it's like to have money.' It was almost an accusation.

'Why do you think I left home?' snapped Grant. 'Seeing what money could do to people. Making them soft, idle. I didn't want that happening to me too. Jonathan escaped that way of life too. And all of you, you know what wealth can do. How it can turn ordinary people into grasping, self-obsessed scum. Why are any of you here?'

'The rich are parasites,' said Jennifer Thomas.

'They deserve to die,' Maria Chalfont echoed.

'They're fucking useless. All of them,' hissed Walton.

'They exploit the poor,' Paul Gardner added.

'Bollocks,' snarled Walton. 'Exploitation has nothing to do with it. You sound like a politician trotting out his clichés. This isn't a fucking political war, Gardner. It's not as if we're a bunch of revolutionaries, that's not what Jonathan wanted.'

'No, he wanted the destruction of the rich,' intoned Paxton. 'Whoever they are.'

'What will we do if Jonathan's convicted?' asked Jennifer Thomas, picking the dirt from beneath her chewed nails.

'You mean *when* not *if*,' Walton said.

'We carry on in his place,' Grant told her. 'It's what he wanted. It's what was planned right from the beginning. We carry on until we've exterminated every rich bastard we can. Trash like this.' He struck the wall with the machete, carving a photo of a politician in half.

'I don't understand why the public think so much of them,' said Maria Chalfont.

'Most people *want* money,' said Grant. 'They don't realize how it fucks up their lives. How it changes them. They live out their own fantasies through these parasites.' He slapped the wall with the back of his hand. 'They watch them on TV, read about them in the papers and they think they're something special. Something different. We'll make them realize they're not.'

'Everyone's equal in death,' chuckled Walton.

Paxton milked the pus from another spot and nodded his agreement.

'So, who's next?' asked Gardner, scanning the photos before him.

'It's not important. Any one of them will do.' Grant

smiled, his dark eyes flicking back and forth. He raised the machete and pressed it against a photo of a man in his early forties. A man with a blonde girl beside him.

He pressed the razor-sharp point into the photo of Frank Harrison.

Nine

The dog heard the sound first.

Or perhaps it wasn't the sound which alerted it but something deeper. It *sensed* a presence. The animal, a cross-breed which was more alsatian than collie, got to its feet and padded across to the bedroom door sniffing the air as it moved. It whimpered slightly, raised one paw and scratched at the paintwork.

Bob Chamberlain sat up in bed, blinked myopically and fumbled for the lamp at the bedside. As he switched it on, pale light flooded the bedroom and he winced, rubbing his eyes.

The dog continued to whimper and paw at the door.

Chamberlain was about to ask what was wrong when he heard something.

The noise came from downstairs.

He swung himself out of bed with a speed and athleticism that belied his sixty-three years, reaching below the bed for the gun. He pulled out a Franchi over-under shotgun and checked that it was loaded.

There was more movement below him. Stealthy and furtive but nonetheless he heard it.

Someone was in the shop.

He'd owned the gun shop for close to thirty years now, taking over the business when his father had died. He'd only had two break-ins in that whole time. The first one had been kids, no more than sixteen. Two of the little bastards. Bob had sent them on their way with a clip round the ear. He hadn't called the law. That wasn't the way in the East End. People looked out for themselves. If you had a problem you dealt with it, you didn't call the Old Bill. The second break-in had been more serious. Bob had been attacked in broad daylight by a couple of black blokes who'd hit him with a metal bar but, despite sustaining a bad cut to his forehead, he'd still managed to fight the buggers off, had even managed to reach his shotgun and aim it at them. It had taken all his self-control not to put some buckshot in the black bastards as they'd fled. Now he hefted the Franchi before him and moved slowly towards the door, careful to avoid the floorboards which he knew creaked. If there *was* someone in the shop, he didn't want them to know he was up there. Bob glanced at his watch.

3.22 a.m.

He reached down with one hand and patted the dog on the head then gripped its collar as he eased the door open with his foot and stepped out onto the landing. He stood for interminable seconds listening to the sounds which drifted to him on the stillness of the night. He heard footsteps below him, heard one of the cabinets which held the pistols being forced open. Whoever was down there obviously didn't care whether they were heard or not. Bob smiled grimly. The bastards would care when *he* got down there.

He began to descend.

He moved without undue haste, gripping the dog's collar

to prevent it rushing away. There was a door at the bottom of the stairs which led to his kitchen and a small sitting room. Beyond that was the shop.

As he reached the door he eased his grip on the dog's collar, patting its head to calm it. But the animal was already scrabbling at the door, anxious to be let loose on the intruders.

'Steady Bitsa,' he whispered to the cross-breed. Bitsa seemed an appropriate name he'd thought, it had bitsa this and bitsa that in it. He smiled to himself. The dog was powerful and eager. Whoever was in the shop was in for a bloody surprise.

Bob paused for a moment and, as he did so, silence seemed to descend.

Had the intruders heard his approach?

He swung the shotgun up across his chest, as if seeking reassurance from the weapon.

Sod them, he thought, his face hardening. If they'd heard him, too bad. Perhaps they'd have the sense to get out while they still could.

He kicked open the door.

'Take them, Bitsa,' he hissed and the dog went hurtling through the kitchen and sitting room, swallowed up by the gloom. It was barking and snarling loudly as it reached the shop itself.

Bob prepared himself, listening to the frenzied barking of the dog.

Then silence.

He swallowed hard and edged forward into the sitting room, aware for the first time of the numbing cold which seemed to have filled the building. It caused his skin to rise in goose-bumps and the hair at the nape of his neck stiffened.

And there was a smell too.

A rank, fetid odour which made him wince. But he pressed

64

on towards the shop, eyes fixed on the open door which led into it.

In the sodium flare from the lights outside he could see that two of the gun cabinets had been forced open, shotguns and rifles removed, pieces of broken glass scattered over the floor.

The stench and the cold intensified but Bob's anger seemed to make him oblivious to these considerations and, wielding the Franchi before him, he advanced into the shop furiously.

'Right you bastards,' he shouted, swinging the shotgun up to his shoulder.

With his free hand he slapped on the lights.

Darkness.

Nothing happened. The shop remained unlit.

Bob's heart began beating faster as he caught sight of the motionless form of Bitsa lying in the centre of the room.

Its head was surrounded by a spreading puddle of blood, its body still twitching slightly.

The bottom jaw had been practically torn off, it hung from the battered skull by just a tiny network of muscles and ligaments.

Bob took a step towards the animal, his attention suddenly wandering, his concern not for the weapons which had been stolen from him but for his dead pet. Bitsa had been a big dog. Whoever had killed him had done it quickly and with incredible power.

Whoever . . .

The hand closed on his shoulder and instinctively he spun round.

It was at that point that the lights came on.

Bob found himself staring into the face of the intruder and as he did his heart increased its speed, its pumping became uncontrollable. He felt white hot pain stabbing at his chest, spreading with incredible swiftness along his left arm, causing him to drop the shotgun.

He opened his mouth to scream but only a low croak came out as the intruder pulled him closer, gazing into eyes which were bulging wide with pain and shock.

And horror.

The intruder was dressed in a two piece suit, filthy, covered in dust, holed in three places across the chest. And, in those holes living things moved. Creatures which writhed and twisted and slid over one another, exuding a noxious liquid. And, where there should have been eyes the intruder sported two more of these holes, holes which were nothing more than seething pits filled to bursting point with parasitic forms. And yet it could still see. Could still look at Bob who now felt as if his head was exploding. The pain in his chest and arm grew, spreading up his neck until it felt as though his upper body had been filled with red hot lead, as if his blood had been transformed into molten metal.

He tried to back away but his legs buckled under him and he dropped to the floor, the pain searing through him, unbearable.

Blood from his dead dog splashed his hand as he tried to drag himself away from the intruder who merely took a step closer, looking down on Bob with something akin to fascination.

Bob tried to suck in a breath but his throat had constricted. His chest felt heavy, his head was spinning. He rolled on to his back, eyes still bulging wide, the whites suddenly reddening as two blood vessels burst and his left eye turned crimson.

And, above him, the intruder peered down through those pits of writhing, reeking shapes, one of which fell and landed on Bob's heaving chest. Then it merely stepped over him and strode from the shop leaving Bob alone again.

The pressure inside his chest seemed to grow ever greater until at last the inevitable happened. His heart simply burst.

Bob Chamberlain lay still as his sphincter muscle opened and allowed his body to empty itself.

The stench of excrement filled the air, mingling with the other, stronger, smell.

The stench of decay.

Ten

The smell of so many flowers was overpowering.

Carter coughed as the sickly sweet scent settled around him like an invisible cloud. The priest paused in his endless ramblings and glanced across at him but Carter merely nodded for the man to continue. For all the effect the words were having, the cleric might as well have been speaking a foreign language.

Carter stood with his arms by his sides, immaculate in a black suit. The slight breeze ruffled his hair and rustled the lower branches of the tree above him.

Birds sat silently peering down at the small gathering below them, wondering what these black creatures were doing. One finally flew off, the movement scattering leaves, sending them to the ground, drifting lazily. One landed on top of the coffin beside a huge wreath of red carnations which carried the tributes:

'To Jim
An ace among Kings
Love Ray'

Carter took a step forward and brushed the leaf aside, careful not to disturb the other floral tributes which covered the lid of his brother's casket.

Everyone in the small gathering had sent flowers of some description. From the small bouquets sent by other members of Harrison's firm, right up to the massive white cross of roses which the boss himself had offered.

He stood beside Carter as the flowers were removed and the coffin was lowered slowly into the ground.

Carter sighed. It all seemed to have happened so quickly.

He'd been discharged from hospital two days before and, on returning home, had been visited by Harrison who'd informed him that all the arrangements for Jim's funeral had been made. He, himself, would pay for everything. That, he'd said, was only right. He'd pay for the coffin, the flowers, whatever was needed.

The cost wasn't important. Jim had been a good boy. One of his best. Harrison's appraisal of his brother's character had done little to relieve the pain which Carter felt. A pain which, after the death of his father, he had not thought he would ever experience again. But now, standing at the graveside, he felt that same hurt and it was all the more acute because of his realization that he was now completely alone. He had no one.

He glanced briefly across at Tina who was looking down at the grass beneath her feet.

No, he had no one.

When the time came, the priest approached him and led him towards the graveside, allowing him to peer down at the polished coffin.

Persuading him to throw in the first handful of earth.

Carter felt, for one ridiculous moment, like a child who had won some kind of fairground competition.

'Go on, sonny, you can be the first one to throw dirt on your

brother's coffin. Go on, just get a handful and throw it in'.

He bent and scraped up some earth, hesitated a second and then dropped it in.

Bullseye, he thought as the dirt hit the brass nameplate. *Anything from the top shelf.*

Carter smiled to himself. Perhaps he was going slightly crazy. Perhaps the pain-killers that the doctors had given him were making him high. Or perhaps he merely couldn't stand the solemnity of the occasion any longer. Fuck it, he thought, stepping back. Jim was dead and all the weeping and wailing in the world couldn't bring him back to life.

Harrison stepped forward and added his own handful of earth to that already scattered on the coffin lid.

The gang boss stood with his back to Carter who looked across at Tina once more and found that, this time, her eyes were on him.

They exchanged a brief glance, aware of Harrison's men all around them. They could afford no tell-tale flicker of emotion in those fleeting looks. She gave him a thin, brief smile and he nodded almost imperceptibly in return.

The other members of the firm filed past the coffin, one or two of them crossing themselves.

Jim had been well-liked by his companions and Carter was gratified to see that there were almost two dozen of them present. Each moved dutifully past the grave, head bowed in reverence until Carter was left alone on one side of the yawning maw. The priest looked at him and then turned to Harrison but the gang boss merely shook his head, motioning for the priest to leave the graveside, to leave Carter alone.

Tina hesitated for a moment but Harrison gripped her hand and guided her away.

She chanced a quick look back as they walked to the waiting cars and saw Carter standing close to the grave looking down into it, as if in silent conversation with his dead brother.

With the wind whistling around him, he stood for what seemed like an eternity, gazing down into the hole, fighting back tears of both rage and grief.

Then, finally, he turned and strode back towards the waiting cortège.

Behind him, the birds began singing in the trees.

Carter held the black suit before him on the hanger, plucking a stray hair from the collar. Then he opened the wardrobe door and replaced it among his other clothes.

Harrison had told him to take the rest of the day off despite the fact that Carter didn't much feel like being cooped up inside his flat alone after the funeral. He returned to the small dwelling in Finsbury, showered and then went for a walk. His seemingly aimless ramblings took him back towards Islington, towards the street where he and his brother had lived most of their lives but when he reached the street he hesitated and turned back, wandering home again. He spent the evening in front of the TV and dropped off to sleep, a bottle of vodka beside him, a glass gripped in his hand.

By the time he woke the sun had fallen behind the jagged skyline of the capital, flooding the twilight sky with crimson, until the heavens resembled a floor cloth soaked in blood. And with the evening came a chill.

Carter pulled on a sweatshirt. He'd jammed the Smith and Wesson 9mm in his belt at the back, the weapon hidden by the folds of his sweatshirt. He stood before the full length mirror in his bedroom, twisting and turning, making sure that the weapon couldn't be seen. When he was satisfied that it was invisible, he wandered back into the sitting room and poured himself another glass of vodka, swallowing half the fiery liquid in one gulp.

The strident ringing of the phone startled him.

He shook his head, as if trying to clear the fog which

shrouded his brain, then he crossed to the phone and picked it up.

'Hello.'

'Ray.'

He recognised her voice immediately and allowed himself a smile.

'Tina. What's wrong?' he asked, the smile suddenly fading.

'Nothing. I wanted to know how you were,' she told him.

'I've been better,' he told her.

'I didn't get a chance to say anything to you this afternoon.'

'Nothing needed to be said. It's over now.' He changed the subject. 'Where's Frank? You're taking a risk calling me.'

'I'm not expecting him until later. I had to speak to you, find out how you were. I wish I could be with you.'

'If you come you'd better bring a bottle,' he said humourlessly. 'The one I've got's nearly empty.' He glanced at the bottle of Smirnoff and at his glass.

'Will I see you tonight?' she wanted to know.

'I don't think that would be a good idea, especially if you're expecting Frank. I'll probably end up in the same hole as Jim if he finds out.' He paused for a moment. 'Tomorrow maybe.'

Silence.

'Tina?'

He heard sounds of movement at the other end of the phone.

Carter frowned.

The phone went dead.

Eleven

She hadn't heard the key in the lock.

Hadn't heard the door swing open.

Only when he pushed it closed behind him did Tina realize that Frank Harrison had walked into her flat.

She turned and smiled at him, trying to hide her fear, praying that he hadn't overheard. At the same time she pressed down on the cradle of the phone, severing the connection.

'Frank,' she beamed with practised sincerity. 'I wasn't expecting you this early.' She replaced the receiver and moved away from it.

'I thought I'd surprise you,' Harrison told her, the bouquet of roses held in one hand so that it bore more resemblance to a club than an offering of affection. He smiled but the gesture never touched his eyes. He held the flowers out before him, as if daring her to take them for him.

She took a pace forward, reaching for the bouquet.

'They're beautiful,' she said, preparing to take the offering.

Instead, Harrison jerked them back from her grasp and gripped her wrist with his free hand, pulling her close to him.

'If you're that pleased with them then prove it,' he said, smiling even more broadly. But, on Harrison's craggy features, the exaggerated smile looked like a mockery of emotion. As genuine as the greasepaint grin of a circus clown.

Tina felt a twinge of fear as his vice-like grip tightened on her wrist. She swallowed hard and leant forward to kiss him.

'Frank, you're hurting me,' she told him.

Still that grin remained plastered across his features like some vile rictus.

He dropped the flowers and snaked his other arm around her waist, pressing her lower body against his groin.

Through the thin material of her skirt she felt the beginnings of his erection pressing into her. He kissed her fiercely, still keeping hold of her wrist, squeezing so tightly now that her fingers began to tingle. She felt his tongue pressing against her lips, trying to force its way inside her mouth and, reluctantly, she allowed him to experience that delight but her response was muted. The pain from her wrist was becoming intense.

She shook loose and looked at him angrily.

'You're hurting my wrist, Frank,' she told him and, with infinite slowness, he released it, revealing white indentations where his finger-tips had been. He held her with his other arm, though, still pinning her to him, enjoying the feel and smell of her body, savouring the build up of his own excitement.

He stroked her long hair, finally winding it into strands, gripping those strands, pulling gently at first.

Then harder.

Harder.

She wore only a thin blouse and skirt and as he tilted her head back he could see her nipples straining darkly against the material.

He kept his grip on her hair but eased her head forward once more, kissing her nose.

She smiled convincingly.

Harrison continued to grin.

'Who were you calling?' he asked, softly, his voice low but full of menace.

'A friend of mine,' she told him, feeling the pressure on her scalp increase slightly as he pulled on her hair again.

'Anyone I know?' he enquired.

'I doubt it,' she said, trying to ease her head forward to relieve the pressure as he continued to pull.

'How do you know?' he asked. 'I know a lot of people.' He held her wrist once more, pushing her hand down so that it was behind her back, allowing him to hold both her arms simultaneously. Then, still with that grin plastered across his face, he began unbuttoning the buttons of her blouse.

Tina stiffened, her eyes fixed on Harrison's face.

'So, who were you calling, sweetheart?' he wanted to know, undoing another button.

'I told you, lover, just a friend,' she explained, trying to inject a note of softness to her voice, to banish the hint of fear which hovered there.

'Male or female?' he persisted, opening her blouse and revealing her breasts. He cupped one in his hand, rubbing it hard, scraping his palm across the nipple which hardened despite her anxiety.

Tina swallowed hard and pushed herself against Harrison, allowing him to explore her upper body more fully. She began to grind her crotch against his leg, hoping that her display of passion would distract him enough to divert him from this line of interrogation.

'It isn't important is it?' she said, feeling his erection grow more prominent.

'After what happened the other night in the restaurant you should be careful who you talk to,' he told her, still rubbing her breasts hard. In fact, his attentions were becoming a little too intense. She felt his nails rake the soft flesh of her breast and held back the whimper of pain. He left three bright red grazes just above her nipple.

'Did I hurt you?' he said softly, almost mockingly, finally releasing her arms.

She pulled away from him, quickly fastening her blouse.

'Bashful all of a sudden?' he said, watching as she brushed her hands over the material.

'We're supposed to be going out tonight aren't we?' Tina reminded him, heading for the bathroom.

Harrison crossed to the drinks cabinet and pulled out a bottle of whisky. He found a glass and poured himself a large measure.

Harrison looked towards the door of the bathroom and heard the sound of the shower sputtering into life.

'Where are we going?' Tina called.

The gang boss didn't answer, he merely glanced at the phone then back at the door.

'Frank, I said where are we going tonight?' she called again, raising her voice to make herself heard over the running water.

'Perhaps we should stay here,' he said. 'It might be safer. If somebody took one crack at me then they might try it again.'

'You can't hide, Frank. They'll think you're afraid.'

Harrison strode towards the bathroom, the drink still in his hand. He tugged back the shower curtain and gazed in at Tina who almost screamed, startled at the sudden intrusion.

'I'm not afraid,' he hissed, watching as the water coursed off her body.

She stood beneath the spray feeling suddenly frightened.

Harrison watched the water running in warm rivulets down her body, from her wet hair over her shoulders and firm breasts, across her lean, flat stomach. Through her triangle of pubic hair and down her slim legs.

They stood like that for long seconds until Harrison took a step backwards to sit on the stool in one corner of the large bathroom.

Tina reached forward to pull the shower curtain across again.

'Leave it,' snapped Harrison, his eyes still fixed on her. 'Finish your shower.' That infernal grin was beginning to form on his face once more.

Tina finished washing hurriedly and stepped from the

shower, drying herself with a towel as Harrison watched.

'I was thinking about you too,' he said, swigging from the glass of whisky. 'You could have been killed when that bomb went off. I don't want that happening again.'

Tina dried her hair then wrapped the big bath towel around her. She padded into the bedroom and sat down at her dressing table, gazing at her reflection in the mirror, glancing towards the bathroom door every so often. Harrison emerged a moment later, a cigarette jammed between his lips, the tumbler still gripped in one large hand. Tina pulled a pair of curling tongs from a drawer and set them on one side to heat up.

Harrison moved to within a couple of feet of her, gazing hypnotically at her, finally catching her eye in the reflection in the glass.

'I think it'd be better if we stayed here tonight,' he said, moving closer, snaking one hand into the damp mass of her hair. 'Just to be on the safe side.'

She felt him touching the back of her neck with his free hand then he put the whisky glass down and began massaging her shoulders. She reached up to touch his hands as his grip grew a little too strong. Again the briefest glimmer of fear flickered across her eyes.

She heard his breathing become harsher as he rubbed and stroked her neck more frenziedly, one of his hands finally sliding forward beneath the towel to grip her right breast. He squeezed hard and she groaned as she felt his nails scratch her once more in that most delicate place. He pulled the towel free, exposing her nakedness, his excitement now almost uncontrollable. She felt his penis straining against his trousers, pressing into her back.

And still he held her firm by the back of the neck as a dog might hold a rabbit.

Tina squirmed as she saw and felt his thick fingers slither

round to her throat where he now stroked and squeezed.

'I wish you'd tell me who you were talking to on the phone, sweetheart,' he crooned, his hand tightening on her throat, his other hand kneading her breast roughly. 'We shouldn't have secrets from each other you know.' He released her breast and began fumbling with the zip of his trousers, finally pulling out his swollen organ which he rubbed against her smooth back. She felt the clear fluid oozing from the head, smearing her skin and she did her best to hide her disgust, more concerned about the force with which he was holding her neck. His fingers dug more deeply into her flesh.

'Tell me who it was,' he whispered, turning her round so that her face was level with his groin, so that she was gaping at his throbbing stiffness.

She reached forward and eased his trousers and underpants over his hips, closing her right hand over his shaft, feeling his strong hand pushing her towards his rampant member.

'Who were you talking to?' he rasped, the softness all but gone from his voice.

'I told you, a friend,' she insisted.

He gripped her by the hair and dragged her up so that she was looking into his face. His eyes blazed wildly.

Tina yelped in pain and tried to struggle free of his grip but he merely twisted her long hair around his fist until she feared the golden strands would be torn from her scalp.

'I know you'd never lie to me,' he said, breathing whisky fumes in her face.

'Frank, for God's sake . . .' she whimpered, the pain now forcing tears from her eyes. She beat at his chest, aware still of his erection throbbing against her.

'You wouldn't lie to me, would you?' he whispered venomously.

'No,' she blurted, tears now running down her cheeks.

He reached for the curling tongs, now almost unbearably hot. He could feel the searing heat as he gripped them, bringing them close to her face.

'Frank, please . . .' The words trailed off as he jerked her head back savagely.

He moved the blistering hot tongs closer to her face and she tried to wrench her head to one side to escape the heat.

'We have to trust each other,' he said, moving the tongs away from her face, further down her body. She felt the heat close to her shoulder then her breast.

Tina was on the verge of screaming. Her breath came in racking sobs and although she tried to speak her throat was dry and constricted.

He passed the tongs close to her nipple. Unbearably close. The swollen bud contracted as the overheated tool missed it by a fraction of an inch.

'I love you,' he said flatly, parting her legs with his knee.

She felt the heat of the tongs between her legs, the searing warmth close to her thighs. Then, with renewed terror, she felt the scorching hotness moving near to her vagina. It hovered there like some blazing penis, held by Harrison's unwavering hand.

'You know I love you, don't you?' he said, glaring at her. 'Don't you?'

She tried to nod her head but his powerful hold on her hair prevented that simple gesture. She was only aware of the blistering heat so close to her pubic mound.

'You wouldn't ever try to leave me would you?' he continued. 'We need each other, especially now.' His own voice was low, thick and mucoid.

He smiled.

'We belong together. I want everyone to know that.'

It was only a fraction of a second.

Less than the time it takes to blink.

He pressed the tongs against her left thigh, close to the soft curls of her pubic hair.

Tina screamed, both from the sudden excruciating pain and from the shock of being released.

Harrison pushed her towards the bed where she lay on her back, unconsciousness slipping over her, the burn on her inner thigh already glistening red. Throbbing as it swelled into a blister the size of a finger-nail.

Harrison was upon her immediately, his face between her legs, lapping at the burn as a cat would lap at milk.

Tina sobbed as she felt his tongue flicking at the red, swollen area. He finally raised his head, that insane grin still on his face.

'My mark,' he said, chuckling. 'That means you're mine. It's important that everyone knows you're mine. We need each other. We need to trust each other.'

He slid between her legs, his penis nudging against her cleft.

'Love me,' he whispered and drove into her.

The room was silent but for the ticking of the clock and Frank Harrison's low grunting as he slept.

Tina lay on her back, gazing up at the ceiling, listening to Harrison's rasping snores.

She finally pulled herself out of bed, wincing as she felt a stab of pain between her legs. Tentatively, she pressed her fingertips to the small blister which had formed on her inner thigh, hissing as she touched the pustule a little too hard. She crossed to the bathroom door, tugged the light cord and fumbled in the medicine cabinet for the bottle of TCP. Soaking a piece of cotton wool she dabbed at the blister, wincing as she did so.

Tina glanced back at the sleeping form of Harrison,

remembering how he had burned her, how he had used her body. She gritted her teeth, the pain she was feeling slowly replaced by anger.

There was a safety razor in the cabinet, along with some spare blades.

Blades.

She looked at them, then back at Harrison who had rolled on to his back, his mouth open.

How easy it would be, she thought. How easy to take one of the blades and slit his throat.

He grunted and began snoring even more loudly.

She looked at the razor blades again.

So easy.

No, she told herself. Not now.

Not yet.

She pulled the cord, plunging the room back into darkness.

There would be another time, Tina thought.

Soon.

Twelve

The door from the cells swung open and two uniformed policemen walked briskly through into Number One court.

Behind them came Jonathan Crawford.

Those occupants of the public gallery turned, as one, to gaze at the young man who had just entered the room.

Mr Thomas Briggs QC gave the defendent only a cursory glance.

Crawford took the stand with all the nonchalance of a superstar making another comeback, enjoying the attention which had been lavished upon him. The stories about him and the murders he'd committed (although Crawford preferred to think of them as executions) still occupied the front pages of most newspapers. It was a notoriety which he found pleasing. The packed public gallery was further proof of the continued interest which his exploits aroused. He regarded the rows of faces impassively, almost disdainfully.

Jonathan Crawford was in his twenty-fifth year. A tall, gangling youth but one who displayed no signs of the clumsiness or awkwardness of some who, like he, approached almost six feet four in height. He was on the thin side of lean, the prison overalls which he wore were woefully short in the sleeves, the trousers too large. His dark hair reached as far as his collar which was open, allowing room for his overly-large Adam's apple. He regarded the occupants of the court from beneath heavy eyebrows and a lined forehead. His eyes sparkled mischievously, darting back and forth with something akin to excited expectation.

Yes, he was enjoying this fleeting infamy, revelling in the attention.

It had not always been like that.

For most of his life he had been treated as a nonentity. Scorned. Humiliated.

The worst time had been at school and for that particular period of suffering he blamed his parents.

His father had worked all the hours God sent in order to send his son to a public school. It wasn't for Crawford's own good, it was just a further indication of his father's idiotic preoccupation with respectability. It had reached a point where holidays abroad, Rotary Club lunches, two cars in the driveway and membership of the Conservative Party were not sufficient. To complete the transition from working to middle class, Crawford's father had decided his son must attend public school. Then university. Then what? To Jonathan Crawford it had seemed as if his future was still to be decided. His parents hadn't yet made up their minds how best to show him off. A position in the firm where his father worked, perhaps? Time would tell.

Time and public education.

He'd been ten when they'd packed him off to the school.

Crawford had been a loner, trying to keep himself to himself. But, as is the way with children, he had not been allowed the haven of privacy.

On the games field he was idle, not willing to extend himself in rugby matches, not prepared to submit to endless poundings around a running track. To his peers he appeared to be totally useless. It was only a matter of time before they found that he himself could provide them with a different sort of sport.

They would hide his clothes, take them from the dormitory. They would spit in his food. Beat him.

Waiting for signs of retaliation which never came.

Not until he was fifteen.

The other boy's name had been Barnes.

One of the many who had subjected Crawford to so much humiliation over the years.

It was in the chemistry lab that Crawford had finally chosen to hit back. It had been no sudden explosion of pent up rage, merely the calm retribution which he'd been nurturing for so long. He'd walked, smiling, towards Barnes who had been taunting him throughout the lesson, cheered by the other boys.

Crawford could still remember how serene and relaxed he'd felt as he'd approached Barnes.

How calm he'd been as he'd picked up the bottle of concentrated nitric acid.

How controlled his actions had been as he'd hurled the corrosive liquid into Barnes' face.

Then, how loudly the boy had screamed as the acid had eaten away his flesh.

How two of the other boys had vomited, others had passed out.

Barnes had screamed so loudly; Crawford had merely smiled down at the festering, pus-oozing wreck which had once been a face.

He'd been lucky to escape criminal charges for that particular assault. Expulsion had brought the full wrath of his parents down on him.

At sixteen he was walking the streets of London, scrounging food from snack bars and restaurants, finally finding work in a book shop in Dean Street. There was a small flat above the shop which he was allowed to use in return for half his wages. The stock was kept up there too. Piles of magazines which catered for all tastes. Paedophilia. Sadism. Masochism. Fetishism. Crawford had found that there was plenty of money to be made selling the stuff in some of the pubs he visited. He usually went out at night with a carrier bag full of it. Always returning with pockets bulging.

Until he returned one night to find the owner of the shop waiting for him.

He'd left that night, his money gone, his back scarred in three places with a Stanley knife as a 'reminder'.

Shortly after that he met Michael Grant.

Thoughts of Grant brought him back to his present situation and he seemed to break free of his trance-like state, looking coldly at Briggs as the counsel for the prosecution approached the dock. The QC by-passed him and approached the bench instead, muttering conspiratorially with Justice Valentine.

Crawford ignored the whisperings and returned to his thoughts.

Michael Grant had been a year younger than him when they'd met but immediately Crawford had found he had a curious control over both his younger companion and the girl who was with him. A raven-haired creature in her late teens who he came to know as Sally Reese.

It was she who had helped Crawford in the killings for which he was now on trial.

Briggs and Valentine finished their conversation and the QC returned to his desk where his clerks had laid out reams of notes. Finally Briggs picked up a wad of papers and cleared his throat. A hush fell over the courtroom as Crawford was called to the witness box.

He ambled over to it, head held high, still glancing around at the curious watchers who eyed him with emotions ranging from curiosity to hatred.

With the preliminary speeches over, Briggs began flicking through his notes.

'You have already told the jury about the murders of Mrs Laura Donaldson and her daughters, Melissa and Felicity. Of how the victims were selected and then butchered.' The QC turned to the jury but his words were directed at Crawford. 'You admitted that Mrs Donaldson was still alive when you cut off her breasts, having already stabbed her sixteen times.'

'I like to be thorough,' said Crawford flatly.

'So it would appear,' rasped Briggs. 'As indeed you were in the murders of Mr and Mrs Harold Trent.' Again the counsel for the prosecution turned towards the jury. 'Mr Trent, as you may know, was a television and stage performer, a comedian.'

'He wasn't very funny *that* night,' Crawford intoned.

'Silence,' Justice Valentine snapped.

'You mean the night you broke into his house and murdered him and his wife?' Briggs said challengingly. 'The night you stabbed Mr Trent to death while his wife watched. Mrs Trent, I believe, was tied to a chair and forced to watch while her husband was butchered in the most obscene manner. She was then killed in a similar fashion.'

'Yes,' said Crawford unflinchingly.

'Mr Trent was stabbed in the face, throat and chest with a sheath knife,' Briggs explained, handing a double-edged blade to the foreman of the jury. The weapon was wrapped in a plastic bag and tagged with an exhibit label. The jury passed it around as if they were playing some bizarre variation of pass the parcel, one of them stopping to inspect the dried blood which still caked the shaft of the blade.

'As you have heard in the police coroner's earlier testimony,' Briggs continued, 'Mr Trent was dead by the time he received the fourth wound. The fatal wound having been one which severed his left carotid artery. And yet, even though it was apparent that death had occurred, you,' the QC spun round to face Crawford, 'you stabbed him another eight times. Correct?'

'I didn't carry a scorecard but I'll take your word for it,' Crawford replied condescendingly.

'And then severed his penis. Correct?'

'Correct.'

'Having done that you then jammed the severed penis into Mr Trent's mouth.'

85

'Correct.'

'What was *Mrs* Trent's reaction to seeing her husband so vilely mutilated?'

'She wouldn't stop screaming at first so I hit her a couple of times and then gagged her. When I stuck the knife into her old man's eye she passed out,' Crawford explained, chuckling. 'So I revived her, slapped her face, threw some water at her. It seemed to do the trick. She was watching when I cut his penis off. In fact she vomited.'

'And, due to the gag, almost choked on her own vomit.'

Crawford shrugged.

'She was going to die anyway,' he said.

'You'd already decided?'

'I'd decided before I got to the house that night, obviously.'

'Obviously,' Briggs echoed. 'And after you'd removed the gag?'

'I cut her throat.'

'Come now, Mr Crawford, you did much more than that. Seven separate wounds were counted on the neck and the face including the one which severed Mrs Trent's head.'

The courtroom erupted in a frenzy of shouts and chatter which even the banging of Valentine's gavel had trouble stilling. Through the chorus of curses and conversation Crawford and Briggs stared at each other, neither breaking the other's stare.

The stenographer swallowed hard and wiped his forehead, glancing first at the QC and then at Crawford as if the two men were about to attack each other. They contented themselves with glaring at one another.

Briggs pulled photos from one of his files and passed them to the jury. The nine men and three women handed the pictures back and forth with distaste, as if none wanted to hold the pictorial record of Crawford's atrocities for too long.

One of the women in the back row of jurors swallowed hard and wiped a hand across her face, watching as the black and white photos were handed down the row towards her.

'And after Mrs Trent's head had been cut off, what then?' Briggs continued.

'What do you mean, "what then"?' asked Crawford haughtily.

'Some slogans were written on the walls of the sitting room where the couple were murdered. Correct?'

'Correct.'

'In blood you wrote "Rich cunts" and "Death to the rich".'

'That's right.'

'Death to the rich is your sworn intention anyway, Mr Crawford, as we've heard previously, is it not?'

'Yes it is. You don't understand that this is a fucking war do you?' said Crawford, his voice still controlled. But now, he was looking around the courtroom, not merely at Briggs. Crawford was addressing his audience. 'I despise the rich and everything they stand for. I've seen wealth, I've seen those with money and they disgusted me.'

'So you decided to embark on a campaign of ritual murder to gratify your warped ideas of revenge,' Briggs stated flatly.

'Those people had no right to live.'

'So you murdered them and mutilated their bodies.'

The woman juror held the photos before her, her hands quivering. She felt her stomach contract, her head began to spin.

'They weren't murdered,' Crawford declared. 'In a war there are no murders. They were executed.'

'So, do you take offence at being called a murderer? Would another name make your crimes more acceptable?' Briggs demanded.

With a low moan the woman in the jury box passed out.

As two policemen rushed to her aid, Crawford smiled at the counsel for the prosecution.

'Yes, I can think of a more apt name,' he said.

'Such as?'

'An assassin.'

Thirteen

'So nobody's heard anything?'

Frank Harrison took a long drag on his cigarette.

'That's bollocks. Somebody, somewhere knows what's going on. I told you lot I wanted them found.'

He walked slowly across the large gaming room of the casino, pausing at one of the roulette tables. The gang boss spun the wheel, watching as it slowly twisted before coming to a halt once more. Apart from himself and the men who worked for him, the place was empty. The large antique clock on the far wall showed 9.35 a.m. The casino was for night people. It came alive after dark. Situated in the centre of Mayfair, it was the most successful of the clubs which Harrison owned. He'd bought it five years earlier and seen it grow both in size and, more importantly, in revenue. Huge chandeliers hung from the ceilings and thick red carpet gave the place a feeling of warmth and sumptuousness. The expensive atmosphere was complemented further by several costly paintings decorating the walls – including two original Goyas which he paid a fortune for in an attempt to prove that he possessed at least some cultural sense. There were some who might have questioned the presence of the Spanish artist's '*The Executions of the 3rd May 1808*' in such supposedly carefree surroundings but that particular canvas was a copy anyway.

Harrison blew out a long stream of smoke, rested both hands on the roulette table and faced his men.

There were about a dozen of them. Varying ages and builds. The youngest was twenty-three, the oldest approaching fifty. There were, naturally, many more in his employ, but those he'd gathered at the casino were the strong arm of his organization.

Those who, if necessary, would do the killing when the time came.

'You can't tell me that not one bastard out on the streets hasn't heard who's got it in for me,' the gang boss said quietly.

'We asked all the usual sources, Frank,' offered Pat Mendham, a thick set, almost brutish man who looked as if he'd been squeezed into his suit with the aid of a shoehorn.

'Then ask the *unusual* sources,' Harrison rasped.

'But nobody's heard,' Lou McIntire added. 'Or if they have, they ain't talking.'

'Then make them talk,' Harrison snarled, spitting a piece of tobacco from his mouth.

Carter watched as the gang leader strutted back and forth puffing agitatedly on his cigarette, his eyes darting to and fro as if he were searching for something inside the room.

A particularly strong ray of sunlight poked golden fingers through one of the windows, bouncing off the crystal chandelier. The light broke up into dozens of coloured beams, as if soft lasers had suddenly burst from it. But, seconds later, the sun was covered by a thick bank of cloud. The colours vanished, seemingly absorbed into the walls.

'First someone tries to kill me,' Harrison began. 'Then two of my betting shops are smashed up and somebody turns one of my pubs over. Don't try to tell me that's a coincidence and don't try to tell me nobody knows what's going on.'

'Who's big enough to have a go at you?' Martin McAuslan wanted to know, his harsh Scots accent cutting through the air.

'There's a few,' Harrison told him. 'That fucking wop, Barbieri, he's been after a few more strip joints up West for a while now. I heard that some of my girls are getting hassled. It might be him.'

'Barbieri's a wanker,' said Damien Drake dismissively, as if his character reference would pacify Harrison.

'I heard he had links with the Mafia,' Billy Weston interjected. Weston was rarely called by his surname but known more readily to his companions as Billy Stripes because of the three razor scars which crossed his face from hairline to chin.

'If every wop in London had links with the Mafia then Al Pacino would be prime minister,' Harrison said.

A chorus of laughter echoed around the room but was rapidly silenced by the wild look in the gang boss's eyes.

'The Mafia haven't got anything to do with this and the closest fucking Barbieri's come to them is watching "The Godfather" on telly,' he hissed.

'What about Cleary?' Joe Duggan offered, his head twitching uncontrollably as it tended to do when he was nervous.

'Could be,' Harrison said. 'The scouse bastard's expanding. He's moving into porn in a big way. I want them all checked out. Barbieri, Cleary, that big fucking mick, Sullivan, and Hayes.'

'What, good old Eugene?' chuckled Mendham, planting one hand on his hip and raising his voice to a higher pitch.

The other men laughed.

Harrison didn't see the funny side.

'I'm glad you lot think it's amusing,' he snapped. 'But just remember where you were less than a week ago. Yeah, at Jim Carter's funeral. Somebody blew his fucking head off, somebody who wanted me dead in case you've forgotten. Let's see you laugh when you've got a .38 stuck up *your* arse.'

'But why would any of the others risk starting a gang war, Frank?' asked Mendham. 'It's not going to do any of them any good. It's not good business. If anybody starts shooting then the police will be all over us like a ton of hot bricks.'

'I don't care about that,' Harrison said. 'If one of those bastards wants a war then he can have it.'

Carter eyed his boss suspiciously. There were murmurs of apprehension from some of the other men too.

'It's been quiet for over two years now,' said McAuslan. 'The last thing we want is a war.'

'Don't tell me what we need,' roared Harrison, his face turning crimson with rage. 'If you haven't got the bottle for what's coming then fuck off. That goes for any of the rest of you too. If you want out then go now.'

'You're talking as if a war had already started, Frank,' Carter interjected.

'Ray, I thought you more than anyone would have agreed with me. Your brother's dead. You were almost killed. Don't tell me you're going to go soft on me too.'

'Fuck it,' said Drake flatly. 'If it's war they want . . .'

Carter interrupted him.

'This is crazy,' he said, looking first Harrison and then at the other men. 'All right, so someone had a go at Frank. He's right, I should want revenge for what happened to Jim more than anyone but that's not going to bring him back is it?'

'They killed one of ours. We should kill one of theirs,' Joe Duggan said, his head twitching madly.

'We don't even know who killed Jim,' shouted Pat

Mendham. 'What are we supposed to do, wipe out everyone else and just hope that we get the right one?'

'Pat's right,' echoed Carter. 'This isn't fucking New York.'

'I wonder what Jim would have said if he'd known his brother was going to turn yellow,' hissed Drake.

'You bastard,' snarled Carter and lunged at the other man.

Restraining hands grabbed him but, even so, he managed to land a powerful right cross on Drake's jaw.

The taller man fell backwards, crashing into the wall. He touched his bottom lip, seeing blood on his fingertips. As he moved forward to retaliate he was grabbed and held still.

'Stop,' bellowed Harrison. 'I don't pay you to kick the shit out of each other.'

Both men were released, Drake dabbing at his split lip with a handkerchief. Carter glared at him for interminable seconds, finally turning to face Harrison once more.

'If you want to do something useful then find out who's behind all this. Find out who wrecked my betting shops and pub. Find out who killed Jim and tried to kill me. And do it quick. Before anyone else gets hurt.' He looked at Carter and Drake. 'You two, shake hands. I don't want trouble in my own firm.'

Carter regarded Drake malevolently, watching as the other man continued to wipe blood from his lip.

'You heard me,' Harrison insisted.

Drake took a step forward, reluctantly extending his right hand.

Carter hesitated then took it, squeezing it in an iron-hard grip.

They finally parted, both turning back to face Harrison.

'All right. For now we wait,' he said. 'We wait and see what happens but I'll tell you this, if the time comes for war then we'll be ready. I'm not having some fucking wop or

92

scouse or bloody mick walking all over me.' His breath was coming in short gasps. 'It took me a long time to build what I've got and I'm not giving it up. I'm certainly not giving it up without a fight. And if anyone wants what I've got then they're going to have to take it by force. And I'll bury any fucker who comes after *me*.'

Fourteen

The place stank of urine as usual.

The dirty tiles were puddled with the substance and close to one of the ticket machines lay a pool of vomit. From the smell rising from it, Adam Giles guessed that it was fresh.

A uniformed policeman was talking to a drunk who had wet himself, the dark stain spreading across the front of his trousers even as he spoke, making exaggerated gestures with his hands. Finally the policeman took him by the arm and led him away. Adam heard a stream of abuse as the drunk was escorted from the underground cavern.

Late night travellers passed the scenes of filth and degradation with scarcely a second glance.

It was business as usual in Piccadilly Circus tube station.

And business was what Adam was looking for.

He'd had a good night so far, nearly one hundred and fifty notes were stuffed into the pockets of his jeans and his leather jacket. He'd managed to find more than enough willing punters tonight. It wasn't always like that. Especially since the AIDS scare, business had slowed down but, nevertheless, there were always customers to be found if you looked hard enough. Adam had been working the area around Piccadilly for the last three months and he knew where to look.

At nineteen he was tall and thin, his face pock-marked, his lips swollen, almost repulsively large. He thought they were one of his best features and he glanced at his reflection in the glass of a ticket window as he passed. The man inside saw him and looked away swiftly. Adam smiled to himself. He had been a customer on more than one occasion. Fifteen quid for a blow job and the ticket seller was more than happy. Most of the punters wanted blow jobs now. They were frightened of AIDS too. Adam was frightened but he had to make a living so he continued playing the game of sexual Russian Roulette, sometimes pulling in up to three hundred pounds a week.

Of course there were others working his patch. Many others and some had resented his intrusion. During his first week he'd been beaten up by two older youths, one of his fingers broken and two front teeth chipped. But it hadn't deterred him. He had sworn from the beginning that, once he had a thousand pounds saved, he'd give up the racket. But he seemed to fritter his money away and the time when he'd be able to leave this particular way of life behind seemed a long way off.

His parents never asked him where he went at night. He'd told them he had a cleaning job in one of the West End's top hotels and they didn't ask questions. He gave his mother fifty pounds a week and lent his father enough to keep him in drink, so they both kept quiet. It probably wouldn't have bothered them if they *had* known how he spent the hours of darkness but, for now, he had chosen to live out the charade.

As he strode through the underground station towards one of the exits he decided that it was time he made his way home, back to Leytonstone. He was carrying too much cash. If one of the other rent boys should decide to have a go at him then he had too much to lose.

It was as he was approaching the exit that he noticed the man standing at the foot of the staircase.

Adam glanced at him, at the dust flecked overcoat, the hat pulled down tightly over his head, the scarf wrapped around his face so that only his eyes showed.

The man caught Adam's eye as he passed, his head turning only fractionally to follow the path the youth was taking.

Adam was half-way up the stairs when he glanced back.

The man was staring up at him.

However, as Adam saw him looking he ducked back out of sight. The youth smiled and turned, heading back down the stairs. Well, maybe just one more job before he went home. He reached the bottom and walked past the man once again, smiling at him this time.

The man remained motionless, his eyes never leaving the youth.

Adam pulled a stick of chewing gum from his pocket, careful not to dislodge a bundle of ten pound notes, and pushed it into his mouth. Then he walked back towards the man in the dusty overcoat and smiled up at him.

'You looking for someone?' he asked.

The man nodded slowly and Adam took the chance to run appraising eyes over him, over that faded overcoat, the hat and the scarf which was wrapped so tightly around his face. What hair he possessed was swept up beneath the hat. His hands were dug deep into the pockets of his coat.

'I don't do business here,' Adam told him. 'Have you got a hotel room or a car where we can go?'

The man nodded once more and turned and walked away towards the exit steps. Adam scuttled along beside him. As they reached the top of the stairs he thought he detected a strange odour, like bad meat, but it faded as a gust of cold wind swept over him.

Adam was about to speak when the man pulled one hand from his pocket and signalled to someone across the street.

His hand, Adam noticed, was encased in a glove.

A Datsun glided across towards them, the driver hidden by the gloom within the vehicle. He reached over and pushed open the back door.

Adam hesitated.

'If there's two of you it's going to cost you more,' he said.

The man in the hat merely held the door open for him and, shrugging his shoulders, Adam slid into the car, scooting across the back seat. His companion clambered in beside him, slammed the door and the car moved away.

The driver did not turn.

The smell which Adam had noticed earlier now seemed particularly powerful and he wound the window down slightly, happy to breathe the traffic fumes. Happy to breathe anything other than the rancid air which filled the car.

The man in the overcoat was gazing straight ahead, as if Adam weren't even in the car.

Perhaps he was nervous, the youth surmised.

'Look, mate, what do you want?' he asked. 'If you've got the money you can have what you like. Wank, suck or anything else. That's what's on the menu.' He chuckled. 'A wank will cost you a fiver, a blow job fifteen, anything else the price varies.'

The man turned in his seat and looked at Adam who, again, recoiled from the vile stench. He glanced quickly at the driver and saw that he too had a scarf wrapped around his face and most of the back of his head. The youth felt slightly uneasy. He also felt sick. The smell was growing stronger by the second, filling his lungs, forcing him to wind the window down to its lowest extent.

'Shall we just get on with whatever you want?' he said irritably.

The man began to unbutton his coat and Adam smiled. At last, he was beginning to lose patience with all this mucking about. He placed one hand on the man's thigh.

The gloved hand shot forward with the speed of a bullet, the fingers fastening around Adam's throat, pulling him forward.

He struggled against the vice-like grip, beating at the hand which held him.

'Get off me you bastard . . .' he hissed, fighting for breath, seeing that the man was slowly unravelling his scarf to reveal his features.

It was like unwrapping an open wound.

Adam felt the bile fighting its way up his throat as he caught sight of the man's features.

Where there should have been a mouth there was just a gaping hole which seemed to stretch from the remains of the nose to the point of the chin. It was surrounded by wisps of grey hair and strands of rotting skin which hung down like obscene raffia curtains over the gaping maw. The lips were little more than pieces of shrivelled flesh which slid back to expel a blast of air so foul Adam almost passed out.

And, from the centre of that reeking hole, a tongue emerged. Blackened and covered by thick yellow sputum which dripped like mouldering pus, it writhed like a bloated worm with a life of its own, twisting and turning in that putrescent gap, flicking in and out.

The gloved hand squeezed Adam's throat more tightly and, despite himself, he opened his mouth.

The intended scream of revulsion was smothered as the tumefied tongue filled his mouth and his body bucked and jerked uncontrollably as he felt the cold appendage tracing patterns inside his mouth, stirring the warm wetness there, ignoring the traces of vomit which had leaked up from his heaving belly. The tongue plunged deeper until it seemed to caress the back of his throat and then the gullet itself.

Locked together in an obscene french kiss, the two figures on the back seat were almost invisible in the gloom.

The driver glanced into the rear view mirror and saw the tableau. Saw that Adam's body had stopped jerking.

'Don't damage the flesh,' he said softly, watching as the youth's lifeless body slid to the floor of the car.

On the back seat his companion nodded and hauled the dead boy upright once more.

The car drove away.

Fifteen

The hinges of the attaché case creaked slightly as it was opened.

The smell of leather mingled with the smell of money.

Nestling in the bottom of the case, in bundles of twenty and fifty pound notes, was close to fifty thousand pounds.

Malcolm Dome glanced indifferently at the money for a moment then closed the case and locked it, slipping it down beside his feet.

Beside him, Steve Joule guided the Astra through the traffic, his eyes fixed on the other cars which clogged the night-shrouded streets. The clock on the dashboard glowed green and Joule looked at it, seeing that it was almost 10.30.

They had one more call to make before they were finished for the night. He saw a gap in the traffic and stepped on the accelerator, narrowly avoiding a Metro which was attempting to turn out of a junction. The driver hit his hooter but Joule ignored him and guided the car into a gap further down the queue of traffic.

Saturday night in London was always busy but tonight seemed to be worse than usual. Usually their calls around Frank Harrison's clubs took them less than two hours. They started their rounds at about seven in the evening and by nine they were back at the Mayfair casino where the cash was counted and then taken to be banked. They began with a different club every week, never using the same routine to move from place to place. Both men had worked in the underworld long enough to know that routine was a dangerous thing.

Dome had been employed by Harrison for six years, Joule a few months longer. Both men had served short terms in prison, Dome for assault, Joule for carrying a concealed weapon (something which he was doing at present) but, upon release, they had found work with Harrison as money collectors. They knew that it was a job which required trust on Harrison's part but also one which, should the takings be light, might well result in them learning to walk with sticks. But Harrison paid well and neither had been tempted to dip into the vast sums of money which the boss's clubs yielded.

As they reached Piccadilly Circus the traffic became even more perilous but Joule sped across the thoroughfare and down Piccadilly itself, past Fortnum and Mason until he came to Duke Street. He swung the car into the turn-off, cutting across the path of a bus.

Neither he nor Dome noticed the Sierra which had been following them since they left the club in Holborn.

Joule slowed down, looking for the yard at the back of the

99

club. He spotted the entrance and swung the Astra in, narrowly missing two pedestrians who had been trying to cross.

The Sierra parked a few yards further down the street on the opposite side of the road.

Waiting.

'I won't be long,' said Dome, picking up the attaché case and hauling himself out of the car.

Joule nodded, lit up a cigarette and watched as his companion headed for the set of metal steps at the rear of the building.

The lower floor was a restaurant, also owned by Harrison, but the top floor was an unlicensed gaming club and it was from there they were to make their last pick-up of the night. Then it was back to Mayfair.

From where he sat, Joule could smell the delicious aromas coming from the kitchen. He climbed out of the car and leant against the side of the vehicle to drink in the delightful smells which wafted to him on the breeze.

High brick walls curtained the yard from the buildings on either side and the car was barely narrow enough to fit. A cat rummaged hopefully amongst the half dozen dustbins outside the kitchen's rear entrance. Joule glanced at his watch then looked up at the top of the metal steps towards the doorway that led into the club. The doorway through which his companion had disappeared a moment before.

The Sierra passed slowly, coming to a halt directly opposite the Astra which looked as if it had been jammed into the small yard.

Joule glanced round and looked at it but paid it no heed, content instead to clamber back inside the Astra. He fumbled under the seat and pulled out a newspaper, flicking disinterestedly through it. He paused at a photo of a half-naked girl and murmured 'Filth' under his breath. He folded the paper and stuck it back under the seat.

The cat was still scrambling about amongst the bins and Joule watched in amusement as the animal tried to tip one of the lids off. It eventually succeeded and the top crashed to the ground with a loud clang, frightening the cat which promptly lost its footing and fell inside. Joule chuckled, not noticing that Dome was emerging from the entrance at the top of the stairs.

He also failed to notice that the Sierra was swinging across the street towards the yard.

Dome raised the case and nodded in silent affirmation that the night's work was complete.

He was half-way down the stairs when the Sierra came hurtling across the road and slammed into the back of the Astra.

Joule felt his head snap forward and he was momentarily stunned as his forehead connected sharply with the windscreen.

The impact of the two cars crashing together shunted the Astra towards the rear of the building and sent it smashing into the row of dustbins.

The cat, still trapped inside one of them, yowled in fear and surprise.

Joule spun round to see men clambering from the Sierra. Two of them.

Dome, momentarily frozen on the metal steps, was the first to see that they carried guns.

Should he try to help his companion or run back up the steps towards the club?

He was still trying to decide when a burst of automatic fire struck the wall beside him. The staccato rattle of a sub-machine gun filled the night as one of the two men from the Sierra tightened his finger around the trigger of an Uzi. The 9mm slugs, travelling at a speed in excess of 1,280 feet a second, spattered the stonework and ricocheted off the metal steps with a high pitched scream.

Bright, blinding muzzle flashes lit the night, turning the yard into a stroboscopic nightmare.

Dome, still clutching the attaché case, finally turned and ran back up the stairs. The next burst caught him in the legs, one of the bullets scything through his thigh, another blasting away one testicle. He screamed in agony and fell forward, rolling over, pulling the .38 from his shoulder holster but finding that his hands were trembling badly both from the intense pain and from fear. His lower body was on fire, searing agony tearing through his legs and groin. He felt blood pouring from the wounds, smelt the rich coppery odour in his nostrils.

Joule was trying to get out of the car, trying to force open the buckled driver's door but he found that it was wedged up against the toppled dustbins.

There was a thunderous blast and the rear window was blown in, showering him with glass which cut his face. He pulled the Beretta from his belt and fired back at the attackers, forced to duck down again as a blast from the Uzi drilled across the stricken vehicle. The driver's seat was riddled with bullets, two of them erupting with sufficient force to smash Joule's left radial bone. A portion of the shattered bone tore through his flesh and he screamed in pain, the pistol dropping from his grasp.

He tried to duck down, to keep clear of the volley of fire which was drawing dotted lines of death across the yard.

Up on the steps, Dome was hauling himself agonisingly towards the door of the club.

It was a shotgun blast which caught him.

The fearful impact exploded the attaché case which he still held beside him and then powered into his side, smashing three ribs and rupturing a lung. He felt the breath torn from him and blood suddenly filled his mouth.

The second blast caught him squarely in the face, slamming his head back against the wall. His features were obliterated by the powerful discharge. The concentrated buckshot stove in his forehead and pulped his eyes before pulverizing the bones at the top of his skull. A huge portion of scalp was blown away, sticky gobs of brain splattering the wall behind him.

Joule decided his only chance was to try and ram the Sierra, to push it back into the road. He started the engine and stepped hard on the accelerator but, before he could complete his desperate manoeuvre, two 9mm bullets hit him in the back, one exploding through his chest, punching an exit hole large enough to hold two hands. Blood and portions of lung spattered the windscreen and, as blood jetted from the gaping wound, he slumped over the wheel.

The Astra shot forward, crashing into the back of the kitchen, the front of the car folding up like a concertina. The steering wheel came back at Joule like a thick javelin, crushing his already shredded chest, cracking bone like matchwood.

Pinned in the devastated car he tried to scream but blood filled his throat.

The two men were running back towards the Sierra which was reversing out into the road, the driver ignoring the curses of passing motorists.

The two men leapt in and the driver put his foot down hard on the accelerator but, as the car sped away, another burst of fire from the sub-machine gun hit the Astra, rupturing the petrol tank.

The car disappeared beneath a searing ball of orange and yellow flame.

Part of the roof was torn off and sent spiralling into the air by the force of the blast. Petrol sprayed from the flaming tank like blazing ejaculate, covering the yard with a spreading puddle of fire. Thick smoke rose into the air like noxious, man-made smog.

The Sierra sped away, tyres screaming loudly as it rounded a corner and disappeared amongst the other traffic.

Money from the shotgun-blasted case wafted lazily on the warm air, some of it drifting down into the conflagration where it too was devoured by the flames.

Sixteen

Both of them were naked.

Both hung from the filthy wall of the supermarket, suspended by the nails which had been driven through their hands and wrists.

A tramp and a rent boy. The dregs of society.

Unwanted.

Unmissed.

The five figures which stood gazing at the corpses were silent, standing in a kind of mock vigil over the bodies. Bodies which now had not one single trace of skin on their faces and necks. The flesh had been expertly removed with knives, cut away with a care and precision which a surgeon would have been proud of. The muscles of Adam Giles' face glistened in the half-light, congealed blood already filling some of the gaps between tendons and gristle. His eyes were open, still wide with terror as if the last thing he'd seen had been indelibly printed on that blind orb for eternity.

The leading figure, a tall man dressed in a dark suit now faded and dirt encrusted, stepped forward and inspected the bodies more closely, prodding first at the skinless mess which had once been Adam's face then at the flayed visage of Danny Weller.

The young tramp's skin sat well on the features of the tall figure. He had smoothed it over his own putrescent face, covering the holes and the sores, hiding the cratered areas where the maggots had bred. The skin was loose around his ears and eyes but portions taken from other parts of the bodies could be used to foster the illusion of normality. And, like his companions, he could always wrap his face with a scarf.

Until the time was right.

Time.

Time seemed to have no meaning any more.

For what was time to a dead man? To him or his four companions? He smiled thinly, his own lips moving beneath the mask of living flesh that was already beginning to mould itself to the rotting musculature beneath.

They had time. Time to complete their task.

And that time was coming closer.

He looked at the two bodies hanging from the wall and nodded.

Seventeen

She had called him more than thirty minutes earlier. Now she sat on the edge of the sofa, sipping at a glass of wine and alternately looking at her solid gold Cartier watch and the large antique timepiece above the marble fireplace.

Eight-forty p.m.

Tina got to her feet and retrieved the bottle of wine, poured herself another glass and glanced out into the night.

The doorbell finally sounded and she turned and hurried to answer it.

Carter stood before her, a slight smile on his lips.

She turned away sharply from him, flicking her long blonde hair so that it fell across her shoulders and neck.

'I called Harrison more than half an hour ago,' she said.

'Is something wrong?' asked Carter, stepping inside the flat and closing the door behind him.

She still had her back to him.

'He said you wanted picking up, that you wanted to be taken to the casino. Wanted to see him.'

'I need something from him,' she said quietly, her head now bowed slightly, still facing away from Carter.

He moved closer, to within an arm's length of her.

'Tina, what's wrong?' he wanted to know.

She turned slowly, allowing him to look at her, using both hands to push her hair back.

'Jesus Christ,' he murmured as he saw the dark bruises on her throat.

She wore a loose fitting red top, the sleeves reaching her elbows but, as Carter watched, she gently pulled the sleeves up to reveal the marks on her upper arms.

'When did it happen?' he said, his voice a combination of

shock and anger.

'Two nights ago,' she told him.

'Harrison?' he enquired.

She nodded and told him about the phone conversation. Or, more to the point, its aftermath.

'He's fucking mad,' hissed Carter. 'The bastard.' He took a step forward and took her in his arms. They kissed fiercely, finally parting their lips but still clinging to each other.

'I didn't want you to know about this,' she told him. 'I would have kept it from you if I'd been able to.'

'I ought to kill him,' Carter snarled. 'It's a pity those blokes who tried to get him the other night didn't succeed. He should have had a bullet in him, not Jim.' He pulled her to him once more. 'And you want to go to him now? After what he's done to you?'

'I don't *want* to, I *need* to,' she said enigmatically.

'And what happens next time he gets mad?' Carter demanded. 'He might kill you.'

She shook her head.

'No he won't,' she assured him. 'He needs me and as long as he does then I'm safe.'

'By safe I suppose you mean he'll have to be content with knocking you about. Is that it?' He shook his head in disbelief.

'It's not only Frank I've got to worry about though, is it?' she said.

'What do you mean?'

'I heard what happened last night. The shooting of two more of his men.'

Carter sighed.

'Yeah, it's getting bad. He's talking about a gang war. Mind you, it looks like one's already started.'

'That's why I want protection,' she said. 'Frank said that

he'd have men watch my flat but that's not enough. I feel like a prisoner in here anyway, I don't want to know Frank's spies are following me everywhere I go, watching everything I do.' She pulled on her coat, pausing before they left to kiss him again passionately. 'Take me to him, Ray.'

Harrison looked up as Tina and Carter entered the room.

Pat Mendham stood up and smiled at the young woman, nodding his head in a gesture of greeting.

'What's wrong, sweetheart?' asked Harrison. Carter felt anger rising within him as he watched Harrison's exaggerated display of affection as he tenderly kissed Tina on the lips. The younger man remembered the bruises which discoloured her arms and neck.

'Can we speak alone?' she asked.

'Of course,' Harrison said and asked Carter and Mendham to wait outside. They dutifully left the room, both of them wandering down to the casino bar.

Tina stood facing Harrison for a moment then sucked in a deep breath.

'Frank, I'm worried about what's happening,' she told him. 'These shootings, what happened the other night at the restaurant. I don't feel safe.'

'I told you, I'll send a couple of men round to watch the flat . . .'

She cut him short.

'No.'

'Then what else can I do?' he wanted to know.

'Give me a gun,' she told him flatly.

Harrison was silent for a moment and then smiled, not sure whether or not he was the victim of some kind of joke.

'Frank, please,' she persisted.

'Why do you want a gun?'

'I told you, I'm scared,' she shouted. 'Is that so difficult to understand?' The tone of her voice softened abruptly. 'If you care about me as much as you say then do that for me. Please.'

Harrison shrugged, held her gaze for long seconds and then turned and crossed to a cabinet on the wall. He took a small key from his jacket pocket and unlocked it, opening the door to reveal what looked like a drinks' cabinet. However, he reached past a couple of the bottles and flicked a switch. The cabinet seemed to revolve, turning slowly to reveal a veritable arsenal of pistols. Automatics, revolvers, even a couple of light SMGs.

The gang boss reached in and pulled out a small pistol which almost disappeared in the palm of his large hand. Then he turned to Tina, the weapon held out for display.

'Take it,' he said.

She picked up the gun, surprised at its lightness and the shortness of its barrel. The pistol was less than four and a half inches long.

'It's a .25 Beretta,' Harrison told her. 'At close range it should do the trick.'

Close range, she thought, looking at Harrison with a smile on her face.

If they lay side by side in bed, she mused, still looking at the gang boss. A smile began to hover on her lips.

Yes, that would be close enough.

She dropped the gun into her handbag.

Eighteen

MADMAN GIVEN LIFE SENTENCE. MASS KILLER
INSISTS THE WAR AGAINST THE RICH WILL GO ON.

The headline screamed at them. Below it was a photo of
Jonathan Crawford being taken from the Old Bailey, surrounded by policemen.

'What does it say?' asked Jennifer Thomas who was seated
in one corner of the room.

The hurricane lamp burned in the centre of the mildewed
floor, bathing the occupants in insipid yellow light. It forced
Michael Grant to squint as he read the story which
accompanied the headline.

'Jonathan Crawford, main defendant in one of the most
sensational murder trials of the century, was sentenced to life
imprisonment today,' Grant began.

The others listened intently as he continued.

'Crawford, 25, was found guilty of five murders and sentenced with a recommendation that he spend not less than
thirty years in prison. However, the defendant was judged to
be seriously disturbed and will spend much of the sentence in
Broadmoor prison which is reserved for inmates who are
classified as criminally insane.'

'Insane?' snorted Phillip Walton. 'Does that make *us*
insane too? For believing in what Jonathan believed in.'

Grant continued reading. 'As Crawford was led away he
shouted to the court, "There'll be more deaths. This war
against the rich will go on." Crawford's co-defendant, Sally
Reese, is due to take the witness stand tomorrow to confess
her own part in the series of killings which Crawford claims
to have ordered. The Charles Manson-like figure claims also

110

to have many other followers who, he says, will continue a campaign of violence against the wealthy and the well-known. Police are still attempting to trace Crawford's associates.'

Grant folded the paper and tossed it contemptuously aside.

'Perhaps we should try to get him out of prison,' said Paul Gardner.

'Don't be ridiculous,' snapped Mark Paxton, scraping the top of a whitehead with his index finger.

'Why should we anyway?' Phillip Walton added. 'We're still here, we can carry on with the work.' He smiled broadly.

Maria Chalfont retrieved the paper from the dirt-clogged fireplace and opened it at the front page, glancing at the photo of Crawford.

'They couldn't break him,' she said, smiling. 'They still haven't won.' She touched the photograph of Crawford lovingly, aware of the moistening between her legs.

'So, who's next?' asked Walton.

'We should choose someone further away this time, perhaps south of the river,' Grant mused, regarding the array of photos and cuttings which decorated the mould-encrusted wall of the room.

'What the fuck does it matter who it is?' snarled Walton. 'They're all going to die eventually. We're not picking them in order of wealth. It doesn't matter which one dies next.'

'The police can't watch everyone,' offered Paxton, coaxing the pus from a particularly stubborn spot. He wiped it on his jeans. 'They won't have any idea who's going to be executed next.'

'There are so many to pick from,' added Jennifer Thomas, flicking at her long dark hair.

'All fucking parasites,' intoned Walton, hawking loudly. He propelled a lump of sputum towards the pictures on the wall, smiling as the sticky mucus struck the face of a large-breasted model.

'What about her?' he asked.

Grant shook his head.

'Oh come on, we might as well draw straws for it,' Walton rasped. 'Are we going to kill one of them or not?'

'The timing is important,' Grant told him. 'We should wait a day or two, until Sally's trial has begun.'

'I hope you can trust her,' said Walton challengingly.

'What do you mean?' Grant demanded.

'I mean, I hope she doesn't crack and tell the police our names.'

'Why should she do that?' asked Jennifer Thomas.

'Well, she was Grant's girlfriend wasn't she?' Walton reminded her. 'She might be missing her lover. She might have forgotten what this struggle is all about.'

'She won't betray us,' Grant replied with assurance.

'She'd better not, otherwise *I'll* kill *you*.' Walton reached for the long knife which was jammed in his belt and pointed the razor-sharp tip at Grant.

'You're welcome to try,' the other man said, his own hand gripping the handle of the machete which hung by a strap from his waistband.

'For God's sake stop bickering will you?' snapped Paul Gardner. 'We're supposed to be united in this fight, not at each other's throats.'

'He's right,' Maria Chalfont echoed.

Walton nodded and slid the knife back into his belt.

Tiring of the spots on his face and neck, Mark Paxton began picking his nose as he watched the other men challenge one another. But then, as if some silent signal had passed between them, the others rose and joined Grant, gazing at the array of photos, murmuring softly as they regarded each one. They knew most of the names. So many to choose from.

Grant pointed at one of the pictures.
The others nodded.
The choice was made.

Nineteen

The keys on the ring jangled noisily as Warden Josephine
Gregory pulled them from her belt and selected the appropriate one. The long key-chain, denoting her years of service
in Holloway, hung almost to her knees.

As she turned the key in the lock, Detective Sergeant Vic
Riley watched her, pulling a cigarette from the packet in his
jacket pocket. He was about to light it when the warden
turned and looked reproachfully at him. The DS shrugged
and slipped the Marlboro back into the box. He thought
about apologising. She made him look as if he should apolo-
gise for even *thinking* about having a fag. Her hair was pulled
back with unnecessary severity and tied in a neat bun. It
looked to Riley as if the flesh of her face had been pulled too,
so tautly stretched over the bones of her skull that her eyes
were slightly narrowed. She reminded him of every sour old
schoolmistress who'd ever rapped his knuckles with a ruler.

She strode through the door and ushered Riley through
behind her, locking the door after both had passed.

The policeman found himself in another long corridor,
flanked on both sides by steel doors. Each one three inches
thick and painted a sickly beige. Paint was peeling off them in

113

places showing rust beneath, as if the scabs had been pulled from badly healed wounds. The observation slots in most of the doors were open and, as he stood waiting for the warden to join him, he could see two or three faces pressed against the slots, peering out at this newcomer.

'Fucking screw,' one shouted.

'Bitch.'

The first voice seemed to start a chorus which echoed around them as they walked.

'Who's your boyfriend, cunt?' one called and Riley found that he was forced to suppress a smile as he caught the look of rage on Warden Gregory's face.

'Bloody cow.'

They walked on.

'Fuck off and die, you bitch.'

Their footsteps were drowned by the continual tirade of abuse.

'Another fucking copper.'

Riley never ceased to be amazed at the ferocity of Holloway's lifers. He'd been into the prison on a number of occasions and, every time, had found the women to be as menacing as any hardened male criminals he'd seen in the Scrubs or Dartmoor.

He wondered what kind of reception he'd get from Sally Reese.

She hadn't been sentenced yet but was still locked up on remand in solitary, for her own protection as much as anything. Her part in the murders of the Donaldson family, particularly the children, had marked her out as the lowest of the low amongst the criminal fraternity. In the pecking order of prison life the greatest hatred and contempt was reserved for child molesters and those who killed youngsters. Even more so in a women's prison. Had Sally Reese been kept in a cell with other women, Riley thought, she might well have been dead by now. Hence the need to keep her in solitary.

It had been more than a week since he'd last questioned her about the murders but, more particularly, about Jonathan Crawford's other followers. At first she'd been full of bluff and bravado, even threatening Riley. But he'd gradually worn her down, telling her that all she could expect after the trial was life in a twelve-foot-square cell. Such a waste for one as young as she, he'd reminded her. Riley had left the twenty-year-old to consider that future, and then he mentioned that she still might be able to get away with a lighter sentence.

If she decided she wanted to name a few names then she might only face a twelve or fifteen year sentence. It was something worth considering. And something that Riley sincerely hoped would strike a chord with her because he and the men on the case were no closer to tracking down any of Crawford's followers and none of them doubted that the insanity which he'd begun *would* continue even after his incarceration. Sally Reese might well be the key to preventing any more slayings.

If she was willing to talk.

Warden Gregory stopped at the door of a cell and reached for her bunch of keys again, sliding one into the lock.

It was as she did so that she noticed that the observation slot had been blocked with a blanket.

The warden tut-tutted.

'She's always doing that,' she told Riley. 'She says she doesn't like being spied on by us.'

The DS nodded, still watching as the key turned.

'All right, Reese,' said the warden, pushing the door open and stepping inside. 'There's someone to see you . . .'

The words seemed to trail off into a whisper and Riley pushed past the warden as he saw the colour drain from her face. He moved into the cell, his eyes widening as he saw what had transfixed the warden.

There was blood everywhere.

On the bare walls, on the floor, on the bed.

And in the centre of the crimson puddles, some of which were beginning to congeal, was Sally Reese.

Exactly how she'd managed to remove the leg from the metal frame of the bed Riley didn't know.

He couldn't begin to imagine how she'd managed to put up with the pain of trying to tug the screws free. He'd noticed that her fingertips were pulped stumps.

But, more than that, he could not conceive of how she'd succeeded in killing herself with that bed leg.

Of how she had driven it into her own stomach and ripped upwards using both hands like some vile parody of a hara-kiri death.

He tried to imagine how long it had taken her to die, her blood jetting from the wound, her entrails spilling from her riven torso like the sticky tentacles of a bloodied octopus.

Tried to understand how she could have inflicted such an agonising end upon herself.

He gazed at the body which was in a kneeling position, his eyes fixed on the length of metal which protruded from her torn stomach like a rigid steel umbilical cord.

'Get help,' he said quietly, glancing at the warden's pale face.

The woman nodded and scurried from the cell, glad to get away from the sight and smell of death.

Riley shook his head, his eyes still rivetted to the dead girl. And, this time, he did light up a cigarette.

So much for Sally Reese, he thought. He spat a piece of tobacco out and cursed under his breath.

Twenty

The girl was barely eighteen.

She was standing beside her car sipping from a can of Coke, the breeze which whipped across the forecourt stirring her long brown hair. She wore an outfit of pure white, a perfect contrast to the unnaturally deep bronze of her tan. The skirt barely covered her buttocks and allowed a glorious view of her long slim legs. Coaxed to hardness by the chill in the wind, her nipples strained darkly against the thin material of her T-shirt which was tied just above the navel, revealing another expanse of tanned flesh. She finished her drink and dropped the can into a nearby waste bin, running both hands through her mane of hair. Then she pulled open the door of the GTi, slid behind the wheel and started the engine.

The car sped off.

'Jesus, did you see that?' murmured Damien Drake, watching the car disappear into the stream of traffic on the motorway below. 'I wouldn't mind a bird like that wringing her knickers out over *my* breakfast.' He sighed wistfully.

Carter, who was filling the Audi's petrol tank, chuckled.

Lou McIntire also smiled and reached for the packet of Rothmans which lay on the parcel shelf. He stuck one in his mouth and was about to light it when he smelled the petrol and remembered where they were. He contented himself with chewing on the filter.

The service station was less than thirty miles from Colchester. Since leaving London just after dawn, they had driven for over two and a half hours.

Another thirty minutes or so and they'd be there.

Then it was a matter of waiting.

Carter tapped the nozzle of the pump against the side of the tank, careful not to waste a single drop of fuel. He re-fastened the petrol cap and headed off across the forecourt to pay.

'See if that bird in white left her sister behind,' Drake shouted after him, smiling.

Carter raised two fingers at him and walked on.

The girl *had* been beautiful and, seeing her had made him think of Tina.

And of the bruises she sported due to Harrison's attentions. The bastard would go too far one day, thought Carter.

Unless someone killed him first.

He knew that the death of the gang boss was the only way he and Tina could ever be together.

Carter paid for the petrol and wandered back to the car, slipping behind the wheel. He started the engine and guided the vehicle down the ramp, onto the slip road and finally out onto the motorway itself.

'What time did Harrison tell us to get there?' asked McIntire from the back seat.

'He didn't say a particular time,' Drake replied. 'We've got to phone him when we arrive.'

'I reckon he's fucking mad,' Carter observed. 'If this doesn't start a gang war then I don't know what will.'

'So what?' Drake said challengingly. 'It might be a good thing. Get rid of some of the bad blood.'

'Just hope that it's not yours,' Carter told him. 'Anyway, what bad blood are you talking about? There hasn't been any aggro for years.'

'Well I'm all for banging a few heads together,' Drake said. 'If somebody's trying to kill Frank then they'll take a few of us with them too.' He looked at Carter. '*You* should know. After what happened to your brother.'

'I don't need reminding,' snapped Carter.

'I still think it's weird,' Drake said, picking his teeth with the nail of his little finger. 'The geezers who had a go at

118

Frank knew exactly where to find him. Same thing when Steve and Malcolm were killed. What if they were tipped off? Frank's talking about other gangs having a crack at him, well, they might be working with one of our own blokes.' He paused for a moment, looking across at Carter who was frowning deeply. 'I reckon there could be a fucking grass in the firm.'

'That's bollocks,' McIntire said.

'Why?' Drake demanded, looking round. 'Like I said, they knew where Frank was that night. They knew where to hit Malcolm and Steve.'

'But no money was taken,' McIntire said. 'Whoever killed them wasn't after the cash. Nothing was taken.'

'I know that, you prat, that's what I'm saying. Somebody's trying to wipe out the firm, right? I reckon whoever it is could be getting tips from the inside.'

McIntire was unimpressed and went back to gazing out of the side window.

Carter sighed, turning over the possibility in his mind.

A grass. But who? He glanced across at Drake and then into the rear view mirror to watch McIntire. Could it be one of the two men with whom he shared the car? Or Pat Mendham, or Billy Stripes? They may have been promised money, maybe a cut of the takings from Harrison's concerns once the boss was removed.

Carter had learned at an early age not to trust anyone and that philosophy looked like being well-founded.

The thought suddenly struck him like a thunderbolt.

There was one person who had more reason than most for wanting Harrison dead.

Could it possibly be true?

Twenty-One

Paxton had left the house in Whitechapel over two hours ago. Now he stood gazing out over the cars parked before the massive edifice of Waterloo Station, his eyes noting number plates but, more importantly, makes of vehicle.

The car he was going to steal would have to be one which would blend in easily with London's traffic. No point stealing the bright red Manta parked close to him or the brand-new silver Porsche which he was leaning against. Cars like that would be too easy to spot.

Besides, the Porsche was too small for his needs.

He continued browsing, as if he were in a vast car showroom.

Paxton smiled as he saw what he sought.

The Range Rover was five or six years old, the paintwork scratched over one wheel arch, the tyres worn and muddy. The exhaust looked rusty but, from where he stood, Paxton could see that it was intact. He moved unhurriedly towards the vehicle, glancing briefly around him and, smiling politely at a woman who was struggling from the station with a suitcase. He finally reached the Range Rover and walked slowly past it, glancing at the driver's door. The owner could be inside the station either bidding farewell to someone or waiting for someone to arrive. Perhaps a loved one, Paxton mused. He would need to work fast.

There were quite a few people milling about around the station entrance but they paid little heed to the spotty-faced youth who leant against the side of the Range Rover.

No one saw him slip the thin piece of bent metal from his jacket pocket and wedge it between the door and its frame.

One quick twist of his wrist and the lock gave way.

He pulled the door open and clambered in, ducking down beneath the steering column, his fingers quickly but calmly prying and searching.

It took him less than a minute to strip the two wires, twist them together and start the engine. The Range Rover purred into life. Paxton let the hand brake off and reversed out of the space.

No one came running after him shouting 'Thief'. He smiled and drove on, guiding the car out into traffic, heading for Waterloo Bridge. Providing the traffic wasn't too heavy he should be back in Whitechapel in less than two hours.

Paxton glanced down at the clock on the dashboard.

3.56 p.m.

The machete felt heavy in his hand as he hefted it before him but Phillip Walton smiled as he ran one thumb along the razor-sharp cutting edge. He suddenly raised the lethal weapon, bringing it down in a wide arc, the whoosh of parting air filling the dank room.

Maria Chalfont turned as she heard the sound, gripping the sheath knife which she held firmly. It had been sharpened on both edges to inflict maximum damage. She felt excitement building up within her as she held the knife and watched Walton slashing wildly at thin air with the machete.

Paul Gardner also carried a knife. The type carried by divers, one edge wickedly sharp and curving up slightly at the end, the back edge serrated.

Jennifer Thomas carried a carving fork, the twin prongs rusty but still needle-sharp. She stood pressing the points gently against her skin, watching the indentations which they made, trying to imagine the effect on human skin and muscle when the fork was applied with force.

Crouching in one corner of the room was Michael Grant, apparently deep in thought. He held a small hatchet in his left hand and there was a long chisel jammed into his belt.

'I'm sick of waiting around here,' said Walton impatiently. 'Let's get going.' He held the machete close to his face, catching a brief glimpse of his own distorted reflection in the steel.

'We can't all leave together,' Grant told him. 'Paxton will pick us up from different places. You all know your own pick-up point?' He glanced around the room, looking at each of his companions in turn. All nodded in affirmation.

'What if he didn't manage to get a car?' asked Gardner.

'Stop worrying, will you?' Grant told him. 'Just go to your pick-up point and wait. He'll be there.'

'He'd better be or I'll take *his* fucking head off,' Walton threatened.

Grant didn't answer.

'You know,' Walton continued, grinning, 'I never thought that Sally would have had the guts to kill herself like that.'

'A long stretch in prison would have killed her anyway,' Grant said quietly.

'Just as well then. She might have talked.'

'She wouldn't have talked,' hissed Grant angrily. 'She was as involved in what Jonathan believed as any of *us*. She knew the risks from the beginning.'

'What do you think they'll do to Jonathan now they've got him locked up?' asked Maria Chalfont.

'What *can* they do to him?' said Gardner. 'They can't wipe out what he's done or what he stands for no matter how long they keep him in prison.'

'I'm sure that'd be a great comfort to him as he counts off the thirty years,' said Walton, swinging the machete once more.

'Walton, you leave first,' Grant said. 'You've got the furthest to go.'

Walton nodded and disappeared into another room. He returned wearing a worn leather coat, badly scuffed on the elbows. However, once buttoned, it hid the machete from view.

'Then you, Maria,' Grant continued, until each of the occupants of the room knew when and how they were supposed to leave the house, attracting the minimum of attention in the process. Luckily the overgrown garden at the rear of the crumbling property led to a rotting wooden fence through which they could leave unseen.

Outside, the gathering clouds hastened the onset of evening and the five young people inside the decaying house welcomed its arrival.

They would need the night to hide them.

Twenty-Two

The inside of the car smelt like a sewer.

There were three of them in the Cortina, all dressed in dark coats, each one with his face shielded.

The car was parked across the street from Harrison's club and the three men inside watched as people came and went.

The taller of the three men reached into the pocket of his jacket and pulled out a cigarette. He stuck it between the flaps of skin which passed for lips and sucked hard. As he removed it a small fragment of liquescent flesh came away on the filter. The odour of tobacco smoke began to mingle with

123

the stench of dead flesh.

'Two years,' said the tall man, his voice low and husky, as if every syllable was torn from his vocal chords. 'While we waited, Harrison thrived. Bastard.'

'He tricked us,' said the driver, the words coming with even more difficulty. His larynx had suffered more damage than that of his former boss. There was a large hole beneath it which, as he spoke, was weeping a thick clear fluid onto his jacket.

The third man did not, could not, speak. He merely sat gazing at the club across the street, eyes which had once carried the spark of life now glaring with dull ferocity at the symbol of their enemy. For these eyes now were no more than festering holes, each one bulging and overflowing with purulent matter that trickled down his cheeks like reeking tears. The remnants of one eyeball had withered and shrunk in the socket.

He shuffled in his seat, gloved hand almost unconsciously touching the butt of the .45 automatic which was jammed in his belt.

The tall man turned and glanced at him, shaking his head gently.

'Not yet,' he croaked. 'Harrison is still too powerful.'

'When, then?' the driver said, mouth opening and closing slowly, just as the hole in his throat did. More of the clear mucus dripped on to his jacket.

'When *we* are ready,' said the tall man, scratching absent-mindedly at his temple with one index finger.

A small sliver of flesh came off and stuck to his glove.

He considered it for a second then pushed it into his mouth, swallowing the fragment of skin.

More people went into the club.

The Cortina remained parked.

The three men inside continued to watch.

And wait.

Twenty-Three

The first of the huge Scanias rumbled past, flanked on either side by jeeps which buzzed back and forth along the short convoy like soldier ants protecting their lumbering queen.

There were six lorries in the procession, all moving at less than thirty miles an hour on the narrow road. The ground shook beneath the massive wheels of the juggernauts.

'Big bastards aren't they?' murmured Carter, watching the convoy through the thick haze of blue smoke which belched from their exhausts. The smell of diesel fumes was almost overpowering and the young driver wound his window up as the trucks lumbered past. The Audi shook, vibrating as the convoy rolled by.

Residents of Colchester continued on their way with scarcely a second glance at the trucks and their escort. The town had been an army base for as long as most of the locals could remember and the sight of military vehicles rolling through the streets was hardly a cause for astonishment. The base itself was about twenty miles outside the town. Carter looked down and checked the map which was spread out over his lap.

Beside him, Drake took another drag on his cigarette, swallowing the smoke.

In the back seat, McIntire was finishing the last few mouthfuls of a hamburger. He finally tossed the carton and the wrapping out of the window, wiping his mouth with the back of his hand. He belched loudly and rubbed his stomach.

Above them, the sky was beginning to darken and Carter had to squint to see his watch in the growing gloom.

'Half-past seven,' he announced. 'We'll give them another fifteen minutes and then follow.'

The three men watched as the last of the trucks rounded a corner and disappeared out of sight. Only the low rumble of the Scania engines echoed through the stillness of the evening.

'I hope to Christ Frank knows what he's doing,' said McIntire nervously.

'It'll be fine,' Drake said.

'Yeah, fine for him. If anything goes wrong, we're the ones who get banged up, not Harrison.'

'You worry too much, Lou. You'll have a heart attack by the time you're thirty-five.'

'I'll have one before the end of the evening if this goes wrong,' McIntire told him.

The three men sat in silence for a moment. Then Drake looked at Carter and smiled thinly.

'How do you get on with Frank's bird? Tina, isn't it?' he wanted to know.

'Why?' asked Carter, a little too sharply.

Drake frowned.

'Just wondered,' he said, catching the look on his companion's face. 'She's a good looker isn't she?'

Carter nodded.

He wondered if Drake suspected anything but then reasoned that there was no way he could know about their relationship. Something would have been said before now. Nevertheless, the driver shifted slightly in his seat.

'You got the money?' Carter asked, anxious to change the subject.

'In the boot,' Drake told him. 'I checked it with Frank before we left this morning.'

McIntire glanced out of the back window and saw a policeman heading towards the car.

'Old Bill,' he said nervously.

'So what,' said Carter, catching sight of the uniformed

126

man in the wing mirror. 'We're not breaking any laws.'

'Yet,' chuckled Drake.

The policeman came within six feet of the car, bending low to look at the men inside.

Carter saw McIntire's hand go to his inside pocket.

'What the fuck are you doing?' the driver hissed.

'He's coming over,' McIntire blurted, hand already closed around the butt of his Walther PPK.

'Get your hand off the shooter,' snarled Carter as the policeman drew nearer.

He was within two strides of the vehicle now.

'Relax, will you,' hissed the driver.

The constable bent low and smiled at the three occupants of the Audi.

'Evening gentlemen,' he said, smiling.

'Evening all,' echoed Drake, trying to suppress a laugh.

'How long do you think it'll take us to reach Norwich if we drive through the night?' Carter asked him conversationally.

'You'd probably be best stopping over unless you're in a hurry,' the constable said, his eyes still flicking around the inside of the car. He looked hard at McIntire who returned his gaze, right hand twitching on his lap. Carter watched the expression on the older man's face reflected in the rear view mirror. Stay calm you stupid sod, he thought. If McIntire lost his bottle and pulled the gun they were all in bother. And not just with the law.

'You driving through to Norwich then?' the policeman asked.

Carter nodded.

'If you want to get there before morning you'd best be off now,' the constable said.

'Yeah, I think you're right,' Carter said, seeing McIntire move uncomfortably in his seat. Carter started the engine, thanked the policeman and drove off, glancing at him in the

127

rear view mirror until they rounded a corner.

'You fucking idiot,' he swore at McIntire. 'You were ready to pull down on that copper weren't you?'

'I thought he was going to start asking questions,' McIntire blurted.

'Yeah, well he didn't did he? Next time keep calm or *I'll* be asking you a question, like how are you going to eat with all your fucking teeth knocked out, because if you ever look like pulling a shooter on a copper again I'll re-arrange your fillings for you.'

Carter saw McIntire pull the PPK from its holster and felt the cold steel against his cheek.

'Yeah?' snarled McIntire.

'Yeah,' Carter repeated and stepped hard on the brake.

The sudden halt caused McIntire to fall forward between the two seats, unprotected as he was without a seat belt. As he sprawled helplessly, Carter pulled his own pistol free of its holster and jammed it against McIntire's face, pushing hard so that the other man's nose was bent back at a painful angle.

'No more shooters, right?' said Carter.

McIntire tried to get up but the driver pulled back the hammer of the automatic, pressing the barrel harder into his companion's face.

'Right,' McIntire said and sat up, rubbing the end of his nose.

Carter holstered his pistol, started the engine once more and drove on.

Drake glanced down the slope at the waiting Audi, the receiver held in his hand. He had a stack of change laid out on the metal shelf before him from which he took out five ten-pence coins and fed them into the phone.

He had to phone Frank Harrison, tell him that so far everything was going according to plan.

His fingers hovered over the buttons and he glanced at the car once again. Then he turned his back as if afraid that Carter and McIntire would see the number he was dialling.

Harrison could wait.

Right now there was someone else he had to call.

He jabbed the digits and waited.

Twenty-Four

John Kenning drove the car into the garage, switched off the engine and slumped back in his seat. The laughter, when it came, was uncontrollable. He jerked in his seat, laughing until tears rolled down his cheeks. Finally he swung himself out of the car and locked it, attempting a chorus of 'We are the Champions' but the words dissolved into another fit of giggles. He could smell the whisky on his breath and thought how fortunate he'd been not to be stopped by police on his drive from the office to his house in Primrose Hill. He'd escaped, he thought and it set him giggling again. Kenning couldn't remember being this happy since the birth of his first child over ten years ago. Naturally there had been many happy times since then but nothing to compare with the exultation he felt now.

He made a mental note to phone his son at boarding school in Buckinghamshire, to tell him the news which had brought him so much joy.

As owner and managing director of Kenning Electronics,

he had, that very day, secured the largest contract his firm had ever undertaken. Namely, to supply electronic scoreboards to no less than nine First Division football clubs up and down the country. Not bad going for a boy who'd been expelled from school and had started his business with less than a thousand pounds borrowed from friends. Now the Kenning empire (as he liked to call it) was worth millions. He chuckled again at the thought and ran a hand through his dark hair. Wait until he told Sharon.

She deserved the success every bit as much as he did. It was she who, in the beginning, had worked at two jobs to help pay for their bedsit in the East End. Like Kenning, she now enjoyed the privileges of wealth, including the five-bedroomed house they had occupied these last six years. Kenning's mother also lived with them. His father had died at the age of just forty-six and he'd made his son promise to look after his mother. It was a task which he was happy to fulfill. There had been disagreements between himself and his wife in the beginning about the arrangement but Kenning's mother had proved to be a great help to them. She also came in handy as a baby-sitter when Craig was home from school.

Kenning tried singing a couple of lines of 'Here We go' but they too trailed off into a chorus of giggles. He approached the door which led through into the kitchen, not bothering to retrieve his briefcase from the back seat of the car. He glanced briefly at his watch, frowning when he saw that it was almost nine o'clock. He'd tried to phone Sharon from the office to tell her that he'd be late but, with the festivities going on around him, he hadn't tried again when she didn't answer his first call. What the hell, he'd take her out for dinner. He could afford it. The thought made him laugh once more. He wasn't sure how much of his joviality was a product of the Glenfiddich he'd consumed but he guessed that a large measure of his light-headedness came from the sheer pleasure he was feeling at what he'd achieved that day. The intoxication was induced not by spirits but by the feeling of success.

He pushed the door open and stepped into the kitchen.

It was like stepping into a Turkish bath.

The room was full of steam. Thick white clouds of it which made him cough. He could smell burning too.

Muttering to himself, Kenning crossed to the cooker and found that the gas was burning under all four saucepans, two of which had boiled dry. The others were caked with blackened contents. He waved a hand before him, reaching up to open a window in an effort to let the steam out. As the white cloud slowly dispersed he looked around the room.

Cupboards had been pulled open, their contents scattered over the worktops and floor.

Drawers had been wrenched out and tossed unceremoniously amongst the other debris.

The kitchen table and several of the worktops had been scored deeply with a knife. A particularly large blade was still embedded in one of the overturned chairs.

Kenning swallowed hard, the joy which he'd felt seconds earlier draining rapidly away. His mind cleared with a speed he would have thought impossible. He stood gazing at the chaos and then suddenly dashed towards the living room, throwing the door open.

The destruction in the other room was even worse.

The leather suite had been overturned, not a single inch of it unmarked by what he took to be knife cuts. Even the wallpaper had been ripped from the walls with sharp instruments. Paintings which had adorned the room were lying in tattered heaps, ornaments had been methodically smashed until not one remained intact.

The television and video had also been wrecked, smashed

with a ferocity that had scattered bits all over the room. The video looked as if it had been forcibly flung from one side of the room to the other. The drinks' cabinet had been overturned, every single bottle inside smashed, the contents soaking into a carpet dotted with faeces.

This final ignominy caused him to gag and he turned away from the sight, his mind in turmoil, his heart thudding madly as he thought of his family. Of his wife. His mother.

Where were they?

The phone in the sitting room had been smashed. He ran for the one in the hall, briefly catching sight of something scrawled on the walls, something in red letters:

RICH FUCK

He ran on, past the upturned armchair, through into the hall, praying that the phone there was working, praying that his wife and mother were still all right.

Praying that the police would arrive quickly.

He reached for the phone, relieved that it was still in one piece.

Praying . . .

The knife was brought down with terrifying force.

All Kenning heard was the swish of the blade then he felt the agonising pain as the knife powered through the back of his outstretched hand, pinning it to the wood of the table as the steel bit several inches into the oak. One of his carpal bones was pulverized by the impact and blood burst from the wound as he screamed his pain, secured to the table by the weapon.

It felt as if his hand were on fire.

Still gripping the knife, grinning at his victim, Phillip Walton leered into Kenning's face.

'Welcome home,' he chuckled.

132

'Come on, come on,' muttered Drake, looking first at his watch and then at the phone box nearby.

'Are you sure you gave the right number?' McIntire asked anxiously.

Carter looked at his watch.

9.58 p.m.

Drake was drumming on the side of the car with his fingertips, the incessant rhythm interrupted only when he looked at his own watch for what seemed the hundredth time since they'd arrived.

The Audi was parked in a lay-by about twenty miles from the centre of Colchester, the road flanked on both sides by trees and bushes which towered upwards in an effort to cut out the weak rays of the watery moon above. Barely five cars had passed them in the forty minutes they'd been sitting here.

'Are you sure you can trust him?' asked Carter.

'Frank set this up himself,' Drake said defensively. 'We've used him before.'

'Maybe he's got cold feet,' the driver insisted, reaching into his jacket for a cigarette.

'He'll ring,' Drake said, gazing at the phone box once more.

Another minute passed.

A car sped past them in the night.

Drake continued drumming on the side of the car.

'He's late,' muttered McIntire nervously. 'What if he doesn't call? We can't go back . . .'

The phone rang.

Drake pushed the door open and scurried across to the booth, snatching up the receiver.

From inside the car Carter couldn't hear what was being said but he saw Drake smile and nod before slamming the receiver down. He ran back to the car and jumped in.

'Let's go,' he said. 'About ten miles down the road. He's waiting for us.'

Carter started the engine and drove off.

The van was parked amongst some trees, about twenty yards from the roadside, completely hidden by the thick foliage and the darkness. As Carter swung the Audi around a corner the driver of the van flashed his headlamps twice.

Carter guided the car towards the waiting vehicle, through the protective undergrowth until he was level with it, both vehicles now hidden from any prying eyes that might pass.

The three men in the Audi got out and stood beside the car, waiting.

The silence was unbroken for a moment.

A moth fluttered close to McIntire's face and he swatted it irritably.

To their left a twig cracked. There was movement in the trees.

Carter reached for his automatic, not liking the darkness. Not trusting the fact that he could barely see more than two feet ahead of him.

The next sound he heard was the metallic rattle of a slide.

Someone else in the woods was carrying an automatic.

Carter turned and saw a man moving towards them, the bulky shape of a Browning Hi-Power gripped in his fist. It was aimed at the trio.

'Are you Vaughn?' Drake asked as the man drew nearer and, as he did, Carter was able to see that he was limping slightly.

The man nodded.

'Drake?' he asked.

He nodded and quickly introduced his companions.

'Excuse the gun,' said Vaughn. 'But you can't be too careful. Have you got the money?'

Drake nodded.

'You got the guns?' he asked.

Quartermaster Andrew Vaughn crossed to the back of the van and opened it up. He pulled a torch from his belt and shone it inside the vehicle, pulling back the blankets which covered three boxes. The other men moved closer to get a better look.

'The best there is,' said Vaughn, motioning towards the boxes as if he were a travelling salesman.

The first box was full to the brim with pistols. .38's, .45's, .357's, semi-automatic and automatic weapons. Carter even noticed a couple of Lugers and a short-barrelled Mauser. Revolvers and automatics of all descriptions. Lying alongside them were several sub-machine guns. He spotted a dozen Ingram's, some Uzi's, a Skorpion machine pistol. Some had the stocks attached.

In another box lay a selection of rifles. Many equipped with telescopic sights. Carter saw some 7.62 GPMG's, 4.85mm rifles and at least half a dozen Ar-18 Sterlings.

'There's enough ammo in here,' said Vaughn patting the third box, 'to fight World War Three.'

'I think that's what Harrison wants to do,' said McIntire, eyeing the weapons.

'I tried to get grenades too but there are limits to what even *I* can manage,' the quartermaster said, smiling.

'And you reckon that no one's going to miss this stuff?' Carter asked, motioning towards the weapons.

'I've been in charge of the armoury for the last seven years,' Vaughn told him. 'I know exactly what goes in and out. *Only* me.' He rubbed the top of his leg and winced. 'Bloody leg,' he muttered. 'Gives me trouble every now and then.'

'Did you get hurt in Northern Ireland?' McIntire asked.

Vaughn nodded.

'It comes and goes,' he said heroically, careful not to mention that the injury had been sustained when his jeep had run into a lamp post and not as the result of the attentions of an IRA sniper.

Carter and the others began loading the weapons and ammunition into the back of the Audi, spreading the load as evenly as they could to prevent the back of the vehicle tilting downwards too much. The last thing they wanted while driving back to London was an inquisitive policeman checking their boot. Vaughn stood watching the men complete the job.

Drake finally crossed to the car and returned carrying a small suitcase which he handed to the soldier. Vaughn laid it on the bonnet of his van and unzipped it.

'You can count it if you like,' Drake told him. 'But it's all there. Two hundred and fifty thousand, like we agreed.'

Vaughn pulled one of the fifty pound notes from its wad and sniffed it. He kissed the note then returned it to its place amongst the other cash.

'Who else do you deal with?' Carter asked.

'Anyone who pays me,' the quartermaster told him. '*This* is my religion, my belief.' He motioned to the money. 'I'd sell guns to the IRA if they made me the right offer.'

'You sold to anyone else from London recently?' the driver wanted to know.

Vaughn shook his head.

Carter locked stares with him for a moment and then climbed back into the Audi. He twisted the key in the ignition, allowing the engine to turn over a few times before stepping on the accelerator and driving off.

Vaughn watched the car disappear down the road.

'Good hunting,' he murmured as he clambered back into his own vehicle and drove off in the opposite direction, the case full of money on the passenger seat beside him.

The woods were quiet once more.

Twenty-Six

The knife came free with difficulty.

Wedged as it was, deep in the thick wood of the table and also through John Kenning's hand, the knife was finally torn out only by a tremendous surge of strength from Phillip Walton. As the blade was removed, Kenning fell to the ground, clutching his bleeding hand and moaning in pain.

Walton was on him in seconds, the steel pressed against his face, the point digging into his cheek.

'Get up you fucking parasite,' he hissed.

Kenning tried to get to his feet but he put his weight on his injured hand and collapsed again.

Walton brought the heel of his shoe down hard on to the bleeding appendage, grinding into the savage gash.

'Get up,' he roared, gripping Kenning by the collar and tugging him bodily to his feet. He shoved the other man hard against the wall and stood against him, the knife pressed at his throat.

'Please,' blurted Kenning. 'I've got money. Don't hurt me. Take as much as you want. My wife . . .'

Walton hawked loudly and spat into Kenning's face. The mucoid lump hit him below the eye and rolled down his cheek like a thick tear.

'You want to see your wife?' hissed Walton.

'Please don't hurt her. Please.' Tears were forming in his eyes, tears of pain and fear. The burning sensation from his ruined hand seemed to be devouring his whole arm. His fingers were already numb. Kenning's breath came in short gasps and, when he tried to swallow, he found that his throat was dry.

'Get upstairs,' Walton snapped, pushing the other man

before him, kicking him hard in the back when he stumbled.

As he dragged himself up to the first floor, Kenning saw, through pain-blurred eyes, that more damage had been wrought.

There was excrement smeared on the walls, the stench making him feel sick. But that nausea was tempered by the terror which engulfed him like a dark glove. He reached the top of the stairs and found himself pushed towards one of the bedrooms.

Inside the room, Sharon Kenning sat tied to a chair with strips of sheet torn from the bed which itself had been subjected to the same orgiastic slashing that the suite downstairs had suffered. Springs protruded through the slashed mattress like the broken bones of a compound fracture.

Next to his wife, Kenning saw his mother, Mary, similarly bound.

Beside her stood Jennifer Thomas, a knife pressed to the old woman's throat.

Both women had been gagged.

'Let them go,' pleaded Kenning, his eyes filling with tears once more.

Walton struck him hard across the back of the neck and he fell to the ground between the two women who both stared down at him, their eyes bulging in fear. Sharon Kenning saw the blood from her husband's injured hand and shook her head. She suddenly thought of their son.

'Please, we have money,' Kenning said, wiping his eyes, trying to regain his composure. 'I'll give you whatever you want, just don't kill us.'

As the others watched, Walton unzipped his fly, hauled out his penis and began urinating on Kenning. The stream of yellow fluid spattered into the businessman who tried to shield his face but, as he opened his mouth to scream, some of the vile fluid filled his mouth. He gagged and then vomited violently. Walton continued urinating.

'Piss on your fucking money,' he said, grinning.

Jennifer Thomas laughed.

So did Paul Gardner.

And Mark Paxton.

Kenning spat the last few bitter-tasting dregs from his mouth and tried to stand up.

As he did, Michael Grant entered the room, followed by Maria Chalfont.

Grant was carrying the machete.

'He says he's got money,' chuckled Walton.

'As much as you want,' Kenning gasped. 'Let me get it.'

Grant nodded.

'What the hell are you playing at?' snarled Walton, glaring at his companion who was watching as Kenning fumbled with a wall safe behind him. He had difficulty turning the combination lock because of the pain from his hand but, finally, he tugged the door open and hauled out bundles of notes and some jewellery. He held them out to Grant as if they were offerings, objects which might pacify him.

'We don't want your money,' Grant said flatly, hefting the machete in front of him.

'Take it, please,' wailed Kenning, Dropping to his knees. 'Please don't hurt us. Please God . . .'

The sentence was cut short as Grant struck him with the machete.

The blade powered into his left shoulder, smashing the clavicle. Blood ran from the savage wound, staining Kenning's urine-drenched shirt.

'No,' he screamed in agony. 'For Christ's sake.' He was sobbing now. 'Oh Jesus Christ . . no . . .'

The machete descended again, cutting deep into his raised forearm.

The money fell to the floor.

'For God's sake .. please . . . no.'

The machete caught him across the top of the head, splitting his scalp, cracking bone. The rent seemed to grow bigger until a throbbing portion of brain forced its way free like a bloated tumour. Blood ran down his face.

He fell forward, still sobbing, his words now more garbled.

'Jesus . . . God Almighty . . . oh God . . .'

His wife tried to scream, her eyes bulging wide, the bile forcing its way up from her stomach as she watched her husband die.

His mother fainted.

Jennifer Thomas slapped the old woman's face, reviving her, ensuring that she didn't miss any of the spectacle.

The machete struck Kenning on the back. On the side.

On the face.

The lower back.

Blood jetted in all directions.

Grant continued hacking at the businessman who was curled up in a foetal position moaning. Low, gurgling noises in a throat filled with blood.

Maria Chalfont felt the wetness between her legs as she watched.

Phillip Walton looked on disinterestedly.

Mark Paxton burst a spot on his neck and sniffed at the pus, tasting it briefly before wiping it on the bedclothes.

'God . . . God . . .'

Kenning's cries were like the agonised lowings of a bullock.

Grant took one last maniacal swipe at him then stepped back, his breath coming in gasps, his clothes drenched in blood.

The killers in the room looked down at the butchered carcass, almost savouring the last spasmodic twitchings, the soft rasp as the sphincter muscle gave out.

Then, they turned on the women.

140

Twenty-Seven

The flat was small but tidy. The damp which was inexorably creeping up the walls had been washed off and covered with emulsion paint, the threadbare carpets had been vacuumed. There was a pleasant smell about the dwelling.

Which was more than could be said for the man who stood in the doorway of Nikki Jones' flat.

She flicked her long curly hair away from her face and turned to the customer who stood motionless in the hall.

'Well, come in, shut the door, you're letting all the heat out,' she told him, trying to disguise the impatience in her voice. She didn't really like the look of this bloke whom she'd picked up just twenty minutes earlier. She liked the smell of him even less. When he'd first approached her she had thought about refusing, such had been the vile odour he gave off. She'd encountered a few dirty sods during her three years as a prostitute and usually insisted they take a bath or shower before they got down to business but, as she'd opened her mouth to turn this latest customer down, he'd flashed a wad of twenty pound notes almost an inch thick and Nikki had had a change of heart. She could always hold her breath. Perhaps she noticed dirtiness so acutely because of her own attention to cleanliness. She kept herself, her flat and her baby spotlessly clean.

The child was sleeping in the other room and Nikki made her way to the door to check on him, slipping off her coat as she did so, revealing the tight, white T-shirt and leather mini-skirt beneath.

'Sit down,' she told her guest. 'I'll get you a drink in a minute.' And a deodorant, she mused, as she passed into her son's room.

In the sitting room, the man in the dark coat sat down, gloved hands folded across his lap, the scarf still wrapped tightly around his face.

Nikki pulled the door of her child's room closed behind her, not wanting to disturb him with the light which was flooding through from the sitting room. He was sleeping, the sheets pulled up to his neck. She leant over and pulled them down, tucking a loose corner around him then she bent lower and kissed his head.

'I love you,' she whispered and stood for long seconds gazing down at the boy. He was almost two years old and Nikki still had no idea who the father was. It could have been one of her customers, or it may have been any one of the half a dozen pimps she'd worked with during the past three years. She didn't know. Didn't *want* to know. He was hers, that was all that mattered. She hated having to bring customers back to the flat but it was her place of work after all. During the day she could afford to send him to a child-minder while she entertained her clients with a 'soothing massage' (that, at least was the wording in the magazines she advertised in). But in the evenings she had him with her in the flat. One of her customers had once asked if the child could be included in the session for a hundred pounds extra. Nikki had told him to leave immediately. Sick bastard. Some people had no morals at all.

She kissed her son once more and then retreated back into the sitting room where her guest was still sitting at one end of the sofa looking distractedly around the room.

'Take your coat off,' she told him, increasingly irritated by his distant attitude. She knew that many of the men she brought back to the flat were nervous but this bloke showed no sign of anxiety, merely an unnerving detachment from the proceedings. Perhaps he was in a hurry, she told herself. Well, if that was the case, fine. The quicker she got the smelly bastard out the better. She crossed to a drinks' trolley and poured herself a small whisky.

'Would you like a drink?' she asked.

He shook his head.

'You don't say much do you?' she smiled and moved across to sit next to him, gritting her teeth as the vile smell assaulted her nostrils once more. She edged closer, her professional skill overcoming her revulsion. She reached for the top button of his coat but he gripped her hand, pushing it down towards his groin instead, guiding it towards the spot between his legs.

Nikki allowed herself to be manipulated, allowed him to press her hand to his crotch. She felt his erection through the material of his trousers and she squeezed it.

The man looked at her, only his eyes visible over the top of the scarf. There wasn't a flicker of emotion in them. It was like looking into the eyes of a fish on a fishmonger's slab. No warmth. No life. The twin orbs seemed to bore into Nikki and she looked away, putting her drink down.

With his other hand he gently touched the back of her head, pushing it down towards his groin.

She hesitated, the hairs at the nape of her neck rising slightly. It felt as if someone were running a freezing feather up and down her spine.

'It's going to cost you more,' she said, realizing what the man wanted.

He dug his free hand into the jacket of his pocket and pulled out five twenty pound notes which he held up for a moment before shoving them down her T-shirt.

Nikki nodded, feeling his hand tightening on the back of her neck. As she lowered her head towards his groin she tried to hold her breath, struggling to undo his zip with her other hand. It came free with difficulty and she slipped her fingers inside, freeing his penis.

It felt cold but she ignored this peculiarity, anxious now merely to finish the job and rid herself of this client.

She bent lower, his erection now pointing up at her, brushing her lips as he pressed harder on the back of her neck.

She closed her mouth around the bulbous head and almost gagged.

There was liquid already seeping from the glans but it tasted unlike any glandular secretion she'd encountered before. It stuck to her tongue like mucus, oozing with greater urgency as she licked the swollen organ. The stench was now almost unbearable and Nikki knew that she was going to be sick. She tried to straighten up but the gloved hand held her firm, her mouth fixed over the throbbing penis which seemed to be swelling even more.

She clutched at his testicles, rubbing them in an effort to finish the vile task more rapidly. She felt them begin to undulate beneath her probing fingers, felt them contract, ready to spill their contents.

Yet above her she could not hear any breathing from her client. He seemed very calm for a man about to climax.

Instead, she was only aware of that stiff, reeking rod which had impaled her mouth and the frightful stench which was almost palpable in its intensity.

She worked her hand up and down his shaft, realizing with relief that he was at his peak. She sucked harder. He thrust violently into her mouth, driving his penis up until it touched the back of her throat.

She retched, tried to straighten up but the hand gripped her and held her. She tasted more fluid on her tongue then the cascade began. His penis jerked violently and the end seemed to open, expelling his emission.

Nikki's eyes bulged madly in their sockets as she felt her mouth fill to bursting point. Her cheeks swelled as she struggled to retain the ejaculation but then she realized that her mouth was filled not with fluid but with dozens of tiny objects.

Objects which were moving.

Twisting and turning on her tongue.

She sat back as the pressure on her neck was released, her mouth opening wide.

The maggots poured from it in a sickly white torrent and, as she looked down, she saw that the penis was still jerking, still spurting, propelling the minute monstrosities from the glans in a thick fountain. Some had already found their way down her throat despite the vomit which now rushed up from her stomach and gushed from her mouth, carrying with it hordes of the parasites.

Then the gloved hand was at her throat again, pulling her closer and she saw that the scarf had fallen from the man's face.

Beneath it his flesh was yellowed, peeling away from his bones like wallpaper, portions of it almost liquescent as it hung from his cheeks and chin.

She felt more of the maggots twisting in her mouth and throat, smelled the incredible stench of decay in her nostrils and, in one last second of consciousness, she gazed once again at the man's penis and saw a bloated, wriggling white shape haul itself from the slit in the bulbous head and drop into his lap.

Nikki Jones blacked out.

Twenty-Eight

Frank Harrison poured himself another glass of Jack Daniels and downed half of the fiery liquid in one swallow. He cradled the expensive crystal tumbler in his strong hand as if threatening to crush it. He looked at the man who stood opposite him.

'I told you when this business first started that I wanted something done and you've given me nothing,' Harrison rasped. 'No leads. No names. Nothing.'

Detective Inspector Peter Thorpe sipped at his own drink and shrugged.

'Look Frank, there are other things going on at the moment. I've got three corpses in a house in Primrose Hill that look like they've been put through a mincer. This nutcase, Crawford, we got him but he's got others working for him. That case takes priority over everything at the moment. I can't carry on making enquiries about who had a crack at you while this other business is still going on.'

'And in the meantime? What am I supposed to do?' demanded Harrison.

'Sort it out yourself.'

Harrison downed what was left in his glass and slammed it on the desk top.

'Fine. Because that's just what I intend to do.' He crossed to a large wooden box in one corner of the room. It was padlocked. 'Open it,' snapped the gang boss and Billy Stripes fumbled in his pocket for the key. He finally pulled the padlock free and lifted the lid.

Harrison reached inside, his back to Thorpe.

When he turned, the DI found himself looking down the barrel of a Sterling AR-18.

'Where the hell did you get that?' he asked, the colour draining from his cheeks. 'That's army issue equipment.'

'Yeah, like you said, perhaps I ought to take care of things myself,' Harrison said. 'So far I've been sitting around waiting for some joker to blow me away. Perhaps it's time *I* did some of the shooting.'

'If you start a gang war, Frank, then I can't protect you. It was all I could do to keep Special Branch away from the murders of Joule and Dome. If you decide to go on a bender you can count me out.' He put down his glass and turned to the door.

The gunshot, when it came, sounded thunderous in the small room. The single bullet from the Sterling hit Thorpe's glass, exploding it into a thousand tiny fragments before hurtling into the desk top, blasting a sizeable lump of wood from the expensive piece of furniture.

'Remember what I pay you, Thorpe. You ain't going nowhere,' Harrison hissed.

The DI turned slowly, trying to remain composed. All around him, Harrison's bodyguards looked on impassively as the gang boss raised the rifle to his shoulder, drawing a bead on Thorpe, fixing his head perfectly in the cross-threads of the sight.

'I own you,' Harrison said, his finger hovering over the trigger. 'Try earning your bloody money. Find out who's having a go at me and do it quick otherwise I'm going to find out myself. And my methods might be a little bit more *direct* than yours. Then I think your superiors might wonder what the hell was going on.' He gripped the rifle more tightly. 'London's set to explode, Thorpe. Just make sure you don't get caught in the cross-fire. You make up your mind who's side you're on but don't take too long doing it.'

'Like I told you,' the policeman said. 'We've got to find whoever killed those three people up at Primrose Hill. That's the case I'm working on.'

147

'Then do some fucking overtime and find out who wants me dead, otherwise it might be you who ends up on a meat-hook.'

Harrison squeezed the trigger.

The hammer slammed down on an empty chamber.

Thorpe let out a gasp of relief, watching angrily as Harrison chuckled and threw the gun to Billy Stripes.

'You've got forty-eight hours, Thorpe,' Harrison told him. 'Then it's *my* turn.'

Twenty-Nine

The flesh had been taken, stripped away from Nikki Jones' face just as it had been from Danny Weller and Adam Giles.

Now there were three bodies nailed to the wall of the derelict supermarket, hanging there like the bizarre trophies of a crazed hunter.

The man who had once been Charles Ross touched the skin of his face and gazed at the trio of crucified bodies before him. His coat was open to reveal the holes in his jacket, holes that had been put there two years earlier. Put there by a Smith and Wesson snub-nose .38 pistol. He gently pushed his index finger into one of the holes and then withdrew it, noting that the digit was dripping with dark, yellowish fluid. He raised it before him, watching as the mucoid substance dribbled down on to his hand.

Beside him, his face still wrapped in a scarf, the man who,

in life, had been known as Liam Kelly stood motionless, eyes fixed on the three bodies. Kelly wore a hat to conceal his mottled scalp. He had never possessed much hair during his short life but now all that covered the patchwork of dark veins were a few silver threads of gossamer.

The one they had called Peter Burton smoothed the flesh over his face as if anxious to remove any creases, ensuring that it fitted as closely as possible over his rotting features.

Ian Massey plucked a piece of dangling skin from his neck, touching the ragged wound in his throat. The bullet which, two years earlier, had killed him, had exploded his larynx and left a gaping gash as large as a fist. Unlike the others he could not utter even the most strained of words.

The fifth man looked on impassively.

Each of them was armed with a variety of weapons but most potent in their armoury was their hatred.

'So why do we have to wait?' Burton wanted to know. 'Why not kill him now? Why not kill Harrison immediately? We've killed some of his men.'

'I want him to suffer,' Ross said. 'I want him to wonder where the next attack is going to come from, never being able to relax, not able to trust anyone, even those closest to him.'

'And the rest of his gang?' Kelly wanted to know.

'They'll die, every last one of them,' Ross snapped. He looked at the fifth man who turned to him and nodded.

Thirty

'Bastard.'

Tina Richardson studied her reflection before the full-length mirror in her bedroom and inspected the scratches on her breasts. She muttered more curses to herself as she stood there in her panties, spotting the bruises which marked her body in numerous places. She raised one shapely leg and placed it on the stool in front of her dressing table. Running her fingers up the inside of her thigh, she felt the small scar where Harrison had burned her over a week ago.

He'd been drunk when he'd arrived at her flat the previous night. At first she'd tried to resist his inebriated advances, trying to persuade him to go to bed and sleep it off but he'd struck her with the back of his hand. She leaned closer to the mirror, relieved to see he hadn't marked her face. It was her back and arms which he'd bruised. Mottled patches of blue skin showed vividly beneath her shoulder blades and on her upper arms. She gently touched the damaged areas, wincing as she did so.

Harrison had pushed her into the bedroom in his drunken rage, frustrated by his own inability to remove his trousers. She'd tried to calm him but it had been useless. He'd managed to wriggle them down as far as his thighs then, tearing her housecoat open, he'd penetrated her, thrusting violently until he climaxed. Then he'd passed out.

She'd lain beneath him, sickened by his very presence, finally managing to roll his heavy form off her. She hadn't attempted to get him into bed, merely thrown a blanket over him and left him on the floor.

The sounds of retching had awoken her that morning but she had not left her bed.

150

Now, Harrison sat in the kitchen drinking coffee and nursing a hangover while Tina got dressed.

She pulled on a leather skirt, stepped into a pair of high heels and sat down to do her make-up.

As she reached into her handbag for her mascara she caught sight of the .25 Beretta in the bottom of the bag.

She looked towards the bedroom door, then carefully took the small pistol out, holding it in her hand, snaking her index finger through the trigger guard and pressing gently. She studied her own reflection in the dressing table mirror for a moment before dropping the gun back into her bag.

Not now.

Not yet.

She began applying her make-up.

'What are you doing today?'

The voice startled her and she caught sight of Harrison standing in the doorway. His voice was even more gravelly than usual and there were dark rings beneath his eyes, as if someone had coloured them with charcoal during the night. He looked ten years older than usual. Closer now to fifty than forty.

'I'm going shopping,' she told him.

'Not on your own you're not,' he replied. 'I'll send someone with you.'

'Frank, I'll be all right.'

He walked towards her, gripping her shoulder a little too hard.

'You've got to be careful,' he reminded her. Then he turned and headed back into the sitting room where she heard him using the phone. He returned a moment later.

'Carter and Mendham are on their way. They'll go with you,' he said.

She suppressed a smile at the mention of Carter's name.

'They'll be bored, trailing round shops with me,' she said.

151

'I don't pay them to enjoy themselves,' Harrison said, moving towards her once more. He began massaging her neck and, again, she winced slightly as she felt his fingers digging just a little too roughly into her flesh. 'Don't want anything happening to my little girl, do I?' He smiled, bent forward and tried to kiss her but she pulled away slightly.

The smile vanished from his face and she saw the anger in his eyes. Tina stroked his cheek placatingly.

'You don't want to spoil my make-up do you?' she said, trying to sound as carefree as she could. She kissed him lightly on the cheek, hoping that simple gesture of supplication would be enough.

The smile returned and he reached for her hand, kissing that instead.

'What about you, Frank?' she asked, relieved as he wandered out of the bedroom. 'What are you going to do with yourself?'

'I've got some business to attend to,' he said. 'I'll probably see you tonight.'

She finished her make-up and pulled on a yellow blouse, leaving the top three buttons undone. Then she walked into the sitting room where Harrison was glancing at the newspaper. He looked up, running appraising eyes over her. He frowned.

'Do your blouse up,' he told her, pointing at her with one accusatory finger. 'I don't want every horny fucker looking at you. It's bad enough that you walk around with no bra.'

She fastened the third button, relieved when she heard the doorbell ring.

Carter smiled broadly as she let him in. He nodded a greeting to his boss and told him that Mendham was in the car outside.

'Billy's on his way to pick you up, Frank,' the driver added.

Carter and Tina turned to leave.

'Carter.'

He froze.

'You take care of her, right?' Harrison said.

The driver nodded, pulling the door closed behind him.

Harrison crossed to the window and watched as Tina climbed into the back of the car and the Citroen pulled away.

But Harrison was not the only observer.

Other eyes had seen them go.

Thirty-One

Pat Mendham felt his cheeks colour as Tina held up the miniscule knickers before him. He coughed and tried to look away, glancing down at his shoes and then across at another of the rows of clothes which surrounded him. A particularly beautiful young woman dressed in only a yellow blouse and a white leather mini-skirt squeezed past him, trailing a long nightdress, on her way to the changing room.

Tina picked out another pair of panties and a matching suspender belt and held them up for Mendham's inspection.

'What do you think, Pat?' she said, trying to hide her smile, something which was even more difficult to do when she saw how deep a shade of scarlet her escort was turning.

He grunted something unintelligible and nodded.

Standing in the lingerie department of Top Shop watching Tina picking out items of underwear was not his favourite way of passing a morning.

'Why don't you go back to the car and wait for me?' she said, smiling, finally taking pity on him.

He shook his head.

'Frank said I was to stay with you all the time,' he said, trying to move aside as two girls pushed past him clutching bras and basques.

'I doubt if anyone will try to attack me in here,' Tina said but her attempts at reassurance were wasted. Mendham merely shrugged.

'I'm only doing what I was told,' he answered.

Tina picked out a couple of pairs of stockings and some more panties and headed for the cash desk. Mendham wandered along beside her like an obedient dog, reaching up to loosen his top button, apologising as he bumped into a woman who was holding a pair of French knickers in front of her.

Tina chuckled and walked on.

Carter slowed the car down as he passed the entrance to the shop, glancing through the hordes of people, trying to catch sight of Tina and Mendham as they emerged from the mêlée. No sign of them yet. He drove on, ignoring the blaring of a hooter when he pulled out into the other lane.

He'd dropped them off about fifteen minutes ago, driven up Oxford Street, swung the car round and come back down again, waiting for them to come out. Twice he'd been mistaken for a taxi, the second time by a large American woman who'd actually got into the passenger seat before he'd had time to tell her to fuck off. Bloody yanks, Carter thought, glancing to either side of him as he drove up the busy thoroughfare. Shoppers clogged the pavements on both sides like ranks of disorderly troops.

Carter turned the car sharply, narrowly avoiding an oncoming bus. He smiled as he saw the driver's furious

154

expression in the rear view mirror. He drove past the shop on the other side of the road, once more gazing towards the entrance. Carter noticed Pat Mendham as he walked gratefully off the escalator which carried patrons up to ground level. Tina followed a few paces behind, her arms full of bags. The driver looked appreciatively at her as she stood with Mendham waiting for the Citroen to pull up.

Carter signalled that he'd seen them, drove on a few more yards and turned, bringing the car to a halt close by.

Mendham opened the door for Tina and she slid into the back seat.

She smiled at Carter who returned the gesture, grinning even more broadly as Mendham slumped, sweating, in the passenger seat beside him.

'Fuck that,' he said, wiping his brow with a handkerchief. 'Next time I'll drive and *you* can go in.'

Tina laughed.

'I don't think Pat approved of my choice of underwear, Ray,' she said. 'Doesn't your wife wear that kind of thing, Pat?' she asked him.

'My Mrs couldn't fit the cheek of her arse inside your jeans, let alone those . . .' he struggled for the word. 'Those knickers. Christ, I've seen bigger napkins.'

Tina laughed again.

'Where to now?' Carter asked.

'Selfridges,' she told him, looking through the bags, pleased with her purchases. She'd paid for everything with the credit cards Frank had given her; it was no less than she deserved she told herself. He'd want to see what she'd bought, to see her model it. And then? She shuddered slightly.

Carter turned the car once more and headed back down Oxford Street towards Selfridges, spotting the flags which flew from its roof as they drew nearer.

There was a set of traffic lights ahead, the red light glowing. Carter slowed down.

The white Astra alongside him slowed down too.

'What are you buying in there?' Mendham asked suspiciously, nodding in the direction of the store.

'Only shoes,' Tina told him. 'Even *your* wife must wear shoes.'

They all laughed.

Carter was still laughing when he saw the back window of the Astra being wound down. He saw the three men inside looking across at the occupants of the Citroen.

The driver was grinning at him, mouthing words that Carter couldn't make out.

He nudged Mendham who also glanced at the other vehicle.

It was he who saw the shotgun.

Thirty-Two

Mendham opened his mouth to shout a warning but his exhortations were drowned by the thunderous retort of the Remington.

Three bursts from the pump action shotgun struck the Citroen in quick succession.

The first blasted a hole in the rear door. The second punched in the back window, showering Tina with glass. Hundreds of tiny shards were blown inwards and she screamed as she felt some of them cutting into the skin of her face and arms.

'Get down,' roared Carter, fumbling for his automatic.

She needed no second bidding. Tina threw herself to the floor of the car, cutting her knees on the shattered glass but covering her head against a renewed assault.

It was the third discharge which did the most damage.

As Mendham pulled the .45 from his shoulder holster the concentrated wad of buckshot caught him in the shoulder. It shattered his clavicle and tore away a large portion of his trapezius muscle. Blood jetted from the savage wound and Mendham moaned as he slumped forward in his seat.

Carter stepped on the accelerator, unconcerned that the lights were still red.

The back wheels of the Citroen spun for a second, screaming on the road, then the vehicle shot forward as if fired from a cannon.

Mendham was jerked back in his seat, the jolt to his ruined shoulder making him yell in pain.

Carter gripped the wheel tightly, guiding the car round and between two other vehicles which were crossing diagonally in front of him. He glanced in the rear view mirror to see that the Astra was following.

All eyes had turned to watch the tableau but Carter had only one thought. To get clear of the men who were trying to kill them. He pressed down even harder on the accelerator until it seemed his foot would go through the floor of the car. It roared on, Mendham still moaning in agony in the front seat, Tina still hunched behind Carter, shaking as she felt a thin trickle of blood running from her cut cheek.

The Astra sped alongside the Citroen once more and Carter glanced across once and saw the shotgun being aimed at them again.

The next blast tore off a wing mirror and peppered the side

157

of the car with buckshot.

Carter stepped on the brake as he turned the car, cutting in front of a taxi as he swung the vehicle left into Park Lane, weaving in and out of traffic in an effort to escape the pursuers.

'Keep your head down,' he told Tina, forced to raise his voice in order to be heard above the roaring of the engine and the sound of the wind rushing in through the shattered back window.

The Astra sped after them, bumping a Metro out of the way as the driver coaxed more speed from the pursuing vehicle.

Mendham stirred slightly and twisted painfully in his seat, the .45 propped against the frame of the window. As the other car drew nearer he squeezed off three shots.

The first struck the windscreen and ricocheted off the glass with a high pitched whine. The second shattered a side window and the third missed completely.

The Astra swerved and moved away from the Citroen, roaring past a Ford that had slowed down, its driver looking on in panic as the two cars shot past him.

Down towards another set of lights the two cars raced, like maniacal Grand Prix cars. The lights were green fortunately although it would have made little difference if they hadn't been.

Carter swung the Citroen in front of another car, trying to thread the vehicle through the traffic in an effort to escape the Astra.

It kept coming.

Mendham moaned, his left arm now completely numb, dangling like a piece of bloodied meat beside him. But he sucked in a deep breath, gritted his teeth against the pain and fired again at the white car.

The bullet smashed a headlight, glass exploding over the front of the Astra.

But instead of pulling back, the driver stepped on the

accelerator and guided the car alongside the Citroen once more.

The Remington roared loudly, two thunderous blasts.

Both of them hit Mendham.

The first caught him in the shoulder again, the impact almost hurling him across Carter's lap. Portions of splintered bone and gobbets of flesh splattered the driver who narrowed his eyes as his companion's blood splashed his face and ran into his eyes.

The second discharge hit Mendham full in the face.

Such was the ferocity of the impact that his head seemed to explode. As if someone had planted a small charge of dynamite inside his skull, the entire cranial cavity erupted, spewing its sticky contents into the car. Mendham's mouth was still open in a scream of pained surprise, his jaw frozen in that attitude as he fell forward in the seat, held by his seat belt, sticky slops of greyish-red brain matter now coating the inside of the Citroen. Blood pumped from inside the pulverized skull, some of it splattering Tina who gritted her teeth and tried not to vomit. Mendham's finger twitched and two more shots from the .45 cut through the air.

Carter spun the wheel savagely, sending the Citroen crashing into the side of the Astra.

The white car skidded slightly but sped on, the driver trying to cut across in front of Carter who merely pressed his foot down even harder on the accelerator and slammed into the vehicle. There was a loud crash as the Citroen's headlights smashed but Carter was satisfied to see a large dent in the white car. It skidded to one side, colliding with another car, giving Carter precious seconds to get ahead.

He twisted the wheel violently, cutting between a lorry and a bus; then, head down over the blood-spattered steering wheel, he guided the Citroen down Sloane Street.

It was as he hurtled through another set of traffic lights that he saw the police car.

Lights flashing madly, it seemed to appear from nowhere, pulling in behind the Astra which was still following with the same mad intent.

Carter saw both vehicles draw parallel and one of the men in the back of the Astra swing the shotgun around towards the police car.

He fired twice.

The windscreen disintegrated under the dual impact, glass flying into the car, blinding the two uniformed men who occupied the front seats.

The police car went out of control, the driver wounded by the lethal shards, peppered with buckshot.

The car hit the pavement, spun twice and then smashed into some tables outside a cafe. The men were catapulted into the air by the force of the crash, one turning over and over before finally thudding down on top of the stricken squad car.

The Astra roared on.

Carter suddenly stepped on the brakes, the tyres spinning madly beneath him. Smoke rose from the scorched rubber as he turned the car into an alley, still desperate to escape the pursuing car. The alley was narrower than he'd anticipated. As the Citroen roared along it, it banged off first one side then the other, sparks flying from the wings, stripping paint from the chassis as effectively as if it had been done with a blow-torch. Carter checked his rear view mirror and noted with horror that the Astra was still following them.

The sound of powerful engines filled the alley for long moments before the Citroen broke clear, skidding once more as it reached another street.

Carter turned the wheel to the left, to the right.

He manoeuvred the car with a deftness born of desperation and, every time it lurched to one side, Mendham's body would swing towards him, splashing him again with warm blood. But he ignored the crimson fluid, more intent on losing the Astra which was still in pursuit. The driver was attempting to draw up alongside once again, enabling the men in the back to get a better shot.

The cars were almost level when they bore down on the zebra crossing.

Carter shouted loudly, perhaps it was meant as a warning to the pedestrians who were running from the crossing.

All but two made it.

The Citroen hit a woman in her thirties, her body flying into the air, suspended there as if on invisible wires before she fell back to the ground, rolling over on the tarmac.

The Astra struck the man with her, catapulting him a full fifteen feet. He rolled over and over, his back broken by the impact.

The two cars sped on into the King's Road.

Carter heard more sirens now, saw two police cars joining the hunt.

Yet still the Astra kept coming.

The men in it seemed oblivious to the presence of the law, so determined were they to kill the other two occupants of the Citroen.

Other cars on the road stopped or pulled into any handy side-street as the procession roared past, the police cars now trying to pull up alongside the Astra, trying to sandwich it between them. But the driver only put his foot down and Carter saw the vehicle coming closer, speeding up as it slammed into the rear of the Citroen.

Tina screamed as the impact almost sent the car out of control but Carter wrestled with the wheel and drove on, slowing down slightly, now allowing the Astra to pull up alongside him.

They roared down the road side by side.

He saw the shotgun poking out of the window, aiming at

him and he realized that he must time his next move to perfection.

As they sped past Chelsea Town Hall, Carter twisted the steering wheel and slammed full tilt into the Astra.

The impact was forceful enough to make the driver lose control.

The car mounted the pavement, scattering those bystanders who had not already taken refuge in the many shops or restaurants which lined the street. The driver fought to control the vehicle but Carter pulled the automatic from his holster and fired three, four, five times into the white car. Bullets struck the windscreen, the side windows and, finally, one hit the driver in the back of the neck.

The bullet severed his spinal cord just below the nape of his neck, shattering bone and cartilage easily, and hurtled out of his mouth, carrying several teeth with it.

The Astra careened out of control, roaring towards a furniture store.

It shattered the front window and ploughed on into the shop itself, massive lumps of glass crashing down around it.

Carter looked round and grinned, his face spattered with blood, the breath rasping in his throat.

Ahead, a lorry was pulling across the road, a massive sixteen-wheeler which had blocked the entire street.

Tina peered over the back seat and saw the lorry.

'Stay down,' shouted Carter and jammed his foot down on the accelerator until the needle on the speedometer nudged ninety.

'No,' Tina shrieked.

But Carter merely pushed her back, ducking low himself over the wheel, heading towards the lorry whose driver had now seen the Citroen. He had leapt from his cab, fearing a collision.

The police cars following slowed down, the occupants

watching the Citroen roar towards the lorry, its speed increasing.

Carter yelled something at the top of his voice.

A prayer perhaps?

The Citroen hit the lorry, passing beneath it, between the sets of massive wheels. There was a scream of buckling metal as the roof of the vehicle was torn free, flying upwards as the rest of the car hurtled on beneath the truck. It skidded twice on the other side and Carter hit the brakes, bringing it back under control, the wind pouring into his face. He was panting like a carthorse as he glanced behind him, satisfied that the lorry formed an impassable barrier. The police couldn't follow for the moment but, he realized, they would already have alerted other units and a bullet-riddled Citroen with no roof wasn't going to take much finding. He slammed on the brakes and jumped out, wrenching open the back door, pulling Tina out. Then he scurried across the street towards a blue Capri whose driver was gaping at him open-mouthed.

Carter aimed the gun at the man's head.

'Get out,' he ordered.

The man was out in seconds, running away from the car. Carter pushed Tina in and clambered behind the wheel. He started the engine and swung the car right, up Old Church Street, heading towards Fulham Road.

They didn't have much time.

He had to find a phone box.

Beside him, Tina was sobbing quietly, her blouse and jeans stained with blood. Carter reached across and squeezed her hand and she leant against his shoulder. He felt her tears soaking his shirt.

As they reached the top of the street he stopped the car and they both jumped out.

There was a phone booth just across the street. Holding Tina's hand, Carter ran across and wrenched open the door.

163

He was still breathing heavily, his throat dry and raw. He pushed the money into the slot, glancing quickly around for any sign of the police.

Or anyone else.

He began to dial.

Thirty-Three

Frank Harrison sat perfectly still in the chair, the glass gripped in his fist. But for the steady rising and falling of his chest and shoulders he could easily have been mistaken for a corpse. His face was deathly white, his eyes closed.

He had arrived at Tina's flat over an hour ago, not long after Carter had rung Billy Stripes and summoned him to take himself and Tina back to the flat in Kensington. There they had cleaned themselves up, she had changed and dressed her cuts, relieved to see that those on her face weren't deep.

Then they had waited for Harrison to arrive.

Carter had told him what had happened.

The chase. The murder of Pat Mendham.

Harrison had begun to drink, small measures at first but gradually the crystal tumbler had become increasingly full. Carter had the uncomfortable feeling that something was about to explode.

He and Billy stood looking at Harrison who had now opened his eyes and was glaring into air, occasionally looking at Tina who sat opposite him on the sofa, touching her grazed knees every so often.

'A fucking grass,' hissed Harrison, so softly the other men barely heard him. 'It had to be a fucking grass. Who else would have known where they were?' He got to his feet. 'Somebody in my firm is a stinking grass.' His breath was coming in short gasps. He looked at Carter. 'And you say you didn't see the geezer that shot Pat?'

'I saw him but he didn't look familiar,' Carter answered.

'I'm going to fucking kill him,' rasped the gang leader. When I find him I'm going to kill him. Whoever's behind this. Whoever tipped those bastards off this morning is the same one who set me up in that restaurant.'

'You can't be sure, Frank,' Billy protested.

'You want to argue with me?' roared Harrison, hurling the glass in Billy's direction.

The other man ducked and the expensive crystal exploded against the far wall.

'I want him found,' the gang boss snarled. 'Do you hear me? I want this fucking grass found.' His eyes were blazing now, the veins on his forehead throbbing madly. He let out a roar of rage and brought his hand down with thunderous force on the table-top.

Carter and Billy could only look on helplessly.

'Well that's it,' said Harrison. 'No more waiting. No more sitting around. I've lost four men in the last two weeks. It's time we started fighting back.'

'But against who?' Billy said. 'We still don't know who's behind the attacks.'

'I don't care,' bellowed Harrison. 'If we can't fight one then we'll fight them all. I want every other gang leader blown away. Fuck it, we take no chances.' A slight grin creased his lips.

The phone rang and he snatched it up.

The others saw him nodding. Heard his grunts.

'Where?' he asked.

Carter saw the boss's eyes blaze once more.

'No. Keep him there,' he snarled. 'You fucking keep him there or I'll have your head too. I'll be there in twenty minutes.'

He slammed the receiver down and turned to face the watching men.

'They've got him,' he said quietly, a smile spreading across his face. 'They've got the grass. Drake overheard him making a call to that fucking wop bastard Barbieri.'

'Who is it?' Carter wanted to know.

'McIntire,' Harrison told him. 'They're holding him at the Mayfair casino.' He laughed quietly, then the façade suddenly changed again and the rage returned. 'You,' he snapped, pointing at Carter. 'You stay with Tina. Don't leave her. Understand?'

Carter nodded.

'Come on, Billy,' Harrison said to the other man. 'We've got some business to attend to.' He started for the door. As he reached it he turned and looked back at Tina and Carter. 'You don't leave this flat, right? You don't go anywhere without my say-so. You take care of her, Carter, or I swear to God I'll make you wish your father had never met your mother.' Those eyes blazed insanely at them for a second longer; then the gang boss was gone.

Carter crossed to the window and watched the car pull away.

So, it had been McIntire all along, he thought.

He was glad Harrison hadn't told him to go to the casino with him.

There were some things he would rather not see.

166

Perhaps he should have been there, Carter thought as he sat down at the kitchen table, drumming gently with his fingers.

Perhaps he should have gone with Harrison to the casino to see what fate awaited McIntire. After all, it had been McIntire who had caused Jim's death. Carter sucked in a deep, almost painful breath. If not for the grass, his brother might still be alive now. He shook his head, realizing that McIntire's death would solve nothing. No amount of bloodshed was going to bring Jim back. And God alone knew there would be bloodshed. Carter touched the automatic beneath his left armpit as he remembered the chase that morning and how Pat Mendham had been killed.

How many more would die before this business was over?

His thoughts were interrupted by Tina.

She appeared in the doorway of the kitchen wearing just a short housecoat, her hair still damp from the shower. She gazed at Carter for a moment, smiling when he looked up at her.

'They'll kill him, won't they?' she said.

'McIntire? Yes, they'll kill him. Eventually,' Carter told her.

She crossed to him, sitting down beside him, reaching for his hand and squeezing it. He responded, gripping her hand tightly.

'You saved my life this morning, Ray,' she said softly.

He shrugged.

'It's a pity I couldn't have saved Pat as well.' He exhaled. 'I was just thinking, that night the restaurant got hit, it might have been me in the car instead of Jim. I was the driver, I *should* have been in the car.'

167

'You can't blame yourself for Jim's death,' she told him. 'You shouldn't feel any guilt.'

'That's easy for you to say, Tina,' he remarked with just a hint of anger in his voice.

She gazed at him for a moment longer before lifting his hand and kissing it, pressing her lips to each finger in turn.

'I'm sorry,' she murmured quietly.

She stood up and moved across to him. Carter rose to meet her, enfolding her in his arms, pulling her tightly against him.

'If *you had* been killed that night . . .' she began, but her words were cut short as he kissed her. Their lips pressed hard together then parted, tongues seeking the warm moistness beyond. Tina gripped the back of Carter's neck, as if not wanting him to break the kiss. He felt the dampness of her hair as he stroked her shoulders through the thin material of her housecoat.

When they finally parted they were both panting, Tina's face flushed. She looked almost imploringly at Carter, taking his hand in hers as she did so. Compliant to her wishes, he allowed her to place his hand on her breast and then it was his own desire which took over. He kneaded the firm globe, feeling the stiffness of her nipple beneath his palm, repeating his actions on her other breast. She gasped softly as she felt him loosen the thin belt of the housecoat. He parted it to reveal her upper body, leaning forward to take first one and then the other nipple between his lips, flicking the erect buds with his tongue.

She felt his strong arms fasten around her waist and he lifted her up on to the table, slipping his own jacket off and allowing it to fall to the floor. He opened the housecoat completely until her entire slender form was exposed to him and, for brief seconds, he allowed his eyes to take in every detail of her body. Her rounded breasts, the nipples hard and upstanding. Her flat stomach and the tiny triangle of hair between her slim legs. Carter had never felt such overpowering desire in his life before. He dropped to his knees before her, his head hovering between her legs for a moment. Then he planted his lips upon her vagina, tasting her wetness, allowing his tongue to flick at her distended lips, slowly taking each one between his teeth before lapping at it gently.

She moaned with pleasure and ground her pelvis against his face, snaking one leg around the back of his neck to draw him in closer.

Tina closed her eyes and surrendered to the expert ministrations of his tongue as he probed and licked at her most sensitive areas, finally fastening his lips around the stiffness of her clitoris, coaxing it from its fleshy hood.

He parted her legs wider with his hands, running his fingers softly along the insides of her thighs, his mouth now working more swiftly, his tongue flicking rapidly in and out of her liquescent cleft.

She wanted him more fully but was reluctant to forgo the pleasure she felt building to a crescendo. As he continued to tease and caress her vagina with his tongue she felt the first unmistakeable feelings of warmth beginning to spread across her belly and thighs. Her breathing became more rapid and she gripped the edge of the table, arching her back to allow him easier access, wanting him to penetrate her even more deeply, needing the release of orgasm.

The pleasure rose to a peak and Tina bit gently at her own fist in a vain attempt to stifle the cry she unleashed as she came.

Carter continued his skilful manipulations, feeling her body quiver violently. Her cries gradually receded into small whimpers of pleasure and she stroked his hair until he slowly rose, his own erection now throbbing powerfully inside his trousers.

Tina sat up, reaching for his zip, pulling it down, loosening his belt so that she could remove his trousers completely. As she did, Carter removed his shirt.

In a matter of moments he too was naked.

He took Tina in his arms, as a man might carry a child and walked through to the sitting room.

There he laid her gently on the floor and slid his stiff shaft slowly into her, savouring the tightness of her muscles as they enveloped him like a slippery glove. He moved effortlessly within her, withdrawing almost to the very limit before pushing deep into her again. She urged him on, knowing that his own climax was close.

Carter felt her hands on his back, her nails scraping gently against the flesh of his spine, trailing down to his buttocks. She gripped him hard, forcing him into her with a ferocity which seemed to overtake them both, an animalistic frenzy which had only one purpose. Their mutual release.

He grunted deep in his throat as he felt that ultimate pleasure sweep over him and Tina too gasped her delight as she felt his hot fluid filling her.

They writhed together, melting into one for brief seconds. As if their two bodies had fused with the heat of their passion. All they felt was pleasure.

For those exquisite moments there was nothing else but love.

Carter stroked Tina's cheek with the back of his hand and she twisted her face to kiss his fingers, taking one into her mouth. He smiled down at her, pushing some hair from her face, enjoying its softness against his fingers.

'I love you,' she whispered, raising her head to kiss him gently on the tip of the nose. As she lay back down he saw that there were tears in her eyes. 'Don't leave me, Ray. Please.'

He shook his head.

'I'll never leave you,' he told her, holding her tightly in his

170

arms, gripping her until it seemed he would snap her in two. 'Never.'

They continued to hold one another, enjoying the touch of the other's body. Lost in a moment which was all too fleeting. But for that reason they savoured it even more. Able, momentarily, to forget everything else. The fear. The pain.

For now there was just love.

Thirty-Five

The second punch broke McIntire's nose.

The nasal bone dissolved under the impact and the fleshy appendage was momentarily flattened by the force of the blow. Blood burst from the smashed nose, most of it spilling down McIntire's chest, colouring his white shirt.

He toppled backwards, slamming his head against the floor, his arms bound behind him tightly to prevent him protecting himself.

Joe Duggan dragged the chair upright again and McIntire found himself gazing into Frank Harrison's face.

The gang boss gripped McIntire by the chin and twisted his head round so that he was looking directly into the older man's eyes.

'Don't pass out on me yet, you bastard,' snarled Harrison and drove another pile-driver punch into the face of the bound man.

The next blow split his bottom lip and loosened one of his

teeth. More blood spilled down his chin.

'How much did Barbieri pay you to set me up?' Harrison demanded, stepping back and lighting a cigarette.

'Frank, I swear to God I didn't set you up,' McIntire burbled, feeling his stomach contract as some blood ran back down his throat. He tried to wrestle his arms free of the rope which held him but the hemp had been fastened so tightly that it cut into his flesh.

'Don't lie to me, you cunt,' Harrison snarled, taking a step closer. He pulled the cigarette from his mouth and, with one swift movement, pressed it to McIntire's right cheek, hearing the hiss as the glowing end burned flesh.

McIntire screamed in pain as his skin was seared by the glowing tip. The skin darkened then rose swiftly into a blister.

Harrison gripped the other man by the hair and wrenched his head back, ignoring the blood which smeared his own hands.

'How much were you paid?' the boss roared.

McIntire could only grunt in pain. A low gurgle escaped him, as if he were gargling with the blood which filled his throat. Harrison snarled angrily and hit him again, this time with the back of his hand. The heavy signet ring which the gang boss wore caught him across the cheek and tore some of the skin.

'You've worked for me for more than seven years,' Harrison reminded him. 'Why, Lou?'

McIntire's head lolled forward on to his chest and he spat blood feebly on to his shirt.

'It was bad enough having a go at me,' Harrison continued. 'But four of my best men are dead and my girl was almost killed. Tell me what that fucking wop paid you or I'll give you pain you could never have dreamed of.'

McIntire shook his head slowly and tried to speak. His lip

172

had already swollen up badly, his nose looked as if it had been repeatedly slammed against a wall. To someone entering the room and glancing quickly at him, he appeared to be wearing a crimson mask. Only his eyes showed white amidst the blood.

'Who killed Joule and Dome?' Harrison asked.

'I don't know,' McIntire told him weakly.

'And Pat Mendham?'

Again the other man merely shook his head as if he were resigned to his fate. Had he known what that was to be, he might well have been a little more forthcoming with his answers.

Harrison looked at Billy Stripes and nodded. The big man crossed to a cabinet behind his boss's desk and pulled something out. An object with a long lead.

It took McIntire only a second to realize it was a power drill.

He watched in terror as Billy plugged it in and pressed the starter button, watching as the bit spun at over 3,500 rpm. The high pitched whine died away as he switched it off again and moved closer to McIntire who now began to struggle even more violently in his chair.

'Hold him,' snapped Harrison and Joe Duggan duly obliged, steadying the captive as Billy moved closer, flicking the drill on again. It gave off a plaintive scream as the drill bit spun viciously.

'Roll his trousers up,' Harrison instructed, watching as Drake knelt by the bound man's legs and tore the material, exposing bare flesh to just above the knee.

'Frank, for God's sake,' shrieked McIntire, struggling madly, his eyes bulging in their sockets.

'Keep the fucker still,' the gang boss instructed, savouring the terror on his victim's face as Billy bent lower, the drill bit aimed at a spot just below McIntire's left kneecap.

173

'Oh Jesus, no,' McIntire bellowed, trying to squirm free. His shouts had become sobs. 'Frank, please call him off, for God's sake.'

The drill was barely six inches from his kneecap.

'Who killed my men?' Harrison demanded.

'I don't know. I swear on my mother's life. Please God stop it, for fuck's sake, please.' The entreaties fell on deaf ears.

Four inches away.

'How much did Barbieri pay you to set me up?'

Three inches.

'I'll tell you, I'll tell you anything. Please stop,' screamed McIntire.

Two inches.

'You've got to learn, Lou,' Harrison said, grinning.

One inch.

'But I said I'd tell you,' screamed McIntire, looking down to see that the drill was still aimed at his kneecap. 'Frank, please. Please . . .'

The last word dissolved into a shriek of agony, the like of which few of the men in the room had ever heard.

The drill bit lacerated flesh then, with Billy Stripes' weight behind it, cut effortlessly through the bone of the patella, churning nerves and ligaments on its way. There was a high-pitched squeal as the bone was pierced then followed by a loud crack as the entire kneecap split in two. Billy began to pull it free, blood flying from the spinning bit.

McIntire felt his leg go numb as pain enveloped it from toe to thigh. It felt as if someone had set light to the whole limb. He screamed but the sound faded as he felt consciousness leaving him. His head flopped forward but Duggan seized his hair and snapped him upright again, slapping his bloodied face to revive him.

Tears of pain and fear were coursing down his cheeks,

174

cutting a path through the crimson fluid which had congealed there.

Harrison looked on impassively.

'I hate fucking grasses,' he said vehemently. 'You talk too much, Lou. Maybe we should make sure you don't keep on babbling.'

Harrison reached behind him into the drawer of his desk.

He held the pliers in his right hand so that McIntire could get a good look at them. Then the gang boss stepped forward.

'Open his mouth,' he said to Joe Duggan.

Realizing what was to happen, McIntire clamped his jaws firmly together, much as a frightened child might do at the dentist.

Harrison nodded at Duggan who gripped the other man's jaws and started to prise them open. McIntire resisted stubbornly, his face, wet with his own blood, was difficult to grip and he managed to jerk away from Duggan's grip for precious seconds but it was only a momentary respite.

Billy Stripes put down the drill and grabbed McIntire's broken nose, twisting the already shattered bone until more blood flowed. The combination of being unable to breath and the agonising pain caused McIntire to open his mouth.

Quick as a flash, Duggan gripped the other man's bottom jaw and weighed down on it causing his mouth to yawn open.

Harrison advanced with the pliers, eyes narrowed, glancing at the terrified McIntire for a moment. Then he fastened the steel grips onto one of McIntire's bottom incisors and pulled.

Such was the force exerted by the gang boss that the tooth cracked under the strain and McIntire screamed again as enamel and pulp spilled back on to his tongue. He retched violently but did not vomit. Excruciating pain thundered inside his head with each beat of his heart and he tried to beg for mercy but, before he could speak, Harrison had taken a firm grip on a molar at the back of his open mouth.

This tooth was stronger and as Harrison tugged, he actually felt it come free of the gum. Blood filled McIntire's mouth but Harrison continued pulling, actually pressing one foot against the captive man's chair to gain more leverage. McIntire tried to struggle but it was useless. Held by a combination of ropes and two of his former colleagues, he was helpless, able only to sit there as Harrison continued wrenching his tooth from its socket.

A little more of the molar came free, tendrils of root dangling from the dripping base.

McIntire felt as if the top of his head was coming off and, incredibly, the pain seemed to intensify as Harrison finally succeeded in ripping the molar out. He gripped it in the teeth of the pliers, like some dripping trophy, blood and sputum hanging from it like thick streamers. He glanced into McIntire's open mouth and saw the hole in the gum left by the tooth. It was a nasty wound, rather like an open sore. It pumped blood steadily.

The gang leader waited for a moment then took hold of another tooth.

This time McIntire blacked out and no amount of slapping roused him.

Harrison ripped the tooth out, snapping it as he did so, leaving a large portion of the root still in the lacerated gum. Then he threw it to one side and looked into McIntire's face. The man was breathing faintly, his chest rising almost imperceptibly.

Harrison stepped back, never taking his eyes from the unconscious individual before him.

'Get rid of him,' he said to Billy Stripes. 'Then clean this place up. I'm going back to the flat to see how Tina is. First I've got to make a couple of phone calls.'

'So what do we do now, Frank?' Duggan asked.

'What we should have done in the beginning,' said the gang boss, reaching for the phone. He dialled, waiting for the receiver to be picked up at the other end. As he stood waiting he wrinkled his nose, aware that McIntire had lost control of his bowels. The phone was finally picked up at the other end.

'Thorpe? This is Harrison,' he said. 'You didn't come up with the goods did you? I had to do the work myself.' He looked at the unconscious figure of McIntire and grinned.

'I've been too busy trying to cover what happened yesterday,' the Detective Inspector said. 'Car chases, gun fights. Where do you think you are, New York? Well fuck you, I've had enough. I told you I couldn't protect you if things went as far as this. You're on your own now, Frank.'

'You were never any use to me, Thorpe,' Harrison hissed. 'But listen to me, you'd better keep your head down in the next few weeks because otherwise you might be going down with the rest of them.'

'The rest of who? What the hell are you planning?' the policeman wanted to know.

'Every other gang leader in London,' Harrison snarled. 'I'm wiping them out. This has gone too far, you're right. Well now I'm going to call a man who can get the fucking job done.'

'A hit man?'

'Bright boy. Well, now you know you'd better keep out of the way otherwise he might have to add one more to his list.'

'You can't do it,' Thorpe protested.

'Don't you ever tell me what I can or can't do,' the gang leader snarled. 'I gave you forty-eight hours. I sat still for forty-eight hours. Well fuck it. No more. You had your chance and you blew it. Now it's *my* turn.'

PART TWO

'I never ask no questions,
I never speak my mind.
I've always found that silence
helps to keep me and my kind alive . . .'

Judas Priest

'Hell is a city much like London . . .'

Shelley

Thirty-Six

'You might attract more customers if you cleaned the place up. It stinks in here.'

Frank Harrison waved a hand in front of his nose and squinted once more at the large ledger laid out before him.

'Oh leave it out, Frank,' Reg Truman said, grinding some cigarette ash into the carpet. 'The old girl who cleans hasn't been round yet. The place is usually cleaner than Mother Theresa's underwear.'

'Well something's making you lose money,' Harrison said, running his index finger down the column of figures. 'Takings are down by a grand from last week. Am I running a strip joint or a fucking charity?'

'The other places have more girls, more specialized acts. We do the best we can,' Truman protested.

'Specialized acts,' Harrison grunted. 'So, what are you telling me, if you had a tart who could pull rabbits out of her fanny you'd get more punters in here?'

Truman shrugged.

'It'd be worth a try,' he chuckled.

Harrison didn't see the joke. He owned five strip clubs in Soho and each one had been losing money for the past month or so. He'd put it down to other gangs muscling in on his manor. Well, if it was, all that would stop once the hit man got his act together. Harrison looked around him. In the harsh light of day the club looked like any other cabaret venue. A dozen or so tables, a small bar and a stage. A considerable p.a. system had been set up, through which music was played to accompany the girls in their on-stage gyrations. As Harrison sat looking at the bank of speakers they suddenly burst into life, filling the club with music loud enough to crack the walls.

'Leroy, for fuck's sake,' roared Truman. The music ceased as abruptly as it had started.

An unmistakeably Jamaican voice came floating over the p.a.

'Sorry Reg, I didn't realize it was on,' said the voice.

'Why don't you get rid of that bleeding jungle bunny? If he's playing that reggae shit, no wonder no one wants to come in.'

'He's a good worker, Frank,' Truman said.

Harrison shook his head and looked at the ledger again.

Carter stood by the door with Damien Drake. Out in the car McAuslan was sitting behind the wheel.

Tina had been left in the care of Billy Stripes for the day.

Just for a fleeting second when Harrison had first called him, Carter had wondered if the gang boss had suspected something was going on between himself and Tina but he'd reassured himself that the boss was still blissfully ignorant of their dangerous affair. If he'd any suspicions at all, Carter thought, then *he* would be floating face down in the Thames by now.

He took a long draw on his cigarette and glanced across at Drake who was scanning the photos of girls that adorned the club's entrance. The beauties in the display case had never been inside the club though, Carter knew that. He wondered how many of them looked at the photo of Joan Collins outside and went home disappointed because she hadn't turned up to do a routine.

He was still contemplating this when he saw a man approach the entrance to the club.

He was well dressed, his suit immaculate. Carter guessed he was in his mid-thirties. About five ten, thickset and very powerfully built. And yet there was a delicacy to his features which belied his build. He nodded a greeting to Carter as he approached and, despite himself, the younger man found himself returning the gesture. He noticed that there was a light covering of whiskers on the man's cheeks and chin.

As the man approached, Drake stepped in front of him.

'Where are you going?' he asked.

'I'm looking for Frank Harrison,' the man said, his voice cultured but without the trappings of pretension.

'And who are you?' Drake demanded.

'My business is with him. Now, if you'd let me pass please,' said the newcomer.

Carter took a step back, watching as Drake put his arm across the doorway to block the man's passage.

'There's always one isn't there?' the man said, shaking his head.

He shot out a hand and gripped Drake by the throat, lifting him off his feet and slamming him against the door frame with a force that almost knocked him out.

Carter raised a hand to reach for his automatic but, without turning round, his hand still fastened around Drake's neck, the man spoke again.

'Leave the gun where it is,' he said softly. 'Now tell Harrison I want to see him, otherwise I'll break this half-wit's neck.'

Carter eyed him malevolently for a moment and then ducked past him into the club.

Harrison, already disturbed by the commotion outside, was on his feet, waiting.

'What the hell's going on out there?' he demanded.

Before Carter could speak, the smartly dressed man had followed him inside, leaving Drake almost unconscious by the door.

'Frank Harrison?' the man asked.

'Yeah, and who the fuck are you?'

'My name's David Mitchell. You sent for me.'

Thirty-Seven

It was as if someone had pressed the freeze-frame button on a video. The little tableau inside the strip club was momentarily motionless as all eyes turned towards Mitchell.

He stood in the doorway a moment longer before stepping forward.

The film was running again.

From behind him, Drake blundered in, clutching his throat, massaging the red marks where Mitchell's fingers had gouged into his flesh. He lunged towards the newcomer but Mitchell merely sidestepped and Drake overbalanced, crashing into a nearby table. He sprawled there for a moment glaring angrily at Mitchell who didn't even spare him a glance.

Drake reached for the pistol beneath his left armpit.

It was Harrison who stepped forward and kicked his hand away.

He dragged Drake to his feet and pushed him aside.

'You're a wise man, Mr Harrison,' said Mitchell. 'You've

lost enough men already, best not to add to the total.' He glared at Drake and the other man saw the fire in Mitchell's eyes. He backed off.

Carter watched the entire scene nervously, wondering if Harrison was going to give the order to start shooting. If this newcomer was as handy with a gun as he was with his bare hands then the cleaning lady was going to need more than a vacuum cleaner.

Reg Truman looked on bewildered, his eyes flicking rapidly back and forth from Harrison to Mitchell who had now fixed the gang leader in an unblinking stare.

'Who are you?' Harrison wanted to know.

'I told you, my name's Mitchell. I understand you need my services.'

'You're a hit man?' Harrison asked, although it sounded more like a statement than a question.

Mitchell nodded.

'You weren't the geezer I spoke to last night,' Harrison insisted.

'Do you need my services or not?' Mitchell said sharply.

Harrison wasn't slow to catch the irritation in the hit man's voice.

'It depends how good you are,' he hissed.

'You won't find better.'

'You're sure of yourself.'

'I can afford to be.'

Harrison finally sat down. Mitchell remained where he was. Drake continued glaring at him.

'Get us a drink,' Harrison said to Reg Truman and the strip club manager crossed to the small bar and returned with some glasses.

'This isn't a social call, Mr Harrison,' Mitchell told him, declining the offer of a drink. 'I understood that you had some work for me. I'd rather discuss that.'

Harrison sipped slowly at his whisky, regarding the new-comer over the rim of his glass.

'I suppose you want to discuss money too?' the gang boss said.

'Not yet. I'll wait until the job's done,' Mitchell told him.

'You'll be needing information then, about the blokes I want taken out.'

'All I need from you is a driver. Nothing else,' Mitchell announced.

'What about a base to work from? Weapons?'

'That's all been taken care of. Like I said, just the driver.'

Harrison looked at Carter.

'Ray?'

Carter nodded, albeit somewhat reluctantly.

'Let's go then,' said Mitchell, turning towards the door.

'Hold on,' Harrison called after him. 'Where do I contact you?'

'You don't. I'll call *you*, when and if it's necessary.'

'Look, Mitchell, I'm not sure I like this arrangement,' snapped the gang boss, getting to his feet. 'You're supposed to be working for me . . .'

Mitchell cut him short.

'You want the job done, don't you?' he challenged. Harrison found himself mesmerised by that icy stare.

'You keep me informed, right?' he said, although some of the bravado had gone out of his voice.

Mitchell hesitated a second longer and then walked out. Carter was about to follow him when the gang boss called him back.

'Ray, you keep your eye on that bastard,' he said angrily. 'I don't know who the fuck he thinks he is. I want to know where he's working from, get me addresses, a phone number, anything. If he farts I want to know about it. You got that?'

Carter nodded and went outside. He found Mitchell standing on the pavement by the club entrance.

'If we're going to be working together, it'd help if I knew your name,' the hit man said.

Carter introduced himself and wandered over to the waiting Volvo Estate. He slid behind the wheel and started the engine. Mitchell climbed into the back seat.

'Where to?' asked Carter, catching a glimpse of the hit man in the rear view mirror.

'Head towards Highgate.'

Carter nodded and pulled out into the traffic. His passenger, he found, wasn't very talkative but seemed content to gaze unseeing out of the car windows. It was as if his mind was elsewhere.

'You been in this game long?' Carter asked finally, tiring of the silence.

'Long enough,' Mitchell told him, non-committally.

'You're not from around here, are you?'

'Very astute,' the hit man answered, the merest hint of sarcasm in his voice.

Carter glanced at him again in the rear view mirror. There was something about this man which made him feel uneasy. It wasn't just his offhand manner. There was something else which was indefinable. A coldness, an indifference which Carter presumed went with the job. Maybe all hit men were like this. He didn't know. He didn't really want to know.

'Do you carry a gun?' Mitchell asked.

'Yes, a 9mm automatic Smith,' the driver replied, both surprised and relieved that his passenger was finally making some attempts at conversation, perfunctory or not.

'It's a good weapon. I prefer a Browning myself. It takes a thirteen shot clip and it's powerful.'

'What about up close?'

'I rarely get close.'

187

Carter swung the car around a corner, narrowly avoiding the back of a van which had braked sharply.

'Stop here,' snapped Mitchell.

'But we're in the middle of the bloody road,' Carter protested.

Mitchell was unimpressed by the cars and other vehicles that drove around them, some sounding their hooters.

'Give me a number where I can reach you,' the hit man said sharply. 'I'll get in touch with you. Tell you where to pick me up and when.'

Carter scribbled his phone number on a piece of paper and handed it to his passenger. Mitchell was out of the car immediately, sprinting across the busy street before disappearing down the entrance to an underground station. The driver watched the dark-suited man descend the stairs out of sight before he put the car in gear and drove on. What the hell was he going to tell Harrison now?

Thirty-Eight

'That's him. The one in the middle.'

Carter nodded in the direction of the three men who had just emerged from the pub called 'The Galleon'.

David Mitchell looked on impassively, his eyes never leaving the overweight, swarthy man Carter had indicated.

Lou Barbieri walked to the edge of the pavement and turned, looking back at the pub.

From where they sat, Mitchell and Carter could see him

pointing at various things on the building, occasionally look-ing at one of his companions. 'The Galleon' was one of several pubs owned by Barbieri in and around the Finsbury Park area and he was considering having it re-decorated. Neither he or the men with him paid any attention to the Volvo Estate parked about thirty yards further up the street, or to its occupants who watched them so intently.

Carter glanced back at his companion.

'You ready?' he said quietly.

Mitchell didn't answer. He merely pulled a black case on to his lap and unsnapped the two clasps. He pulled out the HK33 and the Spas. Within the confines of the car the shotgun in particular looked huge, the muzzle yawning ominously at Carter.

'When I tell you,' said Mitchell, slamming a forty round magazine into the HK33. 'Drive past them slowly.'

'Slowly?' the driver said.

'Just do it,' Mitchell told him. He took four shells from his jacket pocket and pushed them into the Spas, working the pump action to chamber a round. Then, as Carter watched, the hit man pulled a final piece of equipment from his pocket.

The driver looked aghast as he saw Mitchell snap on the headphones of a Walkman. He fumbled in his pocket and produced a tape which he pushed into the machine, pushing the volume up to maximum.

'Music while you work,' murmured Carter.

The second the scream of guitars began to fill Mitchell's ears he smiled broadly and nodded at Carter.

'Go,' he bellowed.

The car moved off, building up speed gradually, drawing nearer to the three men who stood on the pavement.

'*Welcome to the Jungle*,' roared the singer, the second reverberating inside Mitchell's head. '*We've got fun and games . . .*'

The car drew nearer.

'*We got everything you want, honey we know the names* . . .'

Mitchell wound down the rear window and steadied the HK33 against his shoulder.

'*We are the people that can find, whatever you may need* . . .'

Barbieri turned and saw the Volvo bearing down on them.

'*If you got the money, honey, we got your disease* . . .'

Carter saw the look of horror and surprise on the gang leader's face as he caught sight of the rifle aimed at him.

The three men seemed to freeze, not sure whether to throw themselves to the ground or dash back into the pub.

'*In the jungle, welcome to the jungle* . . .'

One of the men pulled a revolver from his jacket.

'*Watch it bring you to your knees* . . .'

The gesture was a futile one.

Barbieri shouted something which Carter couldn't hear.

'*I wanna watch you bleed* . . .'

Mitchell opened fire.

The staccato rattle of the automatic rifle tore through the relative peacefulness of the street. Bullets that missed the three men struck the pub, a couple blasting in a window, another ripping the sign which hung above the door.

Barbieri was hit in the chest and throat.

The first bullet caught him just above the pharynx exploding through his neck with such ferocity that it ripped away a portion of his spinal chord and almost decapitated him. Blood burst from the wound with the force of a high pressure hose, some of it spattering the side of the Volvo. The other shots shredded his chest, splintering ribs and ripping through his lungs, bursting them like fleshy balloons before tearing from his back leaving exit wounds large enough for a man to put his head in. Confetti of pulverized bone, blood and lung tissue sprayed the pavement as the Italian went down.

His companions fared little better. The one with the revolver was hit in the stomach, the bullet bursting his abdomen and macerating most of his large intestine. He dropped to his knees in time to catch another shot in the forehead.

So great was the impact that the top of his head was transformed into liquid. Even bone disintegrated under the terrifying force. Grey brain-matter flew into the air like thick dust.

The third man managed to turn and run for the pub.

Two shots hit him in the back, the blast lifting him off his feet. He was thrown several feet, slamming into the pub doors, blood spurting madly from his wounds. He slid to the floor, his body twitching spasmodically.

There were screams from inside the pub and two women across the street bolted away from the car, fearing for their own lives. But Mitchell was only concerned with the three men lying before him.

He emptied the magazine into them, raking it back and forth across their bullet-stitched bodies, watching as each corpse jerked and jumped when the shells hit it. Lumps of clothing, matted with blood, flew into the air, propelled by the impacts.

The hit-man dropped the HK33 and picked up the Spas, taking aim at Barbieri's body.

He fired twice.

The massive discharges were perfectly aimed.

The first blasted a hole the size of a football between the dead man's legs.

The second tore off most of the left side of his head.

'Go, get out of here,' roared Mitchell and the Volvo sped off.

'It's gonna bring you down . . .'

191

The room looked as if it contained a heavy fog. A bluish haze eddied around the occupants like noxious mist. Detective Sergeant Vic Riley added to the nicotine-stained clouds by lighting up a Dunhill. He blew a stream of smoke and looked towards the head of the table at which Chief Commissioner Frederick Harvey sat.

The Metropolitan Police Commissioner was an imposing sight in his dark suit. A large man with hands like ham hocks and heavy jowls more suited to a bloodhound. He was chewing on the stem of an unlit pipe.

Laid out before him and the eight men who sat around the table were a dozen black and white photos.

Riley glanced at the nearest of them, glad that he hadn't eaten a heavy lunch.

Beside him Detective Inspector Thorpe was picking his teeth with a broken match, gazing through the haze of smoke at the large picture window which looked out towards Westminster although from the fifth floor of New Scotland Yard little was visible apart from the grime-encrusted sides of other buildings.

Harvey finally coughed and rose to his feet. Satisfied that he had the attention of his detectives, he took the pipe from his mouth and laid it on the table-top. He reached, instead, for two of the photos spread out on the large oval table.

'Maureen Lawson and Paul Hughes,' he announced. 'I'm sure I don't need to remind you. She's a presenter on Thames Television or should I say, she *was*. She's lived with Hughes for the last fourteen months. He's an editor, or rather *was*, worked in films and TV. Rich, both of them. Rich and dead, as you can see. Very dead.' Harvey turned towards a small, balding figure on his right who nodded and got to his feet.

Alan Daniels had worked as chief medical examiner at New Scotland Yard for over twenty years. He wiped a hand over his shiny pate.

'The wounds on both bodies were made with a selection of weapons,' he began, a slight lisp tainting his voice. 'I found thirty-seven separate stab wounds on Miss Lawson's body, mostly around the face, neck and chest. Her nipples had been cut off, so had her ears. Mr Hughes' body bore twenty-nine separate wounds, his genitals had been removed and stuck in his mouth.' He held up a photo. 'As you can see.'

Harvey nodded to his companion and the coroner sat down.

'There's no doubt that the murders were committed by the same group of people who killed the Kenning family. There was excrement and blood smeared on the walls of the flat, and some of the slogans were the same as those found at the Kenning place.' Harvey dropped the photos, his mood changing from relaxed detachment to irritation. 'Five murders in a fortnight and we still haven't got a bloody suspect in custody. What the hell is happening out there?'

No one had an answer.

'And if that isn't enough, there's this,' he picked up more of the photos. They showed the bullet-riddled bodies of Lou Barbieri and his two bodyguards. 'Yesterday, in broad daylight, this happened.' He looked at Thorpe. 'What is it, a gang war?'

The DI shuffled uncomfortably in his seat and opened his mouth to speak but Harvey merely pressed on.

'Car chases through the West End, gun fights. Somebody's been watching too many gangster films,' the commissioner said irritably. 'And we've no leads on who painted the pavement with Barbieri either, have we?'

'Not yet, sir,' said Thorpe. 'Presumably it was one of the other gangs.'

'Brilliant,' exclaimed Harvey. 'I didn't really think the Salvation Army sanctioned the hit.'

Some of the other men around the table chuckled but a withering glance from their superior soon banished any humour.

'Whoever did it was very good,' Daniels interjected. 'Very professional too. In most of the hits we've had to deal with, the killer has used a handgun of some description. This hit man obviously didn't intend there to be any survivors; hence his use of automatic weapons.'

'So we can probably expect reprisals,' Riley said.

'Definitely,' Harvey said flatly. He looked at the photos of Barbieri and shook his head wearily. 'One thing we haven't considered is a possible link between the two sets of murders. I want to know if any of the victims of these so-called "rich killers" had underworld contacts.'

'But John Kenning was a respectable business man,' said DS Chris Morrison, a young, slightly-built officer seated across the table from Thorpe. 'And the Donaldson kids were killed, not the old man. I can't see how there could be a link, sir.'

'First thing, son, *no one* is respectable. I've never met a business man yet who hadn't been involved in a fiddle of one kind or another. Christ, it's second nature to most of them,' Harvey insisted. 'Wasn't it Balzac who said behind every fortune there's a crime? Well look into it. Check out their contacts.'

Riley raised his hand.

'But surely, sir, if the "rich" victims *had* been crooked why not just use a hit man to get rid of them? Why butcher their families too?'

'Riley, as I get older I like to indulge in that wonderful pastime known as clutching at straws. Don't deny me that pleasure,' Harvey said wearily and once again a ripple of laughter filled the room. The commissioner sighed and looked at the photos of the dead presenter and the bullet-riddled gang boss.

'We've got a bunch of lunatics running around chopping up everyone with more than twenty pence in the bank and gangland is about to explode. I don't think it would be an understatement to say we had a few problems.'

Forty

The grave was almost joyously ostentatious.

A celebration of manic bad taste.

Two huge marble angels stood on either side, each one with an arm raised aloft supporting a plaque which bore the legend 'MUM'. They looked down on a black stone emblazoned with gold letters and a photo of the deceased. The size and outlandishness of the grave made it all the more incongruous amongst the older and overgrown resting places in Hammersmith Cemetery but it was there to be seen, to be marvelled at.

As far as Eugene Hayes was concerned, nothing was too good for his mother.

He stood by the graveside, his long leather coat flapping in the gentle breeze, the overpowering scent of roses filling his nostrils.

He held before him a massive cross shaped from brilliant red blooms. Pausing for a moment he stooped and laid it across the plinth in front of the stone.

'Happy Birthday, Mum,' he said cheerfully, touching the brim of his grey fedora.

He always wore a hat, mainly to cover his balding head. Hayes was not a vain man but he felt that baldness was somewhat undignified, that it made him look older than his forty-three years. Even though he'd read that it was a sign of virility he had not been persuaded to forsake the sanctuary of headgear. He glanced round to check that the three men who stood with him had removed their hats. He didn't want any disrespect around his mum's grave. She'd brought him up well, struggling to support him through his school years after his father had run off with another woman. Hayes had never forgiven the bastard for that. It was one of the reasons he'd had his father traced eight months earlier and why he'd personally put a bullet through the man's head. It had upset his mum so much when his father had run off and he didn't like to see her upset. She'd died just over a year ago and Eugene had thought it only courteous to wait until she passed on before killing his father. The bastard.

Still, he thought wistfully, what was done was done. At least he'd been able to repay his mum for all her hard work. He'd bought her a three-bedroomed flat in Chelsea and paid all the bills. Anything she'd wanted he'd taken care of. She'd been happy there but, as she'd said to him, she'd have been happy anywhere. As long as her Eugene was doing well. Eugene Hayes was doing very well. With an annual income in excess of five million, Hayes was reckoned to be one of the richest of London's gang bosses. But there were more important things to him than money. He was in love.

He looked at his lover now, smiling across the grave.

Clive Robson smiled back.

They had been together for almost three years since their first meeting in one of Hayes' clubs. Robson had been a barman. He was twenty-three, smooth shaven and powerfully built. The opposite of Hayes who was short. But the difference in height was unimportant. Love was blind to such inconsequential details.

David Mitchell told Carter to wait for him about twenty yards down the street and then swung himself out of the Fiesta and walked towards the cemetery gates. As he walked slowly up the narrow path he glanced across towards the gathering around Louise Hayes' grave.

He spotted Eugene immediately.

Walking slowly, his professional eye taking in the little tableau, Mitchell noted the positions of the men who accompanied the gang leader. The one who stood opposite him and the two who were standing beside an old stone tomb about twenty yards behind.

The church was about a hundred yards to their right. Mitchell looked up at the ancient building and watched as its weather vane turned briskly in the breeze. As he watched he saw the priest emerge from the small church. The man looked across at Mitchell, nodded a greeting which the hit man returned, and then disappeared back inside the building.

Mitchell cut across the grass towards Hayes and his men, stepping around tombstones, apologising inwardly when he stepped on unmarked graves. His quarry was less than fifty yards away now and still hadn't noticed his approach. Mitchell slowed down, pausing beside one grave to pull a fresh flower from the wreath which adorned it. He held the rose to his nose, enjoying the scent. Looping the stem through his buttonhole, he walked on.

Thirty yards away from his quarry he paused again, slipping the Walkman's headphones on to his ears. The tape was already in the machine. He pressed the 'Play' button. The sound of guitars filled his head.

He walked on towards Hayes, one hand now slipping inside his jacket, closing around the butt of the Ingram M-10.

The first of Hayes' bodyguards saw Mitchell approaching and nudged his companion, nodding in the direction of the newcomer.

The second bodyguard, a swarthy individual called Tucker, stepped forward to block Mitchell's path.

Hayes seemed oblivious to the intruder and was contentedly gazing down at his mother's grave, occasionally looking across at his lover.

Hayes reached into his pocket and pushed up the volume of the tape. The music became deafening.

'*Hey, hey, it's coming your way . . .*'

Tucker stepped in front of the hit man and shook his head – a gesture designed to dissuade the newcomer from advancing any further.

'*Dare you to spit on my grave . . .*'

Mitchell pulled the Ingram free of his jacket and gripped it tightly, the barrel lowered at Tucker.

The bodyguard opened his mouth to say something but whatever it was disappeared beneath the staccato rattle of automatic fire as Mitchell opened up.

'*Hey, hey, hell is to pay . . .*'

Mitchell fired in short bursts, raking the sub-gun back and forth.

The blast hit Tucker in the chest, ripping holes in his clothing and his body. Two shells tore through his chest, one of them shattering a rib, the other bursting his heart. He was flung backwards by the short-range discharge, blood spraying wildly from the wounds. He crashed into a gravestone and Mitchell fired two more shots into him, the second of which caught him in the face. The bullet shattered his cheekbone and one side of his head seemed to collapse in on itself. The heavy grain round erupted from the back of his skull, spattering the headstone with fragments of bone and brain.

'*Dare you to spit on my grave . . .*'

The other bodyguard reached for his pistol but Mitchell spun round, dropping to one knee as he opened up again.

The burst of fire from the Ingram stitched a dotted line of holes across the man's chest and he fell backwards, the gun spinning from his grasp. He sprawled in the long grass, blood pumping from his wounds. He tried to drag himself towards the pistol, feeling the cold air hissing through the rents in his lungs. He coughed and blood spilled over his lips. He had one hand on the pistol when Mitchell turned on him again.

A single shot hit him in the base of the skull, bursting his head as if someone had placed an explosive charge inside his cranium. The top of his skull was lifted off, sticky gobbets of brain spraying into the air, propelled by a gout of blood. His body twitched once and then lay still.

'*I will take your sweet dreams with me . . .*'

Mitchell turned towards Hayes who had already used the brief time to turn and run. The gang boss leapt over a gravestone and ran towards the church, with Robson close behind him.

'*Nightmares will come true . . .*'

The hit man tightened his finger on the trigger, raking the Ingram back and forth, the bullets slicing into the running figures.

Hayes felt as if he'd been punched in the side with a red hot sledgehammer. The wind was knocked from him and he pitched sideways, slamming into a tree. He tasted blood in his mouth, felt the sharp end of a rib when he probed the wound with his fingertips. He glanced round to see that Robson had also been hit.

The younger man had taken one shot in the neck and was screaming madly as blood ejaculated from the wound, spurting into the air as if forced from a high pressure hose. He held his hands to the wound until a second blast caught him in the side, one bullet shattering his hip. The strident cracking of bone was audible even above the chattering of the Ingram. Bullets ploughed up the ground around Hayes, tiny geysers of earth erupting on all sides. Others whined off gravestones, blasting chips of marble and granite into the air.

The gang boss clambered to his feet, noticing that Mitchell was reloading.

'When you find the keys to madness . . .'

The hit man slammed a fresh magazine into the sub-gun, pulled back the slide and opened fire again.

Robson was screaming for help, his hand held out imploringly towards his lover who was running towards the church, clutching his side, racing with a speed born of fear.

'Don't leave me,' shrieked Robson, dragging himself along the slippery ground. He still held out one hand, blood dripping from the fingers.

Mitchell fired another burst at him, one which blew off three of his fingers. As the dying man continued to scream, two more bullets hit him in the face, the second catching him in the eye, drilling the socket empty before exploding from the back of his head.

'I will pray for you . . .'

Hayes tripped, fell over a gravestone and rolled twice in the mud. But he dragged himself up and scuttled on, feeling the blood running over his hand as he clutched at the ragged sides of the bullet hole.

Mitchell followed with measured steps.

'If you whisper for my protection . . .'

Startled by the sounds of gunfire, the priest had emerged from the church only to duck back hurriedly inside when he saw the bodies of Hayes' men scattered over the cemetery.

The gang boss himself, face drained of colour, blood

staining his shirt and trousers, crashed into the door and sprawled on the cold stone floor of the church.

'Help me,' he coughed, blood dribbling over his lips.

The priest tried to support him, to drag him inside the building.

He saw Mitchell advancing steadily, the Ingram lowered in readiness.

The priest faced the awful realization that the God he so often spoke of might soon be greeting him personally. He tried to push the church door closed but Mitchell merely drove his weight against it causing the priest to fall backwards as the heavy door swung open.

Hayes had managed to crawl to the altar, where he pulled open his coat and managed to drag the .38 from its holster.

'It will suit me just fine . . .'

'You can't come in here,' the priest shouted, looking down at the gun. 'This is the house of God. You cannot bring weapons into the house of God.'

Mitchell turned and looked at him.

'This *is* God,' he said, indicating the Ingram.

Then he fired.

The priest was hit in the stomach and chest by the blast, hurled off his feet. He crashed into a nearby pew, blood jetting from the wounds which had shredded his torso.

Mitchell moved purposefully up the aisle towards the stricken Hayes who tried to steady himself, tried to fire a shot.

The explosion reverberated around the inside of the church as the pistol was fired, echoing away as Mitchell squeezed his own trigger.

The sound even drowned out the noise of the music which was thundering from his Walkman.

Bullets tore into Hayes, jerking his body as if it had been subjected to a massive charge of electricity. Rounds pierced

201

his chest, his neck, his face, his legs, until he was reduced to little more than a bloodied rag. The stench of excrement mingled with the pungent odour of cordite. Cartridge cases rained from the Ingram like brass confetti, bounding on the stone floor with a loud clank. Only when the hammer slammed down on an empty chamber did Mitchell finally release the pressure on the trigger. Then he turned and walked briskly but unhurriedly down the aisle and out of the church.

'*Dare to spit on my grave* . . .'

Forty-One

As he brought the car to a halt at traffic lights Carter glanced into his rear view mirror and caught sight of Mitchell.

The hit man was carefully wiping the Ingram with an oily cloth, making sure he kept the weapon well hidden from any prying eyes that should happen to peer into the car. Once the task was completed he flipped open a black attaché case and placed the sub-machine-gun inside.

'You enjoy your work don't you?' Carter asked, driving on.

'It isn't a question of enjoying it,' Mitchell told him. 'I do my job well. I take pride in it.'

'How long have you been doing it?'

'Long enough.'

The driver again studied his passenger in the mirror.

'What about you? Have you ever killed a man?' Mitchell wanted to know.

Carter shook his head.

'Never.'

'It isn't as easy as everyone thinks, you know,' Mitchell said, as if he were confiding some staggering revelation. 'Films and TV portray it too cleanly. One bullet sometimes isn't enough. Depending on where you hit a man and with what calibre of shell, you can't be sure of killing him with one shot.'

'Thanks for the lecture,' Carter said acidly. 'I don't suppose you realize what all your work is going to mean, do you?'

Mitchell never answered.

'You may kill the other gang leaders but their firms are going to fight back. No doubt you'll have moved on to another job by then,' Carter muttered.

'Once the other leaders are dead there won't be any more trouble,' said Mitchell with a certain amount of assurance. 'Cut off the head and the body dies.' He smiled.

They rode a little further in silence before Mitchell spoke again.

'Are you afraid of death, Ray?' he asked.

Carter frowned.

'I haven't thought about it.'

All the driver heard was the metallic click of a hammer being pulled back.

The movement had been so swift he was unable to react. Mitchell had pulled the Browning from his shoulder holster, pressed it against Carter's head and pulled back the hammer.

'Think about it now,' Mitchell told him, smiling.

Carter felt his bowels loosen slightly. What was this maniac playing at?

'If you pull that trigger the car will go out of control,' the driver told him. 'You'll end up spread all over this road.'

'Why should I pull the trigger? We're on the same side aren't we?' Mitchell chuckled and the sound sent icy fingers trickling up and down Carter's spine. But as he saw the hit man sit back in his seat he pulled the car over to the kerb.

His own movements were as swift as those of the hit man. Carter pulled his own automatic from its holster and shoved it into Mitchell's face.

'Now,' he hissed. 'Are you scared of death? Because if you ever do that to me again I'll blow your fucking head off.'

Mitchell merely smiled and raised his hands in a gesture of mock surrender. Carter slowly lowered the pistol and holstered it. He turned very slowly in his seat, one eye on his passenger.

Before he could speak, Mitchell had snatched up the attache case, pushed open the door and climbed out. He waved a hand in the direction of a passing taxi and Carter saw the other vehicle's brake lights flare as it came to a halt. Mitchell jumped in and the black cab sped off. Carter shook his head wondering what the hell was going on. For long moments he sat in the car, watching as the taxi disappeared into traffic and then he pulled out as he realized that it was time he contacted Harrison, told him that the hit had been successful. That Eugene Hayes and three of his men were dead. He should have done it when they changed cars earlier but another hour or so wasn't going to hurt.

Besides, thought Carter, he needed to see Tina.

He waited for a break in the traffic and swung the car around and drove back in the direction of Kensington.

Carter parked the car around the corner from the flat and walked the short distance to the building. Once inside he climbed the stairs, running a hand through his hair as he approached her door.

It seemed like an eternity since he'd seen her. Just to see her, to be with her for a few minutes would be enough. Then he'd go and tell Harrison about the hit.

Carter rang the bell and waited.

No answer.

He rang again.

The door opened slowly and Carter smiled a preparatory greeting but the gesture disappeared rapidly.

Frank Harrison was standing in the doorway.

Forty-Two

'What are you doing here?'

There was a hard edge to Harrison's voice and it was all Carter could do to keep his composure.

'The hit,' he said. 'It's done.'

'So? That still doesn't explain why you're *here*?' Harrison said angrily.

Carter saw Tina appear behind the gang boss, wearing only a long shirt. She dared not chance a smile at the driver.

Harrison spun round and snapped his fingers, pointing at her.

'Go and put something on,' he hissed. 'What is this, a fucking whorehouse?'

She hesitated.

'Do it,' snarled the gang boss. Then he turned back towards Carter, grabbing him by the collar of his jacket and

205

hauling him inside the flat. He slammed the door and turned to face the driver.

'Why did you come to Tina's flat?' Harrison persisted.

'I was looking for you,' Carter lied. 'I tried the Mayfair casino, a couple of the strip joints. I guessed you'd be here.'

'Why didn't you ring? Why just turn up?'

Carter shrugged, wondering if his charade was working. God help him if it wasn't.

'I couldn't get to a phone. Besides, I dropped Mitchell off near here so, it was easier to call in.'

'Dropped him off? Where the fuck is he?'

'He jumped out of the car and got in a cab. I don't know where he went.'

'I told you to keep an eye on that bastard. I don't like the way he works. All this secrecy.'

Tina re-entered the room wearing a pair of jeans and a T-shirt. She asked Carter if he wanted a drink.

'No he doesn't,' Harrison answered for him. He noticed that Tina's nipples were prominent beneath the material of her top and he shot her a withering glance. 'I've told you to wear a bra,' he rasped and looked at Carter to see if he had also noticed.

If he had, he made a good job of concealing the fact.

'Get back in the bedroom,' Harrison ordered, as if he were talking to a dog.

Tina swallowed hard, hesitated a moment and then complied. She pulled the bedroom door behind her, leaving just enough space so that she could see through into the sitting room.

'You were looking at her weren't you?' Harrison challenged. 'Don't think I didn't notice.' He got to his feet.

'Give it a rest, Frank,' Carter said, aware that the gang boss was moving towards him, the veins on his forehead bulging.

'Fancy her, do you?' he hissed. 'Do you?'

Tina watched with growing anxiety as Harrison drew nearer.

Carter stood his ground, his eyes meeting those of his boss. The two men locked stares.

'Like to fuck her?'

'I came here to tell you that the hit on Hayes was successful, right?'

'I asked you a question. Do you want to fuck her? It's a simple question.' Harrison's tone had become deceptively soft. 'She's a good looking girl isn't she? Most men would want to. I'm just asking your opinion, Ray.' As he smiled, he became all the more menacing. 'Come on, man to man, give me your opinion. Tina's a good looking girl, isn't she? She's got a good body, hasn't she? If you got the chance you'd fuck her, wouldn't you? Come on, Ray, don't be modest. You've known me a long time. Tell me.' His smile was beginning to fade, the razor edge was returning to his voice.

'Do you want to hear how Hayes went down or not?' Carter said angrily. 'Or do you want to discuss your girlfriend's tits? It's your choice.'

There was a moment of silence and Carter knew that his boss was either going to fly at him or back down.

That moment stretched into what seemed like an eternity.

'Do you know about her tits, then?' asked Harrison, as if he were genuinely interested. 'Have you seen them? Touched them?'

In the bedroom, Tina crossed to her handbag and reached inside.

Her hand was shaking as she pulled out the .25 Beretta.

Had the time come at last? Must she use the gun now?

She opened the door slightly, the pistol gripped in her fist, her index finger curled around the trigger.

'Do you want to hear about this fucking hit?' snarled Carter.

'No, I want to know how *you* know what Tina's tits look like. Have you been here before without me knowing? Is that why you came here today? Hoping you'd find her alone. Hoping you could fuck her. Is it?'

Tina raised the pistol so that it was level with Harrison's head. She steadied the weapon by gripping her right wrist, not sure how much recoil there would be, praying that her shot would bring him down.

'Fuck you, Frank,' rasped Carter. 'What do you want to hear? You want me to say yes? Would that make you feel better?'

Harrison didn't answer.

'I told you why I came here,' the driver continued. 'If you believe me then listen to what I'm saying.'

Harrison's eyes narrowed until Carter found himself looking into two steely slits.

'Mitchell killed Hayes and three of his men. The hit was clean. We ditched the car, picked up the new one and now he's gone again. That's it, end of story, right?'

Tina lowered the gun slightly.

Harrison let out a long, almost painful breath. As he did, he seemed to relax slightly. He took a step back, and that sinister smile returned to his lips.

'You're clever, Ray,' he said. 'Your brother was clever too. But just remember what happened to him.'

It was Carter's turn to feel anger.

'Next time you drop that bastard Mitchell off you tail him,' the gang boss said. 'I want to know where he's hanging out. I'm tired of this hide-and-seek shit.' Harrison sat down and reached for the bottle of Haig on the table in front of him. He poured himself a large measure, then offered one to Carter, who accepted.

Tina exhaled deeply and lowered the Beretta, noticing that her hands were still shaking violently. She returned the pistol

208

to her handbag, sucked in a couple of deep breaths and then padded through into the sitting room where she sat down beside Harrison.

'So, that's Barbieri and Hayes out of the way,' the gang boss said. 'Two down, two to go. Just that fucking scouse bastard Cleary and his mob and then Sullivan.' Harrison chuckled. 'That red-necked mick.'

'And then?' said Carter.

'Then London's mine,' declared Harrison. 'No more sharing. No more competing. It's all mine.' He took a long swig of his whisky. 'Then we take care of Mitchell.'

Forty-Three

'We'll be killed before we get close to him.'

Paul Gardner's voice echoed around the darkened room.

'He's too well protected.'

'That's rubbish, we managed to get at the others,' Maria Chalfont intoned.

'But they didn't have bodyguards,' Gardner persisted.

'This is all bullshit,' hissed Phillip Walton. 'We either go after him or we pick someone else. I'm not sitting around here all night talking about it.'

'I agree with Paul,' Mark Paxton added, bursting a large spot on the end of his nose between his thumb and forefinger. He sniffed the thick yellowish pus then sucked it into his mouth rather like a child would lick the inside of a cake bowl.

Michael Grant looked around the room at his companions.

'Jennifer, what do you think?' he asked.

Jennifer Thomas ran a hand through her hair scratching at her scalp.

'What's the worst that can happen to us?' she asked.

'We could be killed,' Paxton told her.

'Better to die than be locked up for the rest of our lives. The police will find us eventually. I say we kill him,' she decided.

'We need to make the gesture,' Grant told them all, standing in the centre of the small circle they had formed on the mildewed floor of the room. 'We've executed people in the media, in the public eye. We've killed the respectable rich. It's time we struck elsewhere. We have to show that no one is safe from us. We have to kill Frank Harrison.'

'And what brilliant idea have you come up with?' asked Walton, hawking loudly and spitting into the empty fireplace. 'It won't just be Harrison we'll be fighting, it'll be his gang too.'

'Are you afraid?' asked Grant.

Walton regarded him angrily.

'No, I'm not afraid. I'm just being realistic. If we're killed, who's going to carry on the war? Have you thought about that?'

'We won't be killed if we do it right.'

'Our weapons are no match for guns,' Maria Chalfont said, holding up a knife.

'There are other weapons we can use,' Grant said, enigmatically.

'Like what?' asked Walton sarcastically.

The assembled group looked closely at the photo which Grant held up.

The photo of Tina Richardson.

Forty-Four

He spotted Mitchell immediately.

Carter slowed down as he caught sight of the hit man standing in a doorway, the familiar black attaché case at his feet like a sleeping dog.

The driver had received the phone call less than an hour ago. Mitchell had given him instructions tersely, repeating them as if Carter were an idiot. He'd named the place in St John's Wood where he was to be picked up and given Carter a time. The driver had been about to say something about the traffic holding him up when Mitchell had put the phone down.

Carter pulled up at the side of the road and looked across at Mitchell who strode towards the car and climbed into the back seat.

'You're late,' he said flatly. The rebuke only served to irritate Carter further.

'I warned you about the traffic . . .'

Mitchell cut him short.

'Just drive,' he snapped. 'Regent's Park. I'll direct you once we get closer.'

'Who's the bunny this time?' Carter wanted to know.

'Michael Cleary,' Mitchell told him. 'He owns a restaurant close to the park itself.'

'You're not going to hit him inside a restaurant, are you?'

'Just drive.'

'I thought you blokes were supposed to have some kind of code of honour. You never hit anyone in front of their families, you never involve bystanders, that kind of thing.'

'You've been watching too many films,' Mitchell told him scornfully. He glanced into the rear view mirror and saw that the driver was looking at him, eyes narrowed slightly.

'Two hits in two days,' said Carter. 'That's a little risky isn't it?'

'Let me worry about that. 'You just drive the car.'

'But it *does* worry me,' Carter hissed. 'If you fuck up on one of these hits then it's my head that's likely to get blown off too.'

'I never make mistakes.'

'Famous last words.'

'Have faith, Ray. Faith moves mountains,' Mitchell chuckled.

'Yeah, but it doesn't knock over gang bosses.'

'If it's 9mm faith, it does.'

They drove some way in silence then Carter glanced at his passenger in the rear view mirror once again. Mitchell was gazing out of the windows to his right and left like a tourist on a sightseeing trip. As ever, the attaché case was laid across his lap.

'What are your plans when you finish this job?' Carter asked, tiring of the silence.

Mitchell shrugged.

'I don't know. Something will turn up. It always does. You'd be amazed how many people in the world use my services. People you'd never imagine. Politicians, businessmen. Anyone with a grievance,' the hit man explained. 'Killing is my business.' He smiled. 'And business is good.'

Carter was about to speak again when Mitchell leant forward, pointing past the driver to an impressive looking white building about fifty yards ahead.

'Park as close as you can,' Mitchell said, his eyes rivetted to the front of the restaurant, scanning back and forth in search of his pray. He reminded Carter of a terrier that has just caught the scent of a fox.

Carter managed to park the Escort thirty or forty yards

beyond the restaurant. Mitchell turned and gazed out of the back window for a moment and then he flipped open the attaché case.

Inside lay the Spas and the HK33.

Mitchell took the shotgun from the case and pushed in three cartridges, working the slide to chamber a round. Then he replaced it in its case. From his shoulder holster he withdrew a Browning automatic, pulled back the slide and slipped off the safety catch, before he also returned it to the case.

He waited.

And waited.

Carter glanced at the dashboard clock and noted that it was almost 8.30 p.m.

'We've been sitting here for over two hours,' the driver protested. 'What if he's not in there?'

'He's there,' Mitchell said softly, his eyes never leaving the front of the restaurant.

Carter lit up a cigarette, blowing out a long stream of smoke and shaking his head wearily.

'There,' snapped Mitchell, spotting the man he sought.

Mick Cleary emerged from the restaurant in the wake of two other men.

Mitchell smiled as he caught sight of the gang leader.

There was a woman with him. Young, beautiful. She clung to Cleary's arm as if glued to it, like some immaculately coutured leech. The small entourage moved to the edge of the pavement and, as Mitchell watched, a Daimler drew up and Cleary climbed in. The girl scrambled in beside him, careful not to wrinkle her expensive dress. One of the bodyguards got in front beside the driver and the car moved away.

Carter saw it glide past then he started the engine, swung out into the traffic and carefully kept a couple of car lengths between himself and the Daimler.

213

'Don't lose them,' said Mitchell, his eyes never straying from the other vehicle.

Carter didn't answer.

There was a set of traffic lights up ahead. He eased the Escort ahead of the car in front, leaving just one other vehicle between himself and the Daimler.

The sleek vehicle pulled away sharply and Carter had to restrain himself from speeding up to keep close enough to it. Although he doubted if Cleary was aware that he was being followed.

As they drove, the sodium glare of the street lamps shone back off the wet roads. It was like driving over a carpet of burnished gold. The traffic was fairly light and Carter kept his eye on the car in front at all times, afraid that it would speed off and force him into a chase. So far he'd been lucky but a police car passing him in the other direction reminded him that no one's luck held forever.

Mitchell was silent in the back, leaning forward slightly over the seat to keep his own vigil on the Daimler. Then, after a moment or two, he reached into his pocket and produced the Walkman. It seemed to be as much a part of his persona as the weapons, Carter thought, glancing briefly at him as he put on the headphones. He pushed a tape into the machine but didn't turn it on. The time hadn't come yet.

The Daimler turned into Albany Street.

Carter followed.

He could see Cleary in the back of the car with the girl.

She was kissing him. The big Liverpudlian had his arm around her. Both seemed preoccupied with each other. Neither bothered to glance out of the window but, Carter reasoned, even if they had done so they would have seen nothing unusual.

The Escort remained a measured two car lengths away from the Daimler, sometimes dropping back further, allowing other vehicles to filter into the gap.

They turned another corner.

Carter didn't even see the man.

He stepped into the road mere feet ahead of the Escort.

The driver stepped hard on the brake, the sudden halt causing the car to skid slightly.

Carter grunted as he was thrown forward, his seat belt cutting into his shoulder.

Mitchell sprawled on the floor of the car, pitched from his seat by the abrupt jolt.

The pedestrian was unhurt. He turned angrily towards the Escort, slapping the bonnet with the flat of his hand. Then he stalked round to the driver's side.

'You could have killed me,' he shouted, banging on the side window.

In the back Mitchell's hand slowly reached inside his jacket.

'Steady,' muttered Carter, winding down the window a fraction.

'You were going too fast, you stupid bastard,' the man roared.

'And you should look where you're going, you prat,' the driver hissed. 'What's wrong? Did you leave your fucking guide dog at home tonight?'

The man snarled something and grabbed the handle of the door but, quick as a flash, Carter shot his hand through the partially open window and grabbed the man by the collar, pulling his head towards the window, forcing it into the tiny gap. The man grunted in pain.

'Do you remember your birth?' Carter asked him. 'Because we're about to re-enact it.'

He pulled the man a little further into the car then pushed him away. He sprawled on to the wet pavement, looking up in bewilderment as Carter drove off.

'You've lost them you bloody fool,' snapped Mitchell, scanning the road ahead for the Daimler but failing to spot it.

Carter turned into Camden High Street, eyes alert, hitting the wheel angrily when he could not see the other car.

'I told you to be careful,' rasped Mitchell.

'Shut up, for Christ's sake,' the driver retorted.

He'd spotted the Daimler ahead.

It had pulled into a petrol station, the driver and bodyguard had stepped out of the car. The driver was filling the tank. Cleary and the girl remained in the back, still kissing.

A smile spread slowly across Mitchell's face.

Carter pulled into the kerb, the engine still running.

'How do you want to play this?' he asked, his eyes never leaving the other car.

'When I tell you, drive past as fast as you can,' Mitchell told him, slamming a magazine into the HK33. He gripped it tightly in one hand, with the other he pressed the 'Play' button on the cassette. Music filled his head.

Carter waited for the signal.

Waited.

The driver was glancing up at the electronic figures on the petrol pump.

The bodyguard had just pushed another piece of chewing gum into his mouth.

Cleary and the girl hadn't moved from the back seat.

'Well?' said Carter impatiently.

Mitchell didn't answer, words and music were all he could hear now, thunderous in his ears.

'*Behind the smile, there's danger and the promise to be told . . .*'

He gripped the HK33 across his chest.

'*You'll never get old . . .*'

'Go,' he shouted and Carter stepped on the accelerator.

The Escort bore down on the petrol station, passing other cars as it increased its speed.

'Life's fantasy, to be locked away and still to think you're free . . .'

The driver of the Daimler tapped the nozzle against the mouth of the fuel tank, draining the last few drops.

The Escort came roaring towards the garage.

Mitchell rested the barrel of the HK33 on the window frame and hugged it tight to his shoulder.

'So live for today . . .'

The bodyguard shouted a warning to Cleary who spun round.

'Tomorrow never comes . . .'

The girl screamed.

'Die young . . .'

Mitchell gritted his teeth as he opened fire, the recoil slamming the HK33's telescoped stock back against his shoulder.

The barrel flamed as the magazine discharged its deadly load. A stream of bullets tore across the petrol station forecourt, riddling men and machines alike.

The heavy grain rounds punctured the bodywork of the Daimler and shattered its windows, blasting them inwards to shower Cleary and the girl who had thrown themselves down as the roar of automatic fire began.

The bodyguard was hit in the stomach, the impact doubling him up as the bullet ripped through his intestines, exploding from his back, destroying a kidney in its wake. Blood spurted up the side of the elegant car which, in seconds, was riddled with bullets.

As the Escort sped past, Mitchell fired another concentrated burst.

The second fusillade was even more lethal.

Two bullets hit the Daimler's petrol tank.

217

There was a deafening explosion and the car disappeared beneath a ball of orange and white flame. The rear end was sent spiralling several feet into the air, the blazing body of the girl still inside it.

Cleary, his body transformed into a human torch, was hurled from the wreckage. He rolled over half a dozen times on the wet ground, screaming as the flames ate at his flesh.

The driver was catapulted backwards by the blast, lifted by an invisible hand and hurled through the plate glass window which fronted the cashier's office.

But an instant later the blast which had destroyed the Daimler was eclipsed by an explosion of awesome proportions. Half a dozen of Mitchell's bullets hit the petrol pumps and they promptly went off like huge sticks of dynamite, igniting the thousands of gallons of fuel in the tank beneath them.

Plumes of fire fully sixty feet high leapt skyward, colouring the heavens with a hellish red glow. Blazing petrol spouted across the forecourt, spilling into the road beyond. Passing cars were sent skidding across the greasy tarmac by the massive blast. People within fifty yards felt the air sucked from their lungs by the massive conflagration. The very air itself seemed to be on fire.

And, in the midst of it, lay the bullet-torn, twisted remains of the Daimler.

The bodies of Mick Cleary and those who had died with him were scattered around the forecourt in a mixture of blood and burning petrol.

The Escort sped on.

'Die young . . .'

Forty-Five

'Drop me here,' said Mitchell, tapping Carter on the shoulder as they passed a tube station.

The driver hesitated a moment before pulling up and allowing the hit man to get out. Clutching the black attaché case, Mitchell headed for the entrance to the station.

Carter watched him disappear inside and then reversed into a side street and scuttled across the road himself, certain that Mitchell had not seen him follow.

Harrison had said to tail the hit man and that was precisely what he intended to do. As he ran, he felt the 9mm automatic bumping against his side.

Carter hurried down the steps to the ticket machines, grateful for the crowd which hid him from any possibility of detection by the man he was tracking. He saw the familiar black attaché case. Saw Mitchell feeding coins into one of the machines. He passed through the automatic barrier towards the escalators. Carter waited until the hit man had begun to descend then dashed to the ticket machine, rummaging through his own pockets for change.

He had none.

Only a five pound note.

He cursed under his breath and spun round, looking at the ticket office.

There were only a couple of people waiting so he joined the short queue, muttering impatiently as the woman in front of him tried to explain in broken English that she wanted to get to Buckingham Palace. By the time the ticket seller had finished explaining that no tube trains ran directly to the Palace, Carter was frantic. He pushed past the woman, shoved the five pound note through the pay slot and vaulted over the automatic barrier.

Ignoring the shouts of the ticket seller and the flabber-gasted stares of his fellow travellers, Carter ran down the escalators, pushing past a couple of people who chose to ignore the instruction 'Please Stand on the Right'.

At the bottom of the escalator he heard music.

A young man with a white face was energetically tap-dancing in time to a tune which floated from a ghetto blaster. He glanced at Carter as he hurried by, frowning when he tossed no money into the battered top hat which was propped up by the moving staircase.

Carter took the next flight of steps and made it on to the platform.

The air was dry and rank in the subterranean environment. Sounds echoed around the curved walls, litter was scattered beneath the rails like filthy confetti.

Carter glanced down the platform, past two Chinese men who were consulting a street map.

He could not see Mitchell.

Gritting his teeth, Carter moved further along the plat-form, past a drunk who lay on a wooden bench, snoring loudly. Two young girls were staring at him, giggling.

Carter heard the familiar crackle run along the tracks and the gust of wind which ruffled his hair told him that a train was coming. He could hear it rumbling closer.

Still no sign of Mitchell.

Could he have lost him in such a short time?

The train roared out of the tunnel like some swiftly mov-ing, animated worm from the mouth of a dead animal. As it drew to a halt Carter scanned the faces on the platform once more.

He spotted Mitchell.

The hit man stepped into a carriage as the doors slid open.

Carter ran down the platform and jumped into the adjacent

carriage. Through the window of the connecting door he could see that Mitchell had sat down and was gazing abstractedly at the advertisement panels.

The train pulled away and Carter kept glancing at the hit man.

Tottenham Court Road station.

Mitchell didn't move.

Leicester Square.

He rose from his seat.

Carter prepared to step off the train with him but at the last moment noticed that Mitchell had only risen to give his seat to an elderly woman. The train moved on again.

Piccadilly Circus.

This time Mitchell did leave the train.

Carter waited a moment, allowing the hit man time to get clear and jumped out just as the doors were sliding shut.

Mitchell pushed through the crowd, heading for the Bakerloo line.

Carter followed.

A Negro was sitting in one of the passageways, his filthy trousers already stained darkly around the crutch. He was clutching a half empty bottle. Carter smelt the acrid scent of urine as he passed the man.

A train was pulling in.

He slowed his pace, careful not to emerge onto the platform too soon, in case it was sparsely populated. He couldn't risk Mitchell spotting him.

The doors of the train opened.

Carter waited, his breath coming in short gasps.

He turned the corner on to the platform, looked both ways and saw the familiar black attaché case in Mitchell's hand.

The hit man stepped onto the train.

Then off.

Carter ducked back into the walkway, certain now that Mitchell had spotted him.

The doors hissed and began to close.

Mitchell jumped on.

Carter scurried forward and succeeded in squeezing through the narrow gap, trapping the sleeve of his jacket. He tugged it free, careful not to expose the automatic strapped beneath his left arm. He grabbed one of the overhead rails and hung on as the train moved off. Where the hell was Mitchell going?

They passed through Oxford Circus, through Regent's Park.

At Baker Street the hit man left the train once more.

Carter followed, keeping about fifteen yards between them, glancing up every so often as Mitchell stood on the escalators and rose towards ground level. Carter could only guess at his next move.

The hit man passed through the ticket barrier and Carter followed, relieved that there was no one on duty. He couldn't spare the time to explain why he hadn't got a ticket. He scuttled up the steps which led to the street, noticing how few people there were on the darkened stairway. Mitchell must be only ten yards in front of him.

Carter rounded a corner.

He felt a crushing impact on the back of his neck.

Then he felt nothing at all.

Forty-Six

Carter didn't know how long he'd been unconscious.

He felt hands on his face, voices drifting around him. Someone was checking his pulse, feeling his brow.

He snapped his eyes open and sat up, wishing that he hadn't. A stab of pain in the back of his neck made him wince. He groaned and sat back against the cold wall of the staircase. There were three or four people clustered around him, all looking anxiously at him as he struggled to regain his senses. As he screwed his eyes up once more they finally swam into focus.

A young woman was stroking his brow with the back of her hand. She stopped as Carter sat up.

The assembled group seemed to back off slightly as he looked at them, hoping that no one had spotted the 9mm automatic inside his jacket. If they had then they certainly weren't saying anything. Carter slid one hand inside his coat and touched the butt of the pistol to reassure himself that it was still there. Satisfied that no one had found the lethal weapon, he rubbed his neck again and looked at the interested spectators: two youths in leather jackets and a man who was sweating heavily despite the chill in the air.

'Are you all right, mate?' one of the youths asked. 'I saw the geezer hit you. Me and Pete were going to go after him . . .'

Carter cut him short.

'How long have I been out?' he wanted to know.

'Only about a minute,' the youth told him. 'The bloke whacked you and then legged it.'

Carter nodded slowly, painfully, rubbing the back of his neck once more. He tried to rise but his legs felt like jelly. As he swayed uncertainly the young woman moved forward to support him. Carter smelt the perfume she wore and the heady aroma did nothing to hasten his recovery. Maybe if she'd been wearing smelling salts, he mused as he tried to regain control of his legs. That bastard Mitchell, thought Carter as a fresh wave of pain throbbed through his skull.

'Did he take anything?' the sweating man wanted to know.

Carter shook his head.

'You going to call the Old Bill?' the second youth asked.

'No,' snapped Carter. 'No police. I'm OK.'

'We'll get an ambulance,' the young woman insisted.

Carter thanked her but dismissed the suggestion.

People passing by on the stairs glanced at the little tableau with curiosity, glad that they weren't involved. Carter saw the faces gazing at him. He sucked in a deep breath, his senses returning more fully now. He thanked the four people gathered round him and then headed up the steps, leaving them to watch him go.

The sweating man shook his head.

'You're not safe anywhere these days, are you?' he muttered. 'Criminals everywhere. I mean, that poor chap, having a quiet night out and that happens to him.' He shook his head. 'I don't know what the world's coming to.'

'What do you mean you lost him?'

Carter held the phone slightly away from his ear as Harrison rasped the question at him.

'I mean the bastard laid me out,' snapped the driver irritably.

'What about Cleary?'

Carter explained.

There was a moment of silence at the other end before Carter heard a grunt of satisfaction.

'I'm not trekking round London all night trying to find Mitchell,' Carter told his boss. 'I'm going home.'

'Well next time be more careful,' Harrison told him. 'I told you I wanted that bastard found.'

'Look, I'm a driver not a fucking bloodhound. You want him, then put one of your coppers on the job.' He slammed the phone down and stood there for a moment, breathing heavily, massaging the back of his neck with one hand. Then he fumbled in his pocket for more change and fed it into the phone. He jabbed the numbers and waited.

It rang.

And rang.

Carter drummed on the metal shelf, muttering under his breath.

'Hello.'

He recognised the voice immediately.

'Tina, it's me.'

She asked how he was. He explained again, mentioning Cleary only briefly.

'Can you come to my flat?' she asked. 'Frank's been and gone.'

'After what happened last night? You must be kidding,' he said. 'Meet me somewhere.'

They arranged a place and a time. Carter checked his watch, then he hung up. He paused a moment and walked out into the streams of people, pausing by the roadside to call a taxi.

Tina replaced the receiver when Carter hung up. She turned immediately and went into the bedroom, pulling a sweatshirt over her jeans. She stepped into a pair of boots, picked up her handbag and headed for the door. As she paused to lock it behind her she glanced down at the .25 Beretta in the bottom of her bag.

225

Tina took the lift to the ground floor and walked out into the night.

The place where she'd arranged to meet Carter was less than ten minutes from her flat. She set off at a brisk pace, the breeze stirring her hair as she walked.

From across the street, hidden in the shadows of a doorway, Phillip Walton watched her leave.

He smiled to himself and felt the long blade of the knife inside his jacket.

He chuckled.

This was going to be easier than he'd thought.

Forty-Seven

Harrison stood looking at the map of London laid out on his desk, surveying the blueprint of the capital like a general planning his next tactical move. He took a swig of whisky and smiled to himself.

'With Sullivan out of the way, that's it,' he said. 'Barbieri's manor in the north, Cleary's in the south and good old Eugene's in the east. And us right in the middle. Once Mitchell takes care of that fucking Irishman then the whole lot's mine.'

'What about some of the smaller gangs, Frank?' Billy Stripes wanted to know. 'With the big boys out of the way they might start getting ambitious.'

Harrison shook his head.

'The smaller gangs were controlled by Cleary and the other three. The only one who might try something is Cleary's brother but I doubt it. I reckon the scouse bastard will be on the next train back to Liverpool after what happened tonight.' The gang boss and some of the other men in the room laughed.

Billy Stripes didn't see the funny side.

'So you're telling me that these other gangs are going to line up with us, work with us?' he said.

'Why not? It's in their interests. If they don't, they know what the choice is.'

'You can't wipe out everyone in London who's against you, Frank,' Billy insisted.

'Why not?' Harrison demanded with conviction in his words. 'Besides, the law will appreciate it. There'll be peace again.' He smiled.

'When's Mitchell going to hit Sullivan?' Joe Duggan wanted to know.

Harrison shrugged.

'You tell me. I can't even find out where he's staying, let alone what his plans are.'

'He's good at his job, Frank,' Duggan said.

'He ought to be for what he's getting paid.'

The phone rang and Drake picked it up. He nodded then put his hand over the mouthpiece before handing it to Harrison.

'He wouldn't say who he was,' Drake informed the gang boss who took the receiver from him.

'Frank Harrison speaking.'

Silence.

'Who is this?' he hissed.

'I don't like being followed, Harrison.'

The gang boss recognised Mitchell's voice immediately.

'There was nothing in the contract about that. I was to be left alone.'

227

'I don't like all this cloak and dagger stuff,' Harrison said irritably.

'Tough.'

'Now listen, you . . .'

Mitchell cut him short.

'No. *You* listen. Our business is nearly over. Until it is you keep your men away from me, understand? If anyone else tries to follow me or find out where I am then I'll kill them. And if I find out you sent them, I'll kill you too.'

'Who the fucking hell do you think you are?' shouted Harrison into the mouthpiece. 'You're working for *me*.'

The other men in the room looked on bemused. Billy Stripes shook his head slowly.

'You're working for me and you've still got a job to do,' Harrison snarled, gripping the receiver so tightly that it threatened to snap.

'No more tails,' Mitchell said flatly. 'Got it?'

'You can't talk to me like this.'

'The business is nearly completed. Just make sure I don't add you to the list.'

'You bastard,' Harrison bellowed. 'How dare you fucking speak to me like that . . .' It took him a second or two to realize that the phone had been put down at the other end. He glared at it for a moment before bringing the receiver crashing down. His face was scarlet with rage, the veins at his temples throbbing. 'Mitchell,' he rasped. 'Well that settles it. As soon as he's hit Sullivan, I want him found. I want that fucker found and killed.' He looked at the other men in the room, his features still contorted with anger. 'You listening?' he roared. 'I want Mitchell dead. As soon as he's finished this business, I want him dead.'

Forty-Eight

'Dee's Teas' the sign over the door proclaimed in flickering neon letters.

Tina pushed the door open and walked in, aware immediately of the stares she was drawing from two young men seated in a booth at the far end of the cafe. Another youth was playing the fruit machine beside the counter and a series of electrical tunes periodically floated from the contraption, occasionally interrupted by the rattling of change as the machine spewed out some winnings. The youth scooped them up and began feeding them back into the machine, oblivious to everything around him.

The place smelt of fried food and strong coffee. Tina glanced at the youths at the far end of the room and then inspected the other booths.

There was no sign of Carter.

'Can I help you, love?'

Tina turned at the sound of the voice and saw a large woman smiling at her from behind the counter.

'I'm looking for someone,' Tina said hesitantly.

'Well have a cup of tea while you're waiting then,' said the woman, pushing a cup of what looked like steaming creosote towards her. Tina thanked her, paid and sat down facing the door, watching for Carter, wondering why he wasn't already there.

She almost shouted aloud when she felt the hand on her shoulder.

She turned to see Carter standing behind her.

'Where were you?' she said, her heart beating fast.

He nodded in the direction of the toilets behind her.

She relaxed slightly, reaching for his hand and squeezing it.

'How do you feel?' she asked, deciding not to chance the steaming creosote after all.

Carter shrugged.

'I think Mitchell hurt my pride more than my head,' he told her. Their eyes met.

They sat in silence for a moment. Then Tina looked down at the table, glancing at the numerous tea stains and brown rings which covered the formica like a bizarre collage.

'What are we going to do about Frank?' she asked. 'I'm sure he knows what's going on between us.'

'He can't be *sure* or we'd both be dead by now,' Carter told her. 'Although that incident last night was too close for comfort. I don't think he knows.'

'But how much longer is it going to be before he finds out?' she wanted to know. 'Ray, I've had enough of this. Being frightened to speak to you, wondering what Frank's going to do to me. I can't take it anymore. You once said to me that he didn't own us, that we could walk away. You tell me how.'

Carter saw the tears in her eyes. She gritted her teeth, anxious to keep them back.

'There's only one way,' he said flatly. 'Kill him.'

The words hung in the air as thickly as the smell of burned food.

'How?' she wanted to know. 'What about the other members of the firm? Do you think they'd let us walk away after we'd killed him?'

'So, do you want to spend the rest of your life like a prisoner? Because that's what you are at the moment. We both are. I'm offering us a way out. You're right, Tina, it's gone far enough.' As he sat back in the seat his jacket opened slightly and she glimpsed the butt of the automatic in the shoulder holster.

From behind her the fruit machine paid out again to the accompaniment of an electronic fanfare.

230

'Where do we run to, Ray, after he's dead?' she asked.

'It isn't a matter of running,' Carter said angrily. Harrison's a businessman, a gang boss, not the Godfather. And if someone comes after us then . . .'

She interrupted him.

'Then we kill him too?'

'If necessary.'

'And what if it's Mitchell who comes after us?'

'So, he's a hit man, big deal. He's still human. He can be killed.'

Tina ran a hand through her hair and sighed.

'I knew it would have to end like this,' she said. 'I don't know why I'm so shocked.' She opened her handbag and looked at the Beretta. 'I've even thought about killing Frank myself.' There was another long pause before she looked directly at Carter. 'When will you do it?'

He shrugged.

'Let me worry about that,' Carter told her. 'You start getting ready. Once it's done we're going to have to get out of London fast, maybe even out of the country.' He took her hand once more, squeezing tightly. 'When the time's right, I'll kill Harrison.'

Forty-Nine

Tina rose early that next morning. She showered, wrapped a towel around herself, pulled the suitcase from beneath the bed and began packing.

She knew she would have to be careful. If Harrison found any of her clothes missing, if he should chance upon the suitcase, then she would have no way of explaining it away.

She packed the clothes which she rarely wore, putting in a couple of pairs of shoes.

But, could she hide the suitcase once it was full?

She pondered this for a while.

There was nowhere in the flat where she dared leave it. She couldn't take it round to Carter's flat.

The attic.

The flats had a vast communal attic where the residents stored their unwanted possessions. Those which served no practical purpose but which their owners could not bear to part with.

She would store the suitcase in the attic.

Satisfied with her decision she wandered into the kitchen and made herself some breakfast.

She was nervous, nothing she could do could alter that. But, for the first time in months, she felt a sense of anticipation. A feeling that she might still escape.

Across the street, looking up at the window of her flat, Mark Paxton rubbed a throbbing spot on his cheek and waited.

The knock on the door startled Carter.

He didn't get many visitors to his flat, especially not at 8.30 in the morning.

He turned down the radio and crossed to the door.

'What the hell do you want?' he hissed as he saw who stood there.

David Mitchell pushed past him into the flat, looking round like a prospective buyer on a house-hunting expedition.

'I ought to whack you after what happened last night,' Carter said, slamming the door.

'You're welcome to try,' Mitchell said, pulling open his jacket to reveal shoulder holsters on either side. One carried the Browning, the other a 9mm Beretta. 'You should think yourself lucky. I could have killed you.'

'What am I supposed to do, say thanks?'

Carter pulled his own shoulder holster from the back of a chair and fastened it on.

'We've got work to do,' Mitchell told him. 'Derek Sullivan. The last one. Then it's over.'

Carter eyed him irritably, glancing down at the familiar black attaché case which the hit man had put down on the floor beside him. It was like a tool box. A portable genocide kit.

'How much is Harrison paying you?' Carter asked, pulling on his leather jacket.

'I think that's my business, don't you?'

'I just wondered how much it took to ease your conscience.'

'Conscience is something that's never troubled me, Ray,' the hit man said. 'Besides, you're hardly in a position to preach, are you? You may not have killed anyone but you haven't exactly lived the life of a saint.

Carter didn't answer. He merely crossed to the door and opened it, gesturing for the hit man to leave. Mitchell picked up the attaché case and walked out. Carter switched off the radio and followed him, locking the door behind him.

*　　*　　*

'Ray Carter.'

Detective Sergeant Vic Riley nodded in the direction of the driver, watching as he climbed into the Peugeot.

'He's been with Harrison for as long as I can remember. I don't know who the other bloke is.' Riley frowned and took another bite of his Mars bar. His stomach rumbled loudly. It was all he'd eaten since midnight. He'd been sitting in the car with sergeant Alan Larkin for the last eight hours, snatching a couple of hours sleep here and there but, for most of the time, both men had watched Carter's flat.

All over London a similar surveillance operation had been mounted by Riley's men. Six of Harrison's highest ranking employees were being watched.

Riley chewed thoughtfully. Who the hell was the bloke with the case?

He watched as Carter started the engine of the Peugeot, pulling out into the traffic.

Larkin glanced across at his superior and Riley nodded.

The Sierra followed.

'Where to this time?' Carter asked as he drove, glancing in the rear view mirror.

He looked at Mitchell, catching only a momentary glimpse of the Sierra.

'The Elephant and Castle,' Mitchell told him, flipping open the attaché case.

He ran his hand over the Ingram and the Spas, touching them lovingly. A slight smile spread across his face.

In the pursuing Sierra Riley finished the Mars bar and tossed the wrapper out of the window, his eyes never leaving the Peugeot.

'Don't lose them,' he murmured quietly, his right hand reaching inside his jacket.

He pulled the .38 Smith and Wesson from its holster, spun the cylinder and then replaced it carefully.

The cars drove on.

Fifty

It was as they were crossing Blackfriar's Bridge that Carter finally decided they were being followed.

He didn't say anything to Mitchell as he himself hadn't been a hundred percent sure but, the further he'd driven, the more convinced he'd become. The white Sierra had moved rather too quickly through an amber light coming through Holborn, kept its distance almost too methodically. Then, when Carter had deliberately signalled right but turned left, the Sierra had done likewise.

Now as they passed over the bridge, Carter glanced into the rear view mirror once again. No doubt about it.

The Sierra was about two car lengths back, moving steadily.

Beneath the bridge the Thames flowed like a filthy brown tear across the face of the city and Mitchell glanced out, watching a small boat as it chugged through the murky water.

Carter slowed down slightly, his eyes straying to the Sierra once more. There were traffic lights ahead. He was supposed to go straight on. The traffic filtered into three lanes so Carter guided the Peugeot out into the right hand lane and prepared to turn in that direction.

Sure enough, the Sierra did likewise, its driver careful to keep two other vehicles between them.

'What are you doing?' asked Mitchell, glancing at a sign which proclaimed that the Elephant and Castle was straight ahead.

Carter didn't answer. He merely sat, drumming gently on the wheel, eyes on the Sierra.

'We're supposed to go straight on,' Mitchell said. 'What . . .'

'Just shut up, Mitchell,' Carter snapped, jamming the car into gear as the lights changed. He swung it to the right.

The Sierra followed.

'What the hell are you doing?' hissed Mitchell, sitting forward in his seat.

Carter glanced behind him once more to see that the white car was still on their tail. It was moving closer now, overtaking the Mini in front of it so that there were just two cars between it and its quarry.

'You take us to where we're supposed to be going and you do it now,' snarled the hit man, his hand reaching inside his jacket. He gripped the butt of the Browning, preparing to draw the pistol.

'We're being followed,' the driver said flatly.

Mitchell sat back in his seat, not attempting to look round.

'Who are they?' he wanted to know.

Carter could only shake his head. That particular question was one which had been troubling him ever since he'd noticed the pursuing vehicle. Could it be members of another gang? Members of Sullivans' gang perhaps? The Irishman was no fool, he'd seen other members of the underworld gunned down, he didn't need a degree to figure out the gang bosses were being put to sleep and that, eventually, his name would come out of the hat. Maybe he'd decided to strike first.

Carter shuddered slightly, memories of the chase through

236

Mayfair and Chelsea still strong in his mind.

If not another gang then who?

The law?

It was possible. He slowed down slightly, allowing the Sierra to draw nearer, attempting to see its passengers in the mirror.

He swung the car to the right, and took the next left. Manoeuvres designed to disorientate the driver of the Sierra. But to no avail. The unmarked police car kept on coming.

More traffic lights.

Carter slowed up again and another car cruised up alongside him, music blaring from inside. The driver was happily inspecting the contents of one nostril on the end of his finger, digging so deep it seemed to Carter he was trying to scratch his head from the inside. The man looked across at the driver and nodded a greeting, as if they were long lost friends. Carter ignored him, his attention focussed on the Sierra.

The lights changed and Carter allowed his foot to slip off the clutch.

The car stalled.

Not expecting this particular ruse, the young sergeant driving the Sierra pulled forward too quickly, so that there was barely three feet between the bumpers of the two vehicles.

'Come on, come on,' rasped Mitchell. 'Get it going.'

Carter unhurriedly put the car in gear, twisted the ignition and pulled away. As he did so he managed to catch a good look at the men in the Sierra.

He recognised DS Riley immediately.

'That's it, Mitchell, the hit's off,' Carter said.

'What?' the other man roared. 'What the hell are you talking about?'

'That's the law following us. Got it? Now forget Sullivan for today.'

'Like hell.'

'If you try to hit him with the Old Bill up our arse then every copper in London is going to be down on us before the smoke's even cleared. I'm telling you, the hit is off.'

'Fuck you,' snapped Mitchell.

'No, fuck *you*,' Carter shouted angrily.

Ahead of them was a junction, a long stream of traffic strung across it. Carter braked, bringing the Peugeot to a halt.

The Sierra rolled up close behind.

Carter glanced to his right and left, the jam that was blocking the road seemed to stretch for a long distance. Unless some benevolent soul decided to let him out, they were going to be sitting there for quite some time.

Mitchell glanced into one of the wing mirrors and he too saw the two men in the white Sierra. One of them had just lit a cigarette.

He watched them for a moment longer, pushed open the door of the Peugeot and stepped out.

'What are you doing?' Carter asked, turning in his seat.

DS Riley also wondered what the passenger was playing at as he swung himself from the other car.

Mitchell walked briskly towards the Sierra, approaching the passenger side.

Riley looked up at him, the cigarette sticking to his bottom lip.

Mitchell's movements were impressively fast.

He shot a hand inside his jacket and pulled the Browning free of its holster, aiming it at Riley who tried to duck.

'No,' bellowed Carter from the Peugeot.

Mitchell fired twice.

The first bullet shattered the side window and caught Riley in the left temple. His head snapped sideways as the heavy grain shell powered into his skull, obliterating the left temporal bone and most of the parietal vault. It looked as if he'd been hit in the side of the head with a red hot hammer. Blood spouted from the wound, spraying the inside of the car and Larkin screamed in revulsion as he was spattered by a mixture of fragmented bone and sticky grey brain matter. Blood continued to spew madly from the remains of Riley's skull and the second bullet, which shattered his lower mandible, blasting it into a dozen pieces, was an unnecessary extra.

Larkin struggled to unfasten his seat belt and get out of the car but his superior's body had fallen across his lap, pinning him in his seat. Blood from Riley's pulverized head soaked into the younger man's trousers and he felt vomit clawing up his throat as he battled to free himself from the confines of the car. The stench of excrement filled his nostrils, both from Riley's collapsed sphincter and from his own, loosened by terror.

He opened his mouth to scream as Mitchell stuck the Browning inside the car and fired.

The barrel of the GP35 flamed and spat its deadly load at Larkin. The bullet hit him squarely between the eyes exploding his nasal bone and staving in a large portion of the frontal bone before erupting from the back of his head. A reeking flux of blood and brain spattered onto the side window behind him, propelled by the speeding bullet.

Mitchell holstered the weapon turned and scurried back to the waiting Peugeot.

'Move,' he snapped.

Carter turned in his seat, affording himself a rapid glance over his shoulder at the two dead policemen. The Sierra's windscreen looked as if it had been draped with a crimson curtain.

'I said move,' Mitchell repeated angrily.

Carter put the car in gear and drove forward towards the stream of traffic. A car blocking his path hastily reversed, the driver having seen what had happened to the occupants of the

Sierra and anxious not to share their fate. He skidded backwards, ramming into the front of the vehicle behind him.

Carter put his foot down and managed to buffet his way through the narrow gap, slamming on the brakes as a taxi came roaring at him from the other direction. The squeal of tyres mingled with the sound of blaring hooters as Carter twisted the wheel and sent the Peugeot hurtling into the traffic, away from the bullet-blasted bodies in the white car.

He swung left, then right, anxious to put as much distance as possible between himself and the scene of the shooting. The whole area would be swarming with coppers soon. He just hoped that Riley hadn't managed to call any back-up before Mitchell blew his head off. When no sirens sounded and no marked cars came screeching after them, the driver relaxed slightly. He turned into a narrow street at the rear of some shops and stepped hard on the brake, almost causing Mitchell to fall from the back seat.

Carter turned, his face scarlet with rage.

'What the fuck are you doing shooting coppers?' he roared. 'Once the Old Bill find out what happened they'll close up London tighter than a fish's arse. They'll watch every move. You can't kill Sullivan now.'

'All the more reason to hurry,' Mitchell insisted.

Carter shook his head.

'You want to kill him, you drive the fucking car yourself,' he said, pushing the drivers' door open and clambering out.

'Where are you going?' shouted the hit man.

Carter kept on walking, hands dug deep into his pockets.

'Come back,' Mitchell bellowed.

The driver didn't turn. He reached the end of the street and disappeared around a corner.

Mitchell waited a moment, his breath coming in angry grunts, then walked around to the other side of the car, slid behind the wheel and started the engine.

Fifty-One

Carter didn't know how long he'd wandered the streets of London. He'd glanced at his watch only once since leaving Mitchell that morning. Now it was mid-afternoon and Carter sat in the office of the Mayfair casino sipping a drink, glancing around the room at the other men who stood there watching and listening.

Detective Inspector Peter Thorpe had arrived less than twenty minutes ago. The policeman looked angry and flustered and his mood was reflected in his voice as he spoke. Harrison remained on the other side of his desk as if using the piece of furniture as some kind of barrier between himself and the DI.

Joe Duggan slouched in one corner of the room puffing away at a roll-up.

Billy Stripes sat on a chair close to Carter, occasionally touching the three scars which decorated his face like fleshy tattoos.

Damien Drake pulled at the lobe of his ear, his eyes fixed on the tableau before him.

'This killing has got to stop now, Harrison,' Thorpe said angrily. 'What gives you the right to slaughter every other bloody gang boss in the city? I told you I wouldn't be able to protect you if you started anything like this.'

'It wasn't me who started it,' Harrison reminded him. 'It was *me* who nearly got killed when that restaurant was bombed, *my* men who were getting blown away. Someone else started it. I'm finishing it.' He took a sip of his drink. 'Besides, I don't see any coppers beating my door down to arrest me. How can you prove I've got anything to do with it?'

'There's only you and Sullivan left alive,' Thorpe told him.

'Then talk to Sullivan.'

'I don't need to talk to Sullivan,' Thorpe hissed. 'I'm talking to *you* and I'm telling *you*, call that mad bastard off, whoever he is.'

Harrison was on his feet in seconds, one powerful hand grabbing at Thorpe, gripping the policeman's collar.

'I've told you before, Thorpe,' he snarled. 'Don't tell me what to do.' The gang boss pushed the DI away and Thorpe was lucky not to overbalance. He opened his mouth to say something but Harrison continued, 'You tried your way and it didn't work. My way seems to be working very nicely.'

'Knocking over *your* rivals is one thing but when it comes to him blowing away *my* men, that's a different matter,' Thorpe countered.

Harrison merely shrugged.

'I told you to keep them off my back,' he said.

'And I told you I couldn't protect you if you started a gang war. It wasn't me who sent men to cover the members of your firm. I've got the commissioner breathing down my neck for a result on this. I'm telling you, Harrison, if your hit man doesn't lay off, you'll go down.' The policeman turned to look at the other men in the room. 'All of you.'

'Well if we do, you'll come with us,' Harrison assured him.

Carter got to his feet and glared at Harrison.

'He's right, Frank. Mitchell's a fucking nutter,' he announced. 'Everyone knows you don't shoot at the law.'

Harrison turned slowly and looked at the younger man.

'If you don't like it, Ray, then get out,' he said quietly.

The two men locked stares in silence until Billy Stripes spoke.

'I agree with him, Frank. Mitchell should have known

better than to kill a copper. We're not going to be able to breathe after this. The slightest move and the law will be on us like a ton of hot horse-shit.'

Harrison regarded the two men impassively for a moment and then raised his eyebrows, as if that simple gesture were his only acknowledgement of their grievance. He tapped gently on the desk top.

'So, are you trying to tell me I made a mistake?' he said irritably. 'Are you trying to tell me I should have let those other fuckers walk all over me? Take over my manor?' He shook his head reproachfully. 'I always credited you two with a bit more guts.'

'It's got nothing to do with guts, Frank,' snapped Carter. 'Mitchell's a maniac.'

'And I told you that as soon as he'd taken care of things, *we'd* take care of him, didn't I? Look, he's got to come here to get his money, right? Well, he won't be leaving with it.' Harrison smiled and looked across at Joe Duggan who tapped the butt of his pistol and nodded. 'Like I said, when the business is finished so is Mitchell.'

There was a knock on the door.

Harrison shouted for whoever was outside to enter.

McAuslan stuck his head round the door.

'Someone to see you, Frank,' he said, but before Harrison could speak the visitor had pushed past McAuslan into the room.

David Mitchell strode towards Harrison's desk, the attaché case held in one hand, a large plastic bag in the other.

He seemed oblivious of the presence of the other men in the room. The hit man merely looked directly at Harrison and put down his attaché case.

He took hold of the plastic bag and up-ended it.

'It's over,' said Mitchell, stepping back.

The severed head of Derek Sullivan rolled out of the bag

243

coming to rest on the bloodied stump, the eyes still open, fixing Harrison in an unblinking stare.

Mitchell glanced at the head and then back at Harrison.

'You owe me some money.'

Fifty-Two

She thought it must be a wrong number.

Tina had picked up the phone but heard nothing at the other end. She assumed that the caller had realized they'd reached the wrong number and hung up. She replaced the receiver and returned to her bedroom where she continued packing. It was a careful, cautious process but, so far, she'd managed to secrete most of her wardrobe in the attic of the flats. The couple who lived in the apartment opposite her were in Greece for a month's holiday so there were no prying eyes to watch her on her journeys up and down the ladder to the dusty attic, dragging her suitcases with her.

The phone rang again.

Tina crossed the room and lifted the receiver.

'Hello,' she said.

Silence.

She repeated herself.

Still there was only silence at the other end.

She muttered something under her breath and put the phone down once more.

It rang within seconds and she snatched it up, not speaking this time, just listening.

At the other end she heard the unmistakeable sound of low, muted breathing.

'If this is a dirty phone call then you might as well start breathing more heavily than that,' she said. 'And by the way, this phone is attached to an answering machine so everything you say will be recorded . . .'

The line went dead.

Tina smiled to herself, satisfied with her small victory.

The phone rang yet again almost as soon as she replaced the receiver.

She snatched it up angrily.

'Now listen you bastard,' she began but the words trailed off as she turned towards the door, the receiver still gripped in her fist.

The handle of the front door was being turned slowly.

Tina slammed the phone down and dialled quickly, her eyes never leaving the door.

She had to get in touch with Harrison, with Carter.

Anyone.

The phone was dead.

She flicked the cradle.

Dead as a doornail.

The door handle continued to turn.

The line had been cut.

Tina dropped the phone and ran towards the front door. She had almost reached it when she realized she had not locked it. She tried to turn the key in the lock, to slip the bolt, but it was useless.

The door swung open.

Paul Gardner and Phillip Walton burst in, Gardner making straight for her.

Tina turned and fled towards the bedroom, slamming the

245

door behind her, wondering who these intruders were. Terror was filling her now, flowing through her veins like iced water She felt a powerful kick against the door but leaned against it, knowing that she would not be able to hold back the intruders for very long.

Her handbag was lying on the bed.

She could see the Beretta from where she stood.

There was another crash against the door and Tina was almost sent flying. She dashed away, her hand scrabbling inside her bag, her fingers closing around the butt of the .25.

The door splintered under the sustained attack, flying back on its hinges.

Gardner dashed into the bedroom hardly noticing the gun.

Tina fired twice. The recoil, even from such a small calibre pistol, jerked the weapon in her hand. The butt slammed back harshly against the heel of her hand and she winced but kept her finger curled around the trigger.

The first bullet missed and ploughed into the door.

The second hit Gardner in the shoulder, cracked his clavicle and lodged in the musculature of the sterno mastoid. Blood spurted from the wound and Gardner felt searing pain dart up his neck and jaw. He dropped to his knees, clutching at the wound as Tina prepared to fire again.

Walton blundered into the room, ignoring the pistol which was aimed at him.

Tina tightened her finger around the trigger.

The gun jammed.

She pressed the trigger frenziedly but it would not work, the firing pin would not strike the charge in the shell. She did all that was left to her. She threw the pistol at her attacker.

Walton lunged at her, catching a handful of her hair but she spun round and brought her knee up in his groin so hard that she felt it connect with his pelvic bone. He let go of her hair and gripped his throbbing testicles, letting out a strangled cry. But he blundered on, his teeth gritted against the pain, his free hand snatching the knife from his belt.

Tina dashed into the bedroom and locked the door behind her.

Walton drove a powerful kick against it, cursing under his breath.

This wasn't how they had planned things.

Gardner had managed to drag himself to his feet and he pulled his shirt open, inspecting his wound. It throbbed powerfully and the burning sensation was beginning to spread down his arm. Blood had soaked his shirt and jacket and was still pumping rhythmically from the hole made by the .25 bullet. He moaned in pain but Walton ignored him, more intent on kicking down the bathroom door in his efforts to reach Tina.

Inside the bathroom she looked around frantically for something, anything, with which to defend herself. She threw open the medicine cabinet and found a safety razor. One which Harrison had left there. She gripped it in her shaking hand and waited for the inevitable.

Two more powerful kicks and the door exploded inwards.

As Walton came at her she used the razor in a swatting action.

He raised his hand to protect his face and the blade sliced through the palm of his hand. Blood spouted from the torn flesh and Walton grunted in pain but still managed to strike out at Tina, catching her a stinging blow across the face. One of such force that she was lifted off her feet. As she tried to rise he lunged for her once more, his bleeding hand getting tangled in her hair as he dragged her to her feet.

Tina screamed as Walton accidentally tore her ear-ring free.

The lobe of her ear seemed to burst as the fine silver pin ripped through it. Blood spurted down her blouse and she felt burning pain. He drove a fist into her face, smiling as he felt her lip split under the impact. Her head snapped backwards and she slid to the ground, unconscious.

'Bitch,' hissed Walton, glancing at his lacerated palm. The flap of flesh was moving slowly, opening and closing with each pulse like the gills of a fish. He wrapped a towel around the wound and hauled Tina to her feet. She too was covered in blood, most of it from her torn ear. Part of the lobe hung like a raw bud, the crimson fluid still pumping from it.

'Come on, help me,' snarled Walton, ignoring Gardner's moans of pain.

Together they carried Tina from the flat, down the stairs at the rear of the building to the yard at the back of the small block.

Mark Paxton sat behind the wheel of the stolen Capri, milking reeking yellow ooze from a sore on his cheek, licking it away with his tongue like a gourmet. As he saw his companions approaching he pushed open the back door, allowing them to shove Tina on to the back seat.

Gardner got in beside her; Walton swung himself in next to Paxton.

'Move,' snapped Walton, clutching his torn palm, pressing the blood-soaked towel to the gash.

Paxton drove off.

'Do it now,' Walton said, turning in his seat to look at Gardner who was still moaning quietly as the pain from his shoulder wound raged. His face was deathly pale, covered by a thin film of perspiration. He looked ready to black out but Walton snapped at him once more. 'Come on, do it.'

Gardner nodded slowly, painfully and looked down at Tina who'd been thrown across the back seat like an unwanted mannequin. Her face was bruised and bloody, her hair matted with crimson from Walton's and her own injuries.

Walton glared at his companion who finally nodded again, looking down as Tina moaned softly.

He took the knife and prepared himself.

Fifty-Three

The case was slightly larger than Mitchell's attaché case. It was pushed across the desk towards the hit man, sliding in some of the spilt blood which had seeped from the severed head of Derek Sullivan. That particular grisly object had been removed – carried to the furnace in the basement and disposed of.

Now Mitchell looked down at the case before him and slowly lifted the lid.

'Seven hundred and fifty thousand pounds,' said Harrison. 'That was what we agreed, wasn't it?'

Mitchell didn't answer, but merely pulled one of the fifty pound notes from the nearest bundle and held it up to the light, flicking it with his index finger as if to test the crispness of the paper.

Harrison looked across at Joe Duggan who nodded almost imperceptibly and moved towards the door, blocking the exit.

'You don't have to count it all,' Harrison said to the hit man. 'It's all there.'

'I'm sure it is,' Mitchell said, flicking through another of the bundles.

Duggan reached behind him and carefully locked the door. He watched Harrison, waiting for the signal.

Carter glanced first at the gang boss then at Duggan. At Drake too. Both men had taken up positions close to the door. The driver looked at Mitchell, down at the attaché case which carried three of his weapons. Surely Harrison must be aware that the hit man was carrying pistols too. Even if Duggan and Drake managed to get an accurate shot at Mitchell, the chances were that he'd take at least three of the men in the room with him. Harrison for sure.

Carter licked his lips and got to his feet, edging towards one of the windows.

DI Thorpe moved back from the centre of the room.

Mitchell had picked up another of the bundles and was flicking through it.

'What's wrong?' asked Harrison. 'Don't you trust me?'

Mitchell smiled thinly, flipping through more of the brown notes.

Duggan's right hand moved inside his jacket.

'You wouldn't be stupid enough to try and double-cross me,' said Mitchell, still counting.

Carter glanced at Duggan and saw that his hand was actually resting on the butt of his pistol.

Harrison also glanced quickly across at the man, ready to give the agreed signal.

'I'm afraid that Sullivan's driver got rather too heroic,' Mitchell said, matter-of-factly.

'Tough,' said Harrison, edging to one side. He looked across at Duggan again.

Carter moved closer to the window, as if he wanted to be ready to leap from it when the shooting started.

'So, it's all over?' asked Thorpe.

Mitchell turned slightly and looked at the policeman, eyeing him up and down. Then the hit man nodded.

Duggan closed his hand around the butt of the .357, ready to pull it from the holster. Ready to fire as many rounds as necessary into the hit man's back. He hoped that Mitchell would remain where he was.

Harrison moved another step to the right and nodded at Duggan.

The phone rang.

Mitchell continued counting the money.

No one else moved.

Duggan had the gun free of the holster, was standing there like a puppet without a master, frozen. Waiting for his next instruction.

The phone rang again.

Mitchell continued counting.

And again.

Harrison gritted his teeth and finally moved towards the phone. He snatched up the receiver.

Duggan holstered the revolver.

Carter saw the look of fear on the other man's face as he stared at Mitchell's broad back. It looked as though the chance had gone.

Then, suddenly, all thoughts of Mitchell were forgotten as Harrison slumped down in his chair, gripping the phone so tightly that his knuckles threatened to burst through the skin. The colour had drained from his face as surely as water drains from a sink when the plug's removed. He was deathly pale as he sat listening, his lips moving soundlessly as if he were repeating what was being said to him. Finally he sat back in the chair, allowing the receiver to drop from his slack grasp.

'What's wrong, Frank?' asked Drake.

He opened his mouth to speak but no words came forth. The gang boss was gazing straight ahead, his eyes wide, almost entranced. Harrison's shallow breathing became deeper and, gradually, the paleness of his skin began to be replaced by a reddish glow of rage.

Even Mitchell stopped counting the money long enough to look at him.

'Tina,' said Harrison softly and now it was Carter's turn to look aghast at the gang boss.

'What's wrong with her?' the driver demanded, not caring if the concern in his voice was noticeable. 'Frank, who was that on the phone?'

Harrison didn't answer, he merely looked at McAuslan.

'The phone box across the street,' he said quietly. 'Now. Check it out.'

'Frank, what the hell is going on?' snarled Carter as McAuslan unlocked the door and hurried out.

The other men could only stand mystified as the gang boss continued to gaze into empty air, his hands clenched into fists.

Mitchell finished flicking through the bundles of fifties and closed the lid.

'This *isn't* over,' Harrison snarled, looking at DI Thorpe.

'What's it got to do with Tina?' Carter yelled at him.

Harrison turned towards the driver, ready to tell him when McAuslan returned clutching a small package about six inches square, clumsily wrapped in newspaper.

'I found this in the phone box,' he said breathlessly.

Harrison snatched it from him and tore it open.

Inside was a cardboard box.

There was a dark stain on the bottom of it.

Harrison opened it, teeth gritted as he gazed in.

'Oh Jesus,' murmured Drake, who had moved closer to get a better look.

Harrison's breath was coming in short gasps now, his eyes rivetted to the contents of the box.

Carter recognised the ear-ring as Tina's, recognised the lock of hair.

Recognised the severed little finger, hacked off at the second joint.

Spattered crimson where blood had spilled from the digit, there was a note. Crudely written in ball-point. Harrison lifted it from the box with shaking hands and read the words on it. Standing close by him, Carter was also able to make out the scrawl:

RICH CUNT

NEXT TIME IT WILL BE

HER HAND

Fifty-Four

It was Detective Inspector Thorpe who recognised the writing. He took the note from Harrison and scanned the words once more. There was an unmistakeable familiarity about that almost childish scrawl and the aggressive style of the note. He'd seen writing like that inside the houses of the Donaldson and Kenning families and also that of Maureen

Lawson. As Harrison ranted and raved, overturning things in the office, Thorpe turned to look at him.

'I want these bastards found,' roared the gang boss. Then he turned on Mitchell. 'You were supposed to have killed all the others.'

'I killed who I was contracted to kill,' the hit man told him.

'Then who the fuck has taken Tina?' bellowed Harrison. 'I want everyone you can find. Every pimp, ponce, pusher and tuppenny-hapenny little villain working this and every other manor in London. Find out who's done this.'

'It isn't another gang,' Thorpe told him.

Harrison spun round his anger now directed at the policeman.

'How the hell do you know?' the gang boss snarled.

Thorpe explained about the note, about the other killings.

'We've been tracking them for the last few months, trying to find leads but so far we've come up with nothing,' the DI explained. 'They're fanatics. Anti-rich terrorists. They've been hitting at anyone they consider to be wealthy and in the public eye.'

'Then why pick on me?' Harrison demanded.

'You're not exactly destitute, Frank,' said Billy Stripes.

'If they wanted me then why not come for me? Why take Tina?'

'She must be the bait,' Carter interjected. 'Their way to get at *you*.' He pointed at the gang boss.

Mitchell snapped the case shut.

'Well, it seems you have other business to attend to,' he said, matter-of-factly. 'I'll leave you to it.'

Joe Duggan once more moved to block the door.

'Wait,' snapped Harrison. 'You can't leave now. I still need you to help me.'

'My contract is fulfilled,' the hit man reminded him. 'London is yours. You have no rivals left.'

'I need you to help me get Tina back.'

'I don't work for nothing,' Mitchell reminded him.

'This is police business, Frank, you have no right . . .' Thorpe protested.

'Another million on top of that if you get her back alive,' Harrison said.

Mitchell shrugged.

'Very tempting.'

'You don't need him,' Carter protested. 'We can find her ourselves.'

Mitchell smiled and looked almost mockingly at Carter.

'A million,' Harrison repeated. 'Get her back.'

Mitchell nodded.

'You can't do this, Frank,' shouted Thorpe. 'This is official. We're talking about a kidnapping.'

'We'll be talking about a corpse if I leave it to you to find her,' Harrison said.

'I'm going with him,' Carter insisted.

'Fair enough,' Mitchell said. 'I still need a driver. As long as you're not going to walk out on me again.'

The two men exchanged glances.

'But what if she's already dead,' Drake said quietly.

Harrison gritted his teeth and took a step towards Drake, grabbing him by the lapels. He hurled him backwards against the wall, and grabbed him once more as he slammed into the brickwork.

'Don't say that,' snarled the gang boss, his face livid. 'Don't ever say that.'

'He could be right, Frank,' Thorpe intoned. 'From what I've seen of these maniacs so far . . .'

'She's not dead,' roared Harrison at the top of his voice. He stepped away from Drake, standing in the centre of the room, swaying almost drunkenly. 'She's not dead. Now find her.'

Carter looked at the furious gang boss who kept murmuring over and over to himself, like some kind of litany: 'She's not dead.'

Carter prayed that Harrison was right.

Fifty-Five

The first thing she noticed was the smell.

As Tina Richardson slowly regained consciousness she sucked in a painful breath and the stench filled her nostrils. It was the smell of decay, of neglect. Of filth.

She moaned softly and tried to open her eyes but she still felt groggy.

The sharp blow across her left cheek cleared the fuzziness inside her head more swiftly than she would have liked.

Tina gasped, feeling more pain from her ear and from her back. As she tried to straighten up she realized that both her arms were securely tied to a chair behind her, the rope pulled so tightly that the hemp had cut into flesh. Her hair was matted with blood and she could feel her ear throbbing where the ear-ring had been torn out. The wound hadn't been dressed but, as far as she could tell, it had stopped bleeding.

And what of the darkness?

It took her a moment to realize she was blindfolded. The cloth cut deeply across the bridge of her nose, fastened strongly at the back of her head so that it trapped some of her hair.

She raised her head slightly and felt another stinging blow on her other cheek.

The impact snapped her head to one side and almost knocked her from the chair. Tina gasped once more and tried to swallow but her throat was dry.

'Come on you rich slag, wake up,' a voice close to her hissed.

Tina blinked hard beneath the blindfold, trying to clear her mind, trying to concentrate on where she was even though she could see nothing. She could smell the rankness of the room. She could sense that there was more than one person present.

She tried to straighten up but the rope held her firmly, cutting more deeply into her skin as she moved. She felt a trickle of blood run down her hands.

'We should kill her,' snarled Paul Gardner.

He was lying in one corner of the room, his shirt off to reveal the wound he'd sustained earlier in the day. The bullet was still lodged in his neck and every time he turned his head he could feel it grating against his cracked collar bone. The blood had been washed away from around the bullet hole but the injury still looked ugly and it hurt like hell. Gardner sat up, wincing at the fresh wave of pain which washed over him.

'We can't kill her yet,' Michael Grant told him, gazing at their captive. 'She's still useful to us.'

He gazed at Tina. Her face and blouse were covered in blood, her fine blonde hair matted with the crimson gore now stiffened and congealed into a black mess.

'Who are you?' Tina asked quietly.

'Does that matter, bitch?' rasped Phillip Walton, cradling his slashed hand as he stood over her.

'We're your executioners,' Maria Chalfont giggled.

Tina shuddered at the words but did her best not to show her fear though she wondered what was to be gained by such bravado.

257

'Fucking rich cunt,' snapped Walton.

'If it's money you want then there's someone who'll pay . . .' Tina began, but she was cut short by Grant.

'Money's the last thing we want,' he snarled.

'It's your *boyfriend* we want,' Jennifer Thomas added, her voice heavy with contempt.

Tina felt rough hands at the back of her head as the blindfold was yanked free. She frowned, blinking hard to clear her vision, gazing round the darkened room at her captors. She could almost feel the hatred in their stares.

'What do you want with Frank?' Tina asked.

'He's one of the enemy,' Jennifer Thomas told her. 'Just like you.'

'A rich bastard,' added Phillip Walton.

'Why didn't you kill me back at the flat?' she wanted to know.

'Even your sort have their uses,' Michael Grant informed her. 'He'll come to fetch you and we'll be waiting.'

'He won't come alone.'

'You'd better hope he does,' Grant told her, pulling the long-bladed knife from his belt. He pressed it gently to her throat, against the pulse just below her left ear.

Mark Paxton left the room, returning a moment later with a small cassette recorder.

'You're going to send your boyfriend a message,' Grant said.

'Why should I?' Tina said defiantly. 'You're going to kill me anyway.'

As she tried to adjust her position in the chair she felt the rope grating against the skin, felt renewed pain from the remains of her severed little finger. It was throbbing powerfully. In fact, her whole body seemed to ache from her injuries. Her ear seemed to be burning, the portion of the lobe still hanging by a tendril of flesh. Bruises had formed on her face and neck and, as she licked her parched tongue over her teeth, she felt one of them loosen. Tina tasted blood.

'You're not in a position to bargain,' said Grant. 'Send the message.'

He pulled a piece of paper from his trouser pocket and held it in front of her.

Paxton set the tape running and pushed it towards her.

Tina began to read.

Fifty-Six

'Be at St Katherine's Dock at one a.m. tonight. Come alone. If you have anyone with you then the girl will be killed. We will be watching you.'

Frank Harrison snapped off the cassette recorder and sat back in his seat, gazing at the machine, the sound of Tina's voice still ringing in his ears.

'We'd better do what they say, Frank,' said Damien Drake, glancing first at the tape and then at Harrison.

The gang boss was silent, his face drained of colour. He sat forward in the chair, rewound the tape and played it through once more.

Carter could hear the strain in Tina's voice, the harshness. The fear. And though it hurt him to imagine her suffering, he didn't show it in his expression.

The message finished and Harrison jabbed the 'off' button once again. Then with a roar he picked the machine up and hurled it across the room. It shattered against the far wall, circuits and wires spilling from the smashed shell like mechanical intestines from a robotic abdomen. He rounded on Mitchell who had sat through both playings unmoved.

'Well, you're the professional. How do we get her out?' he snapped.

The hit man shrugged.

'They want you to go alone,' he said, quietly. 'And they say they'll be watching. There's no reason to think they'll be bluffing so you'd better play their game.'

'This is no fucking game, Mitchell. Christ knows what they'll do to Tina. What they've already done.' Harrison crossed the room to the drinks cabinet, pulled out a bottle of Haig and poured himself a large measure which he downed in one gulp, wiping his mouth with the back of his hand.

'You asked how we get her out,' Mitchell said. 'That's assuming they're holding her somewhere. The other possibility is that you'll be lured to the dock tonight and murdered there and then.'

'So, what do we do either way?' Carter wanted to know.

'It's *you* they want, Harrison. *You* go,' Mitchell said flatly.

'I offered you a million pounds to get her back. Isn't that enough?' snapped the gang boss.

Mitchell didn't answer.

'Look, we can't follow you if they're watching, Frank,' Carter began. 'But we could be there first. Mitchell and I will get to St. Katherine's dock a couple of hours before, we'll keep well hidden. Wait for you.'

'And blow them away as soon as they show up,' Drake added gleefully.

'Then we'd never find Tina you prat,' Harrison said. He poured himself another whisky and wandered back across the room, interested to hear more of Carter's idea. 'So, you wait for me to arrive, then what?'

'If they've got Tina with them we hit them there and then, if not we follow you. You'll lead us straight to her.'

'Theoretically,' Mitchell intoned. 'What if they try to kill Harrison immediately?'

'Drake will be in the car with him,' Carter expanded. 'Either hidden on the back seat or maybe in the boot.'

Drake nodded.

Harrison exhaled deeply and took a sip of his drink.

'We can't be sure it'll work,' he said tetchily.

'It's all we've got, Frank,' Carter reminded him. 'A slim chance is better than no chance at all.'

Harrison grunted.

'Very philosophical.'

'Look, I care about what happens to Tina as much as you do,' Carter snapped and immediately regretted his words. He saw Harrison's jaw tighten as he turned to face him. The gang boss's eyes narrowed as he glared at the driver.

'Why?' he demanded.

'Whoever's got her must be nutters,' Carter said, trying to edge out of a potentially explosive situation. 'My brother died and I've risked my neck so that you can run London, I don't want some other fucking loonies coming in and stirring up trouble again.'

'What's that got to do with Tina? How come you care so much about her?' Harrison wanted to know.

'Is that really important?' Mitchell wanted to know. 'You want her back, right? Then I suggest you stop arguing and decide exactly what you're going to do.'

Harrison glared at Carter for a moment and then turned and walked towards the window. The street below was quiet, the light from the street lamps reflected in the wet tarmac like puddles of liquid gold.

'We'll go with Carter's plan,' said the gang boss finally.

The driver breathed a muted sigh of relief, angry with

himself for letting his true feelings show. He glanced at his watch.

'We'd better move,' he said.

Mitchell got to his feet, lifting the attaché cases.

'We'll be waiting,' Carter said as they reached the door.

Harrison nodded and glanced at his own watch.

10.38 p.m.

He drained what was left in his glass then crossed to the cabinet on the wall. From it he took a .357 Magnum. He flipped the cylinder out, checking that each chamber was full. Satisfied, he laid the weapon on his desk.

He glanced again at his watch.

Waiting.

Fifty-Seven

The wind whipped across the car park of St Katherine's Dock, tossing pieces of newspaper before it, rattling empty cans across the tarmac. Piles of litter had been blown up against the low concrete walls like heaps of mouldering autumn leaves. The chill breeze stirred these putrid mounds and scattered their contents in all directions.

There were less than a dozen cars in the glistening car park. The lights which surrounded the place were dull, glowing with a sickly yellow light which barely illuminated an area five feet around the concrete poles.

Mark Paxton squinted at his watch, tilting it this way and

that in an effort to see the time in the gloom.

Beside him in the passenger seat of the stolen TR7, Maria Chalfont shuffled nervously and peered into the night.

'He's late,' she said.

'No he isn't, it's not one o'clock yet,' Paxton told her. He yawned and stretched, his bones cracking from the prolonged bout of sitting. They'd been there for just over forty-five minutes and Maria in particular was becoming more restless by the second.

'What if he double-crosses us?' she muttered.

'He wouldn't dare.'

The explanation didn't seem to pacify her. She tried to look at her own watch, remembered she didn't have one and grabbed Paxton's wrist, pulling the time-piece towards her.

12.32 a.m.

She sighed.

'He'll be here,' Paxton assured her, squeezing a spot on his chin. 'We won't have to wait much longer.'

Carter had cramp.

He flexed his right foot, stepping on the floor of the car as hard as he could to relieve the muscular discomfort.

In the back seat, Mitchell was slumped low down, glancing to his right and left, eyes seemingly able to penetrate the gloom which surrounded the Princess. He was watching for the slightest sign of movement from the TR7 that was parked about two hundred yards away.

He and Carter had seen it arrive, park and extinguish its lights but there had been no movement from its occupants. Both men were convinced that the TR7 was the car they sought.

'If we find Tina, be careful with those bloody cannons of yours, Mitchell,' Carter said quietly, still trying to restore some circulation in his leg.

263

'Let's just hope she doesn't get in the way,' the hit man answered and pulled the 9mm Beretta from its holster. He checked that the magazine was full then slammed it back into the butt of the pistol. He repeated the procedure with the Browning.

Carter checked his own automatic.

'*You* be sure you can pull the trigger when you have to,' Mitchell said.

Carter didn't answer, he merely cradled the Smith and Wesson in his hand tracing the sleek lines of the pistol with his eyes.

The wind blew with increased ferocity, whipping a whirlwind of waste paper up around the car like a miniature monsoon before dying away and leaving only the silence behind.

Both men stayed low in their seats, eyes fixed on the TR7.

'There.'

Mark Paxton nudged Maria Chalfont and pointed as the Diamler moved slowly into the car park, its headlamps on half-beam.

'That has to be him,' Paxton said, watching the elegant vehicle finally come to a half about fifty or sixty yards away. The lights were switched off. The car was in darkness.

It was almost one a.m.

Frank Harrison put a cigarette in his mouth but, when his lighter wouldn't work, he tossed the Dunhill out of the side window in frustration. He drummed on the steering wheel, eyes flicking back and forth over the darkened car park, glancing at each vehicle in turn. Coming to rest finally on the Princess which he knew contained Mitchell and Carter.

He murmured something under his breath but it was lost as another powerful gust of wind shook the car.

He looked around once again.

At first he didn't see the girl walking towards the car. She seemed to blend in with the night, dressed, as she was, in black. Harrison thought about turning his lights on to get a better look at her but thought better of it. His hand went to his inside pocket and he felt the .357 there. A comforting bulk.

As the girl drew nearer he stamped three times on the floor of the Daimler.

Huddled in the boot, Damien Drake felt the vibrations, recognised the signal.

He eased the .38 from his belt.

The girl was less than ten feet away now and Harrison squinted through the night to catch a glimpse of her features. But at the last moment she turned and walked around the car to the passenger side.

Before Harrison realized what was happening she had opened the door and slipped into the passenger seat beside him.

'You're Harrison.'

It was a statement rather than a question.

He nodded slowly, looking at her more closely now. About twenty-two he thought, no make-up. Jeans. Sweatshirt. She might have been pretty.

He hardly had time to move as she pulled the knife from under her loose-fitting top and stuck it against his neck.

'Just because I'm a woman, don't try to be clever,' she said. 'We're being watched.' She studied him distastefully for a moment and then pointed with her free hand. 'Drive.'

'Where to?' he asked irritably.

'Where I tell you.'

Harrison smiled thinly.

'I could break your fucking arm and stick that knife up your arse before you could blink,' he hissed.

She moved the blade with practised skill, nicking his ear, slicing part of it away. A thin sliver of flesh fell onto the seat and he yelped in pain as he felt the cold steel cut effortlessly through the membrane. Blood spurted onto his shirt.

'Try,' she challenged.

He was about to say something when she pressed the knife to his throat once more.

'Now drive.'

Harrison started the engine, flicked on the lights and pulled out of the car park.

A moment later the TR7 followed.

Carter, who hadn't taken his eye off the Daimler, waited for several seconds before he pulled out, not turning on his headlamps until he reached the street.

The little procession moved slowly along.

It reminded Carter of a funeral motorcade.

He gripped the steering wheel more tightly.

Fifty-Eight

There was little traffic on the roads. Insufficient to hide a tail thought Carter, careful to keep his distance from the TR7. The driver of the other vehicle, however, seemed too preoc-cupied with watching the Daimler to bother about what was behind him.

As Harrison swung the Daimler into Cable Street he glanced at his passenger.

Maria Chalfont jabbed the knife against his throat a little harder, the point digging into the soft flesh beneath his chin until a small orb of blood welled up and dripped on to his shirt.

She smiled and kept the blade where it was.

'When I get out of here I'm going to kill you,' hissed the gang boss.

'But you're not going to get out,' she told him. 'Not you or your girlfriend.'

'We made a deal. If I turned up alone then you'd let her go.'

'No one mentioned anything about a deal. We don't make deals with the rich.'

'Who's "*we*"?'

'You'll find out.'

'So you intend to kill us anyway?'

'You deserve to die. Just like the others did. All the rich do. You're all the same. Politicians. Personalities. Criminals. There's nothing to choose between you. All rich scum.' She prodded him again with the knife. 'Did you like what we did with your girlfriend's finger?' she chuckled. 'I watched while they cut it off.'

Harrison gripped the wheel tighter, his fury growing.

'She screamed a lot.'

Harrison tried to turn his head to look at the girl but the pressure of the knife prevented even that small movement.

'She's in a bit of a mess, really. Not how you're used to seeing her,' Maria continued, enjoying the verbal tirade. 'We'll let you watch when we kill her. Then we'll kill you.'

'Let her go,' snarled Harrison. 'You've got me, that's what you wanted. Let Tina go.'

'Let a parasite walk the streets? Never.'

She jabbed him with the tip of the blade as if to emphasise her words.

'You don't understand, do you?' she rasped. 'None of you rich bastards understand. You live your lives without a thought for others and until now you've been getting away with it. But not any more.'

'I swear to God I'll kill you if you touch Tina,' the gang boss hissed, his anger now becoming uncontrollable.

'We'll kill her like we killed the others,' Maria told him. 'Slowly. She'll scream a lot. She'll probably beg for her life. That's the best part, when they beg.' Her breath was coming in short gasps and she could feel the growing wetness between her legs. 'Some of them try to be quiet but most shout out in pain. It takes some of them hours to die.'

'Shut up,' snapped Harrison.

'It depends where you cut them you see.'

'Shut up.'

'How deep the knife goes, how much they bleed.'

'I'm telling you.'

'It'll take a long time for your whore to die.'

'NO.'

He roared at the top of his voice, twisting the wheel of the Daimler so that the vehicle skewed across the road and skidded to a halt.

The sudden violent movement caused Maria to overbalance, and she slammed heavily into the side of the car and Harrison felt the pressure of the blade against his neck relieved. With lightning speed he turned in his seat, grabbing Maria's wrist in a vice-like grip, slamming her hand against the dashboard until the knife fell from her grasp.

She lashed out with her other hand and gouged the skin of his face, tearing three deep furrows with her nails. But Harrison ignored the attack, pressing forward his advantage. He gripped a handful of her hair and slid across towards her, driving her head against the side panel of the door with crushing force.

'Where is she?' he roared, smashing Maria's face into the panel once again.

Her nose splintered under the repeated impact, the bones disintegrating. Blood spilled down her sweatshirt but Harrison kept up his maniacal pounding. A split opened below her hairline and a fresh crimson stream began coursing down her face. Two of her front teeth broke, one of them tearing through her upper lip.

'Where's Tina, you fucking bitch?' he roared, pulling the .357 from his belt.

He drove Maria's head against the window with a force that threatened to smash the glass, blood smearing the clear partition. She merely burbled feebly, blood and pieces of shattered tooth filling her mouth.

Harrison pulled her hair hard, yanking her back so her head lolled against the seat. He shoved the barrel of the revolver into her mouth and thumbed back the hammer.

'Tell me where she is,' he snarled, his face purple with rage.

Maria tried to speak but her throat was full of blood and bile.

'Cunt,' roared Harrison and pulled the trigger.

The close range impact was devastating.

The bullet blew most of her head away, showering the roof of the car with brains and pulverized bone. It was as if a charge of dynamite had been detonated inside her skull. The top of it merely erupted, spewing its sticky contents upwards like a reeking fountain.

He still had the gun pressed to the back of her throat when he saw the TR7 overtake him.

Mark Paxton had heard the shot and as he drove past he saw Maria's dead body.

He knew what had to be done.

Carter and Mitchell also heard the shot, but the driver was

more concerned about the fact that the TR7 was streaking away into the night.

'We've got to catch him,' he said, pressing down on the accelerator. The Princess shot forward, speeding towards the Daimler where Harrison was struggling free, waving the other car to slow down, to pick him up.

Carter ignored his boss's frantic gestures and continued in pursuit of the fleeing TR7.

Harrison bellowed something at the swiftly moving car but soon it was nothing more than a blur of rear lights in the gloom.

Carter pressed down harder on the accelerator, coaxing more speed from the Princess, anxious not to lose Paxton as he sped through Whitechapel.

In the back seat, Mitchell checked his pistols once more. He knew that they would soon be needed.

Carter hunched low over the wheel, squinting through the darkness to catch sight of the TR7's tail lights. Even if the driver of the vehicle had realized he was being chased, Carter was determined that he should not escape.

But, as they sped through the night, Carter was gripped by the unshakeable feeling that if Tina were not already dead, she shortly would be.

The cars roared on.

Fifty-Nine

Mark Paxton knew he was being followed and, as he drew nearer the house in Whitechapel he became more afraid. He knew that he should have led his pursuers away from the house but his instinct had been to reach safety, to surround himself with his companions and destroy those who were chasing him.

He spun the wheel violently. The car skidded, slamming into the kerb. It bounced back into the road and he regained control knowing that he was less than half a mile from the house.

There was no way of warning Grant and the others, no way of telling them that things had gone wrong, that Maria was dead.

Paxton turned into the next road, slowing down slightly. He swung the TR7 across the street and blocked it. Then he jumped out and ran as fast as he could towards the black derelict houses where he and his companions hid.

If only he could reach the house . . .

The Princess came hurtling round the corner and Carter saw the running man pinpointed in the headlights of the car like a target in the cross-threads of a rifle sight. The driver put his foot down.

He drove around the TR7, up onto the pavement, and sped straight for Paxton.

The car was doing about sixty when it hit him.

The impact catapulted the running man into the air where he hung for long seconds as if suspended on invisible wires. Then he crashed down on to the roof of the Princess, spun round, and fell into the street, his right leg broken by the collision. Burning pain enveloped him and, as he reached for the injured limb, he felt a sharp piece of bone against his finger tips. His shattered femur had ripped through the flesh of his thigh like a skeletal dagger, tearing the skin to shreds. Blood poured from the agonising wound and Paxton tried to stifle a scream as he pressed the ragged edges of the laceration together against the spear of bone.

The Princess skidded to a halt and Carter leapt out, scurrying back towards the fallen figure.

Paxton lay flat on the cold stone pavement, his free hand slipping inside his jacket. His fingers closed over the hilt of the dagger.

He was lying on his stomach when Carter got to him.

The driver immediately dug his hands beneath Paxton's body and flipped him over on his back.

As he did, the injured man struck out with the blade.

It parted the air inches from Carter's face and he was lucky to avoid the vicious swing.

He jumped back, aiming a kick at Paxton, seeing the glistening white bone protruding from his torn thigh, the sharp end having ripped his trousers too.

Yet, amazingly, Paxton dragged himself upright and stood balanced on his one good leg, facing Carter, the knife brandished before him.

'Where's the girl?' Carter asked, pulling the 9mm Smith and Wesson from its holster and aiming it at Paxton.

'Dead,' the other man hissed.

Carter frowned but there was no conviction in the voice of his foe. Yet dare he take the chance that Paxton was bluffing? He had to know where she was.

Mitchell had joined him now and the two of them faced the crippled Paxton who was growing weaker by the minute. Carter glanced round to see Mitchell screwing a silencer into the barrel of the Beretta.

'No sense in letting them know we're here,' said the hit man, raising the pistol. He fired once.

There was a dull thud as the gun spat out its load.

The bullet hit Paxton in the right eye, the impact pitching him backwards as it carried away a sizeable portion of his skull.

He fell into a nearby hedge, blood spouting from his empty eye socket.

'Come on,' said Mitchell turning towards the deserted houses. He unscrewed the silencer and dropped it into his jacket pocket. The two men scurried towards a tall, over-grown privet hedge which guarded the front of the derelict property. There was a rusty iron gate set on wooden posts in the hedge and they both passed through cautiously, Carter wincing as the metal groaned and creaked.

The house was in darkness, a gaunt black shape rising like a tangible portion of the night, formed from the very blackness itself.

Mitchell glanced at the front door with its blistered paint and mould but was distracted by Carter who nodded in the direction of two bulkhead doors around the side of the building. They obviously led down into a cellar. It seemed a more sensible way of entering than by the front entrance. As yet the two men had no idea how many people they would face once they got inside the house. Their problem at the moment was to gain access.

The grass which grew around the house had not seen a mower for close to a year and it stood waist high. The men waded through it as if passing through water, heading for the bulkhead doors.

The wood was rotten, the rusty padlock which secured the doors all but useless. Using the butt of the Browning, Mitchell punched a hole through the rotting timber, tearing away more planks until he had opened up a hole big enough for them to enter.

A rank and fetid odour of damp and decay wafted up from

below and Carter raised a hand to shield his nose from the powerful odour. He peered down into the gloom, unable to tell how far the drop to the ground was. The driver fumbled in his pocket for his lighter and flicked it on, waving it about in the darkness. It was still almost impossible to tell how far the drop was. Carter guessed it couldn't be more than ten feet.

He snapped off his lighter, dropped it back into his pocket and eased himself through the hole, gripping on to the edge of the bulkhead for support. His lower body seemed to be enveloped by cold and the smell grew almost unbearable. He felt as if he were lowering himself into a cess pit. Taking the weight on his arms, he hung there for a second or two and then let go.

The floor rushed up to meet him and Carter grunted as he hit it.

It was soft and spongy and he realized that he had landed on earth. Wet, rancid earth.

Something crawled quickly across his outstretched hand and he had to stifle a cry of surprise.

He looked up to where Mitchell was peering in through the gap.

'Come on,' whispered Carter, watching as the hit man swung himself carefully over the edge and dropped, landing heavily. He cursed and rubbed his ankle but the pain soon passed and, with Carter's help, he straightened up.

They couldn't even see their hands in front of them. The darkness was like a living thing. Thick and cloying. And there was that ever-present stench around them. Carter reached for his lighter again, flicking it on and holding it above his head. The makeshift beacon scarcely made any impression on the impenetrable blackness but, inch by inch, the two men made their way across the cellar floor, relieved when the ground began to grow firmer. Another two steps and they were on concrete. Carter lifted the lighter higher, wincing as it began to get hot.

Ahead of them was a flight of stone steps.

Carefully, they began to climb.

Sixty

1.46 a.m.

'They should have been here by now,' said Michael Grant looking at his watch.

Jennifer Thomas looked at the selection of knives which lay on the table before them.

'We'll give them another ten minutes,' Grant said. 'Then we'll kill the girl.'

His words filtered through to the next room where Paul Gardner sat with his back to the wall, his watery eyes fixed on the bound form of Tina.

'Did you hear that?' he said. 'Another ten minutes and I'm going to slit your throat.' He winced as he felt fresh pain from his injured shoulder. 'You hear me?'

Tina didn't answer, she was moving her hands slowly behind her back, trying vainly to loosen the ropes which held her. Every movement brought renewed discomfort but she persevered, ignoring the fact that skin was chafing away from her wrists and lower arms as she worked to free herself. Blood had congealed on the hemp and her hands felt numb but she continued her slow, steady movements. If she was going to

275

die, at least she would not die helpless.

Downstairs, Phillip Walton was sitting in what was once a kitchen, his feet propped up on the rotting table, a bar of chocolate held in one large hand. He sat in the gloom, quite comfortable in the darkness, waiting for Paxton and Julia to return with their captive. Walton pulled the long-bladed knife from his belt and ran one thumb over the wickedly sharp edge, pressing so hard that it sliced through the skin. He smiled and wiped the blood on his trousers, imagining what that knife would do to Frank Harrison's face. Then, when that part of the ritual was over, there was the girl to attend to. Walton smiled again.

Carter was the first to reach the top of the cellar steps.

He peered through the crack in the door, noticing that there was light filtering down from the stairway directly ahead of them. He assumed it came from some kind of hurricane lamp on the landing above. The ground floor seemed to be in darkness.

Mitchell pulled the Browning from its holster and then, with his other hand, turned the rusty door knob.

The door was locked.

Carter cursed under his breath.

There was no way in without crashing through the partition.

He pulled the Smith and Wesson Automatic from inside his jacket and waited.

'This is going to have to be fast,' whispered Mitchell, steadying himself.

'Set?'

Carter nodded, his heart thudding powerfully against his ribs.

Paul Gardner moaned as he moved, trying to re-adjust his position to relieve the pain from his shoulder. He gripped the machete with one hand and glared at Tina.

She sat as still as she could, her hands moving behind her back, one of the biting thongs finally coming free. She managed to ease it over the bone in her wrist, satisfied that she could now free herself completely given time. Except that time was one thing she didn't have.

Across the landing Michael Grant looked at his watch again.

It was almost time.

He picked up one of the knives which lay in front of him.

Mitchell drove a powerful kick against the door and the entire partition was ripped free of its rusty hinges. It fell to the ground, throwing up a cloud of dust. Both men dashed from the confines of the cellar, not quite sure what awaited them.

Silence.

It was as if time had been frozen.

They both stood in the hallway, turning slowly, glancing at each doorway in turn, looking up towards the landing.

Nothing moved.

Carter glanced at the hit man who seemed to be listening for something unseen.

A floorboard creaked across the hall and, suddenly, the silence was replaced by a bedlam of shouts and yells. But above all the sudden noise Carter heard one sentence more clearly than any other.

From above came the order:

'Kill the girl.'

Sixty-One

Carter took the stairs two at a time, ignoring the protesting creaks and groans of the wood which threatened to collapse beneath him.

Below him Mitchell spun round and saw Phillip Walton hurtling at him from the kitchen.

The hit man ducked beneath Walton's mad charge, using his attacker's own momentum to his advantage. As Walton struck at him with the knife, Mitchell drove his shoulder hard into the younger man's midriff, rising quickly, lifting him into the air. Walton somersaulted over the hit man and landed with a bone-jarring thud on the floor behind.

He rolled over, trying to lift himself up, hurling the knife at Mitchell who was lucky to avoid the spinning blade.

He dropped to one knee and fired twice.

The first bullet hit Walton in the chest, tearing through his pectoral muscle above the heart and shattering a rib. The impact threw him back against the wall where he staggered for a moment, blood running freely from the wound.

The second shot caught him in the stomach. It ripped into his intestines, part of which burst through the entry wound like slippery, swollen worms, gleaming with blood. He moaned and tried to push them back into the large cavity opened by the bullet but his hands were shaking violently and all he could do was drop to his knees, blood now spilling over his lips.

He opened his mouth to shout his rage and pain but Mitchell's third bullet silenced him as it shattered his pharynx, snapping his head backwards. He collapsed in a spreading pool of crimson which soaked into the thick dust on the floor like ink into blotting paper.

As Carter bolted up the stairs the three shots sounded thunderous within the confines of the house but he didn't look back. His only concern now was to find Tina.

So preoccupied was he with his task that he didn't even see Jennifer Thomas appear from a door behind him.

Carter heard her footsteps and then all he felt was burning pain in his arm as she drove the knife into his shoulder. It felt as though he'd been punched with an icy fist. The blade grated against bone and Carter groaned, twisting to face his opponent.

She clawed at his face with her nails but he managed to bring the automatic up, using it like a club which he slammed into her face. Her nose crumbled under the impact and she fell back, dazed, her features distorted by the blow which had made her face a crimson mask. Yet she ran at him again as he tried to pull the knife from his shoulder.

Jennifer lunged at him again but Carter stepped back, hooking one foot around her ankle as she swept past him. She was jerked off her feet, losing her balance at the top of the stairs. She clutched at empty air for a moment and then pitched forward, rolling over and over, bumping down the steep steps, her head slamming against the wood as she tumbled over.

Carter dropped his pistol and took hold of the hilt of the knife, gritted his teeth and pulled.

The steel came free of his shoulder with some difficulty as he grunted in pain, dropping the bloodied blade to the floor.

The bullet which struck the balustrade close to him shocked him back into awareness. He looked down to see Mitchell aiming the Browning up towards the landing, apparently at Carter.

As he turned he realized that he was not the hit man's target.

Michael Grant threw himself towards Carter, knocking

him off his feet. They landed heavily, Grant on top, using his advantage to fasten his hands around Carter's neck.

Mitchell moved up the first three steps to get a better shot, stepping over the twisted body of Jennifer Thomas in the process. He glanced down at her, not sure if she was dead or not, unable to spare the time to find out.

Weak from the wound in his shoulder, Carter could not fend off Grant's attack and he felt the other man's thumbs digging into his throat.

Grant lifted Carter's head an inch or two and slammed it down, almost knocking him out.

Carter brought his knee up and drove it into Grant's back. The impact was enough to make him loosen his grip slightly and Carter used his good arm to strike upwards, catching Grant a stinging blow across the face. He toppled to one side and Carter rolled over, his hand scrabbling for the dropped automatic.

Another shot exploded nearby. Then another.

Carter saw Mitchell advancing up the stairs.

Grant got to his feet, realizing he couldn't fight two armed men. He turned to run into one of the bedrooms but Carter reached his gun. He swung the Smith and Wesson round and fired twice. The first bullet struck the wall beside the running man, blasting a huge piece of plaster from it. The second hit him in the shoulder, the impact spinning him round as blood sprayed the mouldy paintwork.

Grant overbalanced but kept moving, crawling into the enveloping darkness of the bedroom.

'Find Tina,' Carter shouted as Mitchell reached the landing.

The hit man turned to his left, into another ill-lit room. Carter raised himself up and moved cautiously towards the bedroom into which Grant had disappeared. He paused at the door, not venturing over the threshold into the gloom, aware that his wounded adversary might be waiting to pounce on him.

The scream distracted him.

It came from deeper inside the house. From the direction that Mitchell had gone.

Carter stupidly turned slightly and, in that split second, Grant struck at him again, kicking him hard in the stomach.

Carter dropped like a stone, winded but still holding on to the pistol. Grant drove another kick into his opponent's side and Carter felt a rib crack. He rolled over in an effort to escape the onslaught, trying to bring the automatic to bear on Grant. The floor was spattered with blood, both Carter's and his adversary's. Carter finally reached the wall and tried to rise but Grant ran at him once more, driving his shoulder into Carter's chest, slamming him up against the wall. Carter gasped for breath, the pain from his shoulder almost unbearable now, but he gritted his teeth and gripped Grant by the throat. Then, with lightning speed, he drove his head forward. His forehead connected with Grant's nose, splintering the nasal bone, stunning the other man who backed off a few paces, dazed.

It was all the respite Carter needed.

He levelled the pistol and fired repeatedly.

Bang.

The bullet tore through Grant's right lung.

Bang.

As he put up a hand to shield himself, the heavy grain shell blasted off two of his fingers.

Bang.

The third shot hit him in the chest, lifting him off his feet as it stove in his sternum, the loud crack of shattering bone audible even above the roar of the pistol.

Grant sprawled on his back, spreadeagled, blood spilling from his wounds, forming a crimson cloak around him.

The stench of cordite in the air mingled with the smell of

281

excrement but Carter seemed to ignore the odorous confirmation that his opponent was dead. He fired two more shots into Grant's head, watching with relish as the cranium was ripped apart by the staggering impacts. The skull exploded as the bullets entered it, Grant's corpse jerking as the lethal loads struck him.

Carter sucked in a deep breath and staggered past the body, almost slipping in a thick puddle of brains and blood. But he blundered on, trying to find Tina.

Trying to trace the scream he'd heard, praying he wasn't too late.

Sixty-Two

She hadn't screamed when she'd heard the door being broken down.

She hadn't even screamed when she heard the gunshots.

But now, as Paul Gardner rose and staggered towards her, the machete gripped in his fist, Tina had finally found the breath to scream in terror.

Gardner moved slowly, clumsily, the large-bladed weapon moving menacingly before him. He was grinning, but the smile of triumph was tempered by fear. The gunshots had startled him. The sounds of struggle had alarmed him. He knew that he must kill Tina and do it fast. He had no idea who the intruders were but he did realize that they would soon reach him.

Tina continued to struggle with the ropes which held her, openly trying to free herself as her would-be executioner drew nearer.

He steadied himself, raising the machete as if to strike.

She lashed out with her left foot, bringing it up hard between his legs.

Gardner grunted in pain and dropped the machete, one hand clutching his throbbing testicles. With the other he struck Tina, a blow which knocked her off the chair.

'Fucking bitch,' he wheezed, reaching again for the weapon, determined now to finish the job as she lay helpless, her hands still twitching, trying to remove the rope which held her to the chair.

Gardner moved closer, turning slightly as he heard footsteps approaching.

He raised the machete again, his eyes bulging wide with rage and frustration. She must die. She *would* die.

Tina screamed.

The sound was drowned by the deafening retorts of the Browning and the Smith and Wesson.

Tina saw both Carter and Mitchell silhouetted in the doorway guns flaming as they pumped shot after shot into Gardner.

Four. Five. Six.

Bullets continued to hit him even as he was sent skidding across the room by the deathly impacts, each fresh one blasting a new hole in him. Each wound spraying blood into the air, on to the walls. On to Tina.

Eight. Nine. Ten.

The sound of gunfire was deafening and Tina wanted to scream again as the crescendo of explosions throbbed in her ears and skull. The barrels continued to flame. Smoke wafted like a dirty curtain across the dusty room and the smell of cordite filled her nostrils.

Eleven. Twelve.

Carter felt the hammer of the 9mm slam down on an empty chamber but he watched as Mitchell put one more shot into the body which now resembled a sieve. The hit man finally released the trigger and re-holstered the pistol, the afterburn of the muzzle flashes still seared on to his retina, the thunderous roar of the pistols still reverberating inside the room.

Carter crossed to Tina and untied her, helping her to her feet.

'Are there any more of them,' he asked.

She shook her head.

'What about Frank?' she wanted to know. 'Is he dead?' There was a note of anticipation in her voice but Carter merely shook his head almost disappointedly. He helped her up and the three of them moved back towards the landing. Tina looked at Carter's injured shoulder with concern but he seemed oblivious to the raging pain from the stab wound, more concerned with the injuries which Tina had sustained.

Mitchell followed them on to the landing, Carter turning towards the stairs.

He had taken just two steps when he realized that the body of Jennifer Thomas no longer lay where it had fallen.

He heard movement behind him, heard the arc of the wood as it came crashing down onto his head. Heard the roar of Mitchell's Beretta.

Then the floor was rushing up to meet him.

Pain was forgotten.

Darkness.

Sixty-Three

Daylight was flooding through the half-drawn curtains, touching his face as if trying to coax him from his stupor.

Ray Carter felt the warmth on his skin and opened his eyes slowly. He blinked hard and rolled over.

Sudden savage pain shot through him as he flopped on to his side. His shoulder felt as if it was ablaze and he hastily moved on to his back once more, relieving the pressure. He reached up tentatively towards the injured shoulder and was surprised to feel a large pad of gauze covering the wound, held in place by a bandage which had been expertly applied.

Carter blinked again, trying to clear the fog which seemed to cloud his memory. He had another bandage on his head and, as he sat up, he felt a dull ache at the back of his neck. Events slowly came back to him.

The chase through Whitechapel. The gunfire. The stabbing. The shattering blow across his head.

And Tina.

She was alive, or at least she had been last time he'd seen her. He hauled himself further up in bed, suddenly realizing that it was *his* bed. He was in his own flat, cleaned up and bandaged as if by some phantom nurse.

'I thought you were dead,' a voice snapped, close to him.

Carter rubbed his eyes and turned to see Frank Harrison standing in the doorway, holding a cup of coffee in his hand.

'What are you doing here, Frank?' Carter wanted to know, wincing as he sat up, swinging his legs over the edge of the bed.

'Looking after your *nurse*,' said the gang leader, emphasising the last word with irritation.

As he spoke, Tina appeared beside him.

285

'Are you all right, Ray?' she wanted to know, taking a step towards him.

'He's fine,' snapped Harrison, extending an arm to block Tina's advance.

'How did I get back?' Carter wanted to know. 'I remember being laid out by one of those bloody nutters, then nothing at all.'

'I told Mitchell to bring you back here,' Tina explained. 'I dressed your wounds.'

'What else did you do?' Harrison wanted to know, gripping Tina's shoulder. 'You were alone here for a couple of hours before you called me.'

'I was unconscious for fuck's sake,' Carter rasped. 'Talk sense, Frank.'

Harrison took a step forward, one finger pointing menacingly at Carter.

'Don't pop off to me, Carter. I want to know what happened here last night. I want to know what you two got up to before I arrived.'

'Like Ray said, he was out cold.'

There was an uncomfortable silence while Harrison took a sip of his coffee, glaring first at Tina and then at Carter.

'What happened to Mitchell?' Carter wanted to know.

'He's waiting for us now,' Harrison said. 'He called here to say he'd be at the Mayfair casino to pick up his money.' The gang boss glanced at his watch. 'That was an hour ago.'

Carter nodded gently, pain throbbing inside his head but, nevertheless, he began to unwind the bandage around his cranium, feeling the large bump at the back of his skull.

'What are you going to do about Mitchell?' Carter wanted to know.

'Kill the bastard,' Harrison said flatly. 'I said I would when all this was over.'

'That might be easier said than done,' Carter reminded him.

'Well it better work because you're going to help me. Get your clothes on and let's go.'

The driver glared at Harrison before reaching for his shirt and pulling it on, wincing as it slid over his injured shoulder,

'And Tina? What about her?' Carter asked.

'She comes with us.'

'It could be dangerous . . .'

Harrison cut him short.

'I'll worry about that,' he rasped. 'She's *my* concern not yours.'

Harrison downed what was left in his coffee cup and turned towards the kitchen, leaving Carter to dress. The driver glanced briefly at Tina who chanced a smile and then followed Harrison.

Carter reached for his pistol, strapping it on, ensuring that the 9mm automatic nestled beneath his left armpit. Then he pulled on his jacket.

'Come on,' Harrison snapped. 'I want to get this over with.'

Carter glanced at his watch.

It was 11.36 a.m.

Sixty-Four

'He's late.'

David Mitchell glanced at his watch and then at the clock on the wall of Harrison's office.

'That's not my fault,' Damien Drake protested.

'Maybe I'll just take the money and go anyway.'

'You can't do that.'

Mitchell raised one eyebrow quizzically and looked at Drake.

'Why? Who's going to stop me? You?' The hit man's voice was low but full of menace.

'I don't know the combination of the safe. I can't get to the money. You'll *have* to wait for Harrison to get here.' There was a note of concern in Drake's voice. Even the pistol beneath his left armpit didn't give him the reassurance he needed in Mitchell's presence. The hit man got to his feet and began pacing the room slowly.

He stopped abruptly as he heard footsteps outside the office door.

Drake smiled thinly, relieved that Harrison had finally arrived. However, there was a moment of silence outside the door, the handle was turned slowly, almost tentatively.

The figure which entered was not Harrison.

This man was taller, older. Dressed in a dark coat which reached as far as his knees. Both hands were tucked into his pockets. As the man entered the room Drake and Mitchell became of a growing chill in the air and also of a rank odour which made the hit man frown.

The newcomer remained motionless, eyes flicking slowly back and forth between the two men.

Mitchell took a step backwards, his fingers flexing slightly.

'How the fuck did you get up here?' Drake wanted to know. 'The casino's closed. This area is private.'

'You're Damien Drake,' said the figure, his voice low and rasping, as if his throat was clogged with mucus.

Drake frowned.

'How do you know me?' he demanded.

'We met. Once. A couple of years ago. In the East End.'

'What do you want?' Drake asked but some of the bravado had gone from his voice, replaced instead by uncertainty. Fear?

'You could say I've got some unfinished business.'

'Who are you?'

'Charles Ross.'

Drake frowned; then his mouth began to curl up at the corners in a smile. But the gesture never touched his eyes.

'Ross,' he chuckled humourlessly. 'Charlie Ross is dead.' The smile faded.

'Yes. And so are you.'

The movement was swift. So swift that neither Drake nor Mitchell had time to reach for their own weapons.

Ross pulled open his coat, both hands closed around an Ingram M-10, the normally compact sub-machine gun looking huge because of the bulbous silencer attached to the barrel. He tightened his finger on the trigger and opened fire, spraying the stream of bullets back and forth across the room, the deadly fusillade drawing dotted lines of death across both Drake and Mitchell.

Mitchell was hit four times in the chest, flesh and shattered bone propelled from the wounds by the impact. He was catapulted back over the desk, crashing against a wall, his blood spurting from the holes.

Drake shouted in pain as the first of the bullets hit him in the left shoulder, powering through the scapula as it exited. The next caught him on the point of the chin, shattering his jaw and causing splintered teeth to fly into the air. Another shot took off most of the right side of his head and he was thrown backwards, slamming into the wall where he remained upright for several seconds as Ross pumped more shots into him. Then Drake slid down to the floor leaving several thick crimson trails on the paintwork behind him.

The smell of cordite filled the room and Ross stood motionless for a second, glancing at the two dead men. Then he jammed the Ingram into his belt and walked across to the twisted body of Drake, kneeling beside it.

Ross grabbed a handful of hair and lifted the man's head so that he was gazing into the blank eyes, tilting his pulverized skull backwards to expose the throat.

Then he slid the knife from his pocket.

Sixty-Five

As Carter brought the Daimler to a halt across the street from the casino he saw Billy Stripes come scuttling towards the vehicle.

'What the hell is going on?' asked Harrison, flinging open the door and clambering out. Tina followed him.

Carter walked behind, puzzled by the look on Billy's face, the concern in his voice.

'We don't know how it happened? Or who it was,' he blurted as Harrison strode towards the main entrance of the club. 'They'd been dead about half an hour when me and Joe found them . . .'

'Who's dead?' snarled Harrison, grasping Billy by the lapels.

'Someone hit Drake and Mitchell. In your office,' Billy said, shaking loose of his boss's grip.

Harrison pushed past the younger man and ran into the club, past Joe Duggan and Martin McAuslan who were standing in the main games room of the club.

Carter pushed Tina back and sprinted after Harrison. She hesitated a second before following. Billy also tried to restrain her but she continued up the stairs.

Harrison reached his office and paused on the threshold. Even from there he could smell the stench of death, see the blood spattered on the carpet and walls. There were bullet holes in the far wall, the desk had been drilled full of the lethal projectiles. Carter and Tina caught up with him as he paused in the doorway, his face drained of colour. Then, slowly, he stepped inside.

'Who knows about this?' Harrison wanted to know.

'No one,' Billy told him. 'We haven't even called the law.'

'Well don't. Get rid of the bodies yourself.'

'Who could it have been?' Tina wanted to know, looking away after glancing at the bullet-torn corpse of Mitchell.

'Mitchell was supposed to have killed them all,' Carter added. 'There aren't any gangs left.'

'Then who the fuck did this?' snarled Harrison, his voice cracking. He looked down at Drake's body, at the bullet holes. At the savage gash which ran from ear to ear. Blood had spread out in a thick dark pool around the dead man.

'We found this,' Billy said softly, reaching for the door. It had been pushed back on its hinges, hiding part of the wall but now, as he pushed it forward Harrison swallowed hard, felt his bowels loosen as he read the words, written in Drake's blood, which covered the wall:

SEPTEMBER 3RD
IN MEMORIAM
CHARLES ROSS

The gang boss opened his mouth to speak but no words would come. He merely stepped back, eyes still fixed on the words, and perched on the edge of his desk, ignoring the spots of blood which spattered it.

Tina read the scrawl and glanced first at Harrison then at Carter.

'Who's Charles Ross?' she wanted to know.

'You mean who *was* he?' Carter said softly, his own eyes also rivetted to the wall. 'He's dead. Him and his men. Dead for two years now. Two years to the day.' He nodded at the date scrawled in blood on the wall. 'Ross and four of his boys were taken out on September 3rd two years ago.'

'The bastard was dangerous,' said Harrison quietly, as if he had difficulty speaking. 'He was always a mad fucker. Ran wild after I ordered a hit on his brother. He swore he'd kill me.' The gang boss's voice had mellowed and become almost reflective. 'There was a building development being started in the East End, I forget the name of it now, something Towers I think.' His face was very pale as he spoke, his eyes never leaving the bloody letters. 'I called Ross, told him and his blokes to meet me at the building site, told him I wanted to make peace. The gang war was fucking up business for everyone, the law were down on us all. He turned up with four men. We were waiting for him. Me, Drake, Joule and Pat Mendham. We took them all. Waited until they were lined up and then shot the fucking lot. We put the bodies in the foundations of one of the tower blocks, they were due to be filled in the next day. We figured no one would ever find them inside thousands of tons of concrete.' He smiled humourlessly. 'They disappeared. Like they'd never existed. The other gangs knew what had happened, and none of them bothered me after that. London was mine.'

'So who's done this?' Carter demanded. 'Barbieri's dead, so are Cleary, Sullivan and Hayes.'

'Someone trying to put the frighteners on you, Frank?' Billy offered.

'Like who?' Tina asked, but her question went unanswered.

'There's something else, Frank,' Carter observed. 'You said that you, Drake, Joule and Mendham did the killing that day, right? Well, the other three have already been murdered.'

'One of Ross's gang?' Billy offered.

Harrison shook his head.

'After he was killed the others left London. Besides, why wait two years? If any of them had been left, they'd have come after us sooner.'

'I know that place you're on about, there was something about it in the paper,' said Carter. 'Langley Towers it was called. It's being demolished.'

'So?' Harrison said.

'Maybe they found the bodies,' Billy suggested.

'I told you, no one would know who they were, there's no way of linking the deaths of Ross and his men with me,' Harrison muttered.

'Well somebody knew Charlie Ross,' Carter added. 'Someone with a grudge against you, Frank. My bet is you're next on the list.'

The gang boss glared at Carter.

He was about to say something when the phone rang.

Harrison hesitated before picking it up.

'Yeah,' he barked.

Silence.

'Hello, who is this?'

There was a soft, gurgling sound at the other end and then a liquid rattle.

'Harrison,' the voice said and the gang boss almost dropped the phone. 'Did you see my message? Did you see it, you fucker?'

'I saw it,' he replied. 'Who is this?'

'Who do you think?' There was anger in the words but something more. Triumph? 'You're going to die, Harrison. Soon. You won't know when but I want you to look into my face before I kill you, something you never had the guts to do before. Do you hear me?'

The gang boss gripped the receiver hard, his knuckles turning white.

'Now listen to me, you cunt, if you think you can scare me . . .'

He was cut short.

'I'm not trying to scare you,' the voice rasped. 'I just want to kill you. I've waited long enough.'

The line went dead.

Harrison slammed the receiver down, his hand shaking. His face was deathly white and he was forced to lean against the desk for support. Tina stood watching as he spun round to face Carter and Billy.

'Carter, you and Billy, you go to Langley Towers, understand?' he hissed. 'You search it. Search every fucking inch of it. Take Duggan with you.' His breath was coming in low, quick gasps. 'Find those bodies.'

Carter frowned.

'Frank, what the hell are you talking about?' he asked,

294

irritably. 'Ross is dead. That message is from someone trying to wind you up.' He pointed at the blood-drawn words on the wall.

'Find the bodies,' Harrison bellowed. 'I have to see them. I have to know he's dead.'

'You killed him yourself,' Carter roared back. 'Charlie Ross is dead and buried.'

'Check that site, got it?' Harrison snarled. 'I'll be at my flat with Tina. You report back there.'

'This is fucking crazy,' snapped Carter.

Harrison lunged forward, grabbing him by the collar, but Carter gripped his boss's wrists and threw him backwards. Even as he staggered two or three paces, Harrison slid his right hand inside his jacket and pulled out the .357. He aimed it at Carter's head and thumbed back the hammer.

'You check that fucking site or so help me I'll kill you,' the gang boss rasped.

Tina looked anxiously at Carter and at the gaping barrel of the revolver.

'So, we go looking for dead men?' Carter mused.

Harrison didn't speak, he merely lowered the gun slowly and then carefully released the hammer, disarming the .357. He slid it back into its holster. The gang boss grabbed Tina by the arm and pulled her towards the door.

'Clean this fucking place up. Then do what I told you,' Harrison snapped. Then he was gone.

Carter looked at Billy Stripes and shrugged.

'He's fucking mad,' said Carter, shaking his head.

'So, who do you think it is, Ray?' Billy wanted to know.

Carter crossed to the body of Drake and looked down at it.

'I'm not paid to think, Billy,' he said quietly.

Drake's eyes gazed at him blindly.

They called McAuslan and began their task.

The words of blood on the wall remained in plain view.

An accusation.

A challenge.

Sixty-Six

2.49 p.m.

Harrison looked across at the wall clock and muttered under his breath. He downed what was left in the glass, crossed to the cabinet and poured himself another large measure of Haig.

Tina sat on the sofa, one leg drawn up beneath her, watching as the gang boss paced agitatedly back and forth pausing occasionally to glance at the phone.

'What the hell's taking them so long?' he hissed. 'They should have been there by now.'

'Give them time, Frank,' Tina said, her own nerves frayed after the events of the past few days. 'Why don't you just sit down and . . .'

'Sit down,' he snarled, turning on her. 'Sit down and what? Relax?' He took another large gulp of whisky. He'd already got through half a bottle since they'd arrived at the flat two hours earlier and now, as he paced up and down, his steps weren't so assured. Once or twice he almost stumbled, cursing when he spilled the whisky.

'You're getting yourself worked up,' she told him.

'Somebody's trying to kill me,' he rasped. 'What the fuck

do you expect me to do, have a sing-song?' He finished what was left in the glass and hurriedly poured himself some more.

'Drinking isn't going to help,' Tina protested.

'Button it,' Harrison growled. 'Just shut up.' The bottle cracked hard against the glass, almost chipping the delicate crystal. He could smell the drink on his own breath.

Tina got to her feet, tired of Harrison's abuse.

'Where are you going?' he demanded.

'Into the kitchen,' she told him.

He snaked out a hand and gripped her arm, squeezing hard. Tina tried to shake free but Harrison held on, finally pushing her back on to the sofa.

'You stay with me,' he said, lurching over to the sofa and slumping down beside her.

She slid to one end, anxious to get away from his whisky-smelling breath.

'What's wrong with you, Frank?' she wanted to know.

'Somebody's trying to kill me, have you forgotten that? If I'd been in the casino this morning the bastards would have had me then.' He rubbed his forehead with a thumbnail. 'That fucking Charlie Ross, he always was a devious sod.'

'Ross is dead. Ray said that the message was from someone trying to scare you . . .'

'Ray. Ray. Ray said. I don't give a fuck what Carter said,' Harrison growled. 'So, you believe *him* and not *me* do you? Why? What makes him so fucking special?' He gripped a handful of her hair in his fist and pulled her towards him.

Tina recoiled both from the pain and also from the stink of liquor on Harrison's breath. He finally pushed her aside.

'Why should Carter be right?' the gang boss wanted to know.

'Frank, be sensible about it,' she said, irritably. 'If Ross is dead . . .'

'Yeah, *if* he's dead,' Harrison interrupted.

'But you said you killed him yourself, and buried his body. How could it be Ross who's after you now? Be logical for Christ's sake.'

He glared at her.

'You weren't like this after the restaurant attack,' she told him. 'You were angry not scared.'

Harrison chuckled humourlessly.

'And you think that when they come for me they're going to leave you alone, is that it?' he asked. 'Is it?'

'When who comes for you?'

'Ross,' he bellowed, jumping to his feet.

'Ross is dead. For the last time, he's dead.'

'I won't believe that until I see his fucking body.'

Ray Carter took a long draw on the cigarette and held the smoke in his mouth for a moment before blowing it out in a long bluish stream.

He watched as the JCB's and the bulldozers rumbled over the piles of rubble which had once been Langley Towers, crushing stone beneath their huge caterpillar tracks, scooping debris up in their buckets, dumping it into the huge Scania lorries which waited obediently on the site.

Beside him Billy Stripes looked at his watch and sighed.

'How much longer do you think they're going to work?' he mused.

'A couple of hours,' Carter said, scanning the ruins.

Most of the first block and at least half of the second had been demolished. The third stood as a last defiant monument to the idiocy of modern planning, the late afternoon sunshine reflecting off its windows as if it were bouncing off so many blind eyes. The buildings which surrounded the three blocks were also still intact. Carter glanced at the supermarket, watching it for a moment before taking a last drag on his cigarette and tossing the butt out of the window.

298

'Shouldn't we tell Frank we're here?' asked Joe Duggan from the back seat.

Carter didn't answer. He merely glanced into the rear view mirror at Duggan.

'We'll call him if we find anything,' Billy said.

'Amongst all that rubbish,' said Carter, nodding towards the mountains of debris, a note of desperation in his voice. 'And what the hell are we supposed to do even if we do find Ross's body? Take it back to his flat?'

Billy reached for the packet of cigarettes lying on the parcel shelf. It was empty. He swore and screwed it up.

'Fuck this,' said Carter finally, starting the engine of the car. 'Let's go and get a cup of tea. We'll come back when the site's quiet.' He put it into first gear. 'If Ross is there he's not going to go far anyway, is he?'

The other two men chuckled as Carter spun the wheel and drove away.

Behind them, the destruction continued.

The sun sank lower in the sky.

It would be dark in three hours.

Sixty-Seven

The skies above London were mottled grey with cloud, the approaching rain combining with the night to make the gloom totally impenetrable.

Thousands of lights glowed like grounded stars in the buildings which surrounded the derelict site. Across the water the lights of the City itself seemed to cast a glow up towards the lowering heavens as if trying to keep the darkness at bay.

But, on the wreckage of Langley Towers, there was only blackness.

Except for the spear-like shafts of torch-light which swept back and forth over the rubble like hand-held searchlights.

Carter, Billy Stripes and Joe Duggan moved down the steep incline from where they had parked the car, picking their way over piles of shattered masonry, endeavouring to keep their balance. Duggan cursed as he slipped and twisted his ankle on a piece of rock.

Carter gave him only a cursory glance as he kicked the offending stone to one side, hissing once more as he stubbed his toe on the lump of concrete. The torch beam waved erratically through the air as he struggled to prevent himself falling.

The earth movers now stood unattended, metal carcasses amongst the carnage they had wrought. The wind moved the bucket of a JCB and it squeaked rhythmically, adding a background to the steady crunching sound made by the men's feet as they continued to struggle over the bricks and concrete.

'Where the hell do we start?' said Duggan, surveying the huge expanse of desolation. 'We could be here all night.'

'The bodies were buried in concrete weren't they?' Billy added. 'How deep?'

Carter could only shrug.

'Christ knows,' he grunted. 'Even if we find them we'll probably need a bloody JCB to dig them out.'

'I reckon Harrison's gone mental,' Billy added.

'You mean it's taken this long for you to notice,' Carter muttered cryptically. 'He's always been a fucking headcase.'

'We must be pretty bloody stupid, wandering around a demolition site looking for blokes who've been dead for two years,' Duggan added.

'Tell Harrison that.'

The three men came to a halt, gazing around them.

'We might as well split up,' said Carter. 'I'll look around here, you two try over by the other blocks.'

'How long are we going to look?' Duggan wanted to know. 'Until we find something?'

'Bollocks,' snapped Carter. 'We'll meet back at the car in three hours.'

'But what if we don't find anything?' Duggan protested. 'Frank isn't going to be very happy.'

'Then let him come down here with a shovel and look for his bloody self,' Carter snapped.

The men stood in the silence of the night for a moment and then Billy and Duggan picked their way over the rubble, visible only by their torch beams. Carter turned and began shining his own torch over the pockmarked ground, picking out pieces of broken glass and masses of pulverized rock in the process. It was like walking through a huge quarry. As he moved about he shivered, saw his breath clouding in the air. He would pause occasionally, overturning large lumps of concrete as if expecting to find Ross or one of his men beneath it.

His search continued.

301

On the other side of the site Duggan and Billy were having no luck either. They, like Carter, weren't even sure what they were looking for but, nevertheless, they continued their vigil, moving amongst mounds of rubble.

'I feel a right prat doing this,' said Duggan.

'Join the club,' Billy added wearily. He nodded in the direction of the half-demolished second block. 'I'm going to try in there. You stay here, have a scout round through the crap.'

Duggan nodded and shone his torch over the ground while Billy headed off towards the second of the towers. As he walked a fine shroud of dust rose up around his feet, settling like mist as he moved towards the building. The place was thick with dust and Billy coughed as he entered, waving a hand in front of him. Dust particles swirled and danced in the torch-light and he moved slowly across what had once been the lobby, avoiding cracks in the floor as best he could, stopping to peer down into them every now and then. Maybe Ross or one of his men would be down there waiting to be discovered, he thought and chuckled to himself.

Unknown to him, his every movement was being watched.

Carter traced the outline of what he took to be the foundations of the first block with the torch, pausing once to light a cigarette. He sucked hard on it, the end glowing red in the darkness as he walked. What a waste of time, he thought irritably. Wandering around freezing his nuts off just to satisfy his idiot boss. Harrison was cracking up, his outburst earlier in the day had convinced Carter of that. Sending them out to hunt for dead men. Jesus, the bastard was ready for a straitjacket. Carter shook his head and walked on, his thoughts turning to Tina. She was alone with Harrison. What if he got impatient? Roughed her up? Carter gritted his teeth and tried to push the thoughts to the back of his mind. If Harrison dared to hurt her again . . .

The weight of the automatic beneath his left armpit felt comforting.

He paused by a particularly large hole in the foundations and shone his torch into it, scanning the cracked concrete for anything vaguely human. Bones, clothes, anything.

The hole was empty.

He walked on, taking another suck on his cigarette.

He turned and headed back in the direction he'd seen Billy and Duggan take, wondering if they'd had any joy in what he was convinced was a fruitless search.

It was as he was climbing over a mound of debris that he saw something move.

A figure?

It was difficult to tell in the gloom.

Carter shone his torch in its direction but picked out only more bricks.

'Billy,' he called, his voice echoing in the stillness. 'Joe.'

Silence.

Carter shook his head and continued scrambling over the ruins.

More movement, to his right this time.

He spun round, torch cutting through the gloom.

Nothing.

'If either of you two silly sods are having a joke . . .' he called, allowing the sentence to trail off.

Ahead of him a pile of bricks fell, slowly at first then with a dull thud.

Carter sprinted forward towards the rubble. Dust was still rising from it. It had been only recently disturbed.

If one of his colleagues was pissing about he'd be mad. It was bad enough trekking about in the cold looking for the remains of dead men without them playing tricks on him.

Carter advanced towards the supermarket.

He was within fifty yards when he saw the figure slip

through one of the open doors.

'Right, you bastard,' Carter muttered under his breath. He'd get his own back now. See how the other two liked a bloody joke. Ducking low, hidden by the shadows, he flicked off his torch and scuttled towards the supermarket, pausing at the door, listening.

There was no sound from inside.

He pushed the door with one hand and stepped in.

The smell which hit him was like an invisible wall. So rank and putrid in its intensity that he was forced to put a hand over his mouth. All thoughts of the figure vanished as he concentrated on trying not to vomit. The smell was incredible. He took a step inside, pulling a handkerchief from his pocket to cover his nose and mouth.

Broken glass crackled beneath his feet, dust swirled up around his shoes.

Carter played the beam of the torch over the huge empty shelves which seemed to stretch for miles, so far that the beam could not reach the end of the aisles. The check-outs stood long abandoned, covered by dust nearly an inch thick. He stood motionless, torchlight bouncing off the dirty shelves, squinting to catch any movement in the gloom.

He saw nothing.

It was then that the hand closed on his shoulder.

Sixty-Eight

Carter's heart raced madly as he felt the hand touch him and he spun round, reaching for the automatic.

His torchlight illuminated the face of Joe Duggan.

'Jesus Christ,' gasped Carter, sucking in a deep breath. 'What the hell are you playing at? I nearly shit a brick.' He raised the torch in mock anger, as if to hit Duggan who recoiled momentarily.

'Sorry, Ray,' his colleague said.

'I saw you come in here. I followed you. I thought it might have been someone . . .'

'What are you on about? *I* followed *you* in here,' Duggan explained.

'But I saw someone come in.'

'It wasn't me.'

'Where's Billy?' Carter wanted to know, glancing now not at Duggan but around him, up and down the endless aisles of the supermarket.

'He was having a look round the other block. It might have been him you saw come in here.'

Carter nodded slowly. He hoped Duggan was right. For some unexplainable reason he felt a shiver run down his spine and, now his initial shock had subsided, he was once more aware of the vile stench which filled the building.

'Smells like something *died* in here,' said Duggan wrinkling his nose.

'There've been reports of packs of wild dogs and cats around this area. Maybe they've been in here.' Carter shone his torch over the dusty floor noting that the thick covering had been disturbed in many places up and down several of the aisles. 'It looks as if someone's been in here.'

Duggan advanced towards the closest aisle, his torch beam alighting on an object in the dust.

He bent to touch it.

A broken bottle.

'Somebody's been in here recently,' he observed, noting that there was hardly any dust on the top surface of the bottle.

'Brilliant work, Sherlock,' Carter said sarcastically. He was still shining his torch over the aisles. 'Let's check this place out, find Billy and fuck off. It's getting too cold to be poncing around here for much longer.' So saying, he moved briskly up the first aisle, shining his torch to the right and left. Still the beam wouldn't reach the end of the shelf, but disappeared into the inky blackness beyond.

Duggan moved up the adjacent aisle, hidden from Carter's view by the blackness and the height of the shelves.

Neither of them saw the figure approaching from the opposite direction.

Carter was in aisle three, Duggan in four.

The man who, in life, had been known as Liam Kelly was moving slowly and purposefully down the fifth aisle, Ian Massey behind him. Both carried shotguns.

'You see anything?' Carter called, his voice lancing through the darkness.

'No,' came the reply.

Carter shone his torch over the dusty floor and paused.

There was a dark stain in the thick carpet of dust and grime.

He knelt quickly and pressed one index finger into it.

'Blood,' he whispered, wiping the sticky red fluid on his jeans. He shone the torch ahead, realizing that he was coming to the end of the shelves.

In aisle two Charles Ross eased back the bolt on the Ingram, priming it. Beside him Peter Burton hefted the .45 automatic in one gloved fist.

306

'Ray, there's something up ahead,' called Duggan from aisle four.

'I see it,' Carter replied, his eyes now fixed on the sight before him. His torch beam wavered slightly as it illuminated the apparitions ahead of him. If only they had been apparitions.

'Oh Jesus,' murmured Duggan, emerging from aisle four level with Carter.

The stench was now quite intolerable.

The sight which met them, even more so.

The bodies of Danny Weller, Adam Giles and Nikki Jones, nailed to the wall of the supermarket, were in advanced stages of decomposition, particularly their faces from which every last trace of skin had been stripped away.

Carter shone his torch slowly up and down the hanging body of Weller, noticing that other parts of his body had been flayed but not as expertly as his face. Lumps of muscle had been gouged from his lower body, particularly the stomach where the cuts were so deep that portions of shrivelled intestine poked through the rents.

Nikki Jones' breasts had been slashed repeatedly, the left one hacked off completely. It lay in the dust beneath her like a punctured, fleshy balloon.

Adam Giles' scrotum had been carefully opened with one single knife cut, his testicles removed. His shrivelled penis too had been ripped away. Carter was sure there were bite marks around the dead boy's thighs.

'What the fuck is this?' gasped Duggan.

Carter had no answer.

There was a movement to his right, from a doorway.

A man emerged, or at least what had once been a man.

His face was covered in a mask of flesh, ill-fitting but still stretched tautly enough over his own rotting features to give him some semblance of humanity.

He was holding an Uzi 9mm machine pistol in his ravaged hands, the barrel levelled at Carter and Duggan.

He was smiling.

'Where's Harrison?'

The question came from Carter's left and he looked to one side, still aware of the other man.

The man who had once been Charles ross stepped into view, the Ingram pointing at his two living adversaries.

'Was the bastard too frightened to come?' Ross hissed through lips which seemed to flap like sails in a high wind.

Pete Burton stood alongside him.

'Charlie Ross,' murmured Duggan.

'Yeah, that's right. Been a while hasn't it? Two years to be precise,' the gang leader rasped, taking a step forward. 'Maybe you recognise my friends too?'

From behind Duggan, shotguns levelled, Massey and Kelly emerged.

In the doorway ahead John Campbell continued to smile, a thick clear mucus oozing from one corner of his mouth.

'This isn't real,' Duggan said, his eyes bulging, his heart thudding madly against his ribs. 'You're dead.'

Ross smiled.

'Now where have I heard that before?' he chuckled.

Carter knew it would be pointless to reach for his gun. His mind struggled to grasp what was happening. He and Duggan were being held at gunpoint by five corpses. Five living corpses? He almost laughed.

Pinch yourself, my son, he told himself, *and the bastards will disappear*.

Just like the three crucified corpses on the wall?

Would they disappear too?

He wondered for one fleeting second if he'd gone insane. If this entire vile tableau was the product of some psychotic nightmare. Perhaps he was still lying in bed at home recovering from that bang on the head. Perhaps he was dreaming.

Perhaps . . .

He knew he was going to die.

The five men who in life had been his enemies now raised their weapons, drawing a bead on himself and Duggan.

If Carter had believed in God he might have said a prayer. As it was, all he could do was shake his head.

Then the gunfire started.

Sixty-Nine

The report of the pistol inside the supermarket was thunderous.

The muzzle flash seemed to illuminate the darkness with uncanny brilliance and in that moment of searing brightness Carter saw Billy Stripes standing at the top of aisle six, the .357 gripped in both hands. He fired off three rounds, two of which hit Campbell.

The first heavy grain shell hit him in the chest, propelling him backwards through the door, dark fluid spurting from the gaping hole in his chest. The second one ricocheted off the frame but the third hit him in the face, ploughing through brittle bones and staving the face in as surely as if it had been hit with a sledgehammer. Campbell's head seemed to fold in upon itself and he hit the ground with a thud, the gun dropping from his twitching fingers.

The brief respite was enough to save Carter and Duggan

from death at least but not from the ferocity of the fusillade unleashed by Ross.

The dead gang boss tightened his finger on the trigger of the Ingram and the air was filled with the staccato rattle of automatic fire.

Two bullets caught Duggan. One in the shoulder, one in the thigh. The muscular part of his leg seemed to explode in a cloud of blood and broken bone and as he saw the crimson fountain spouting from the wound he realized with horror that his femoral artery had been severed. He screamed in pain and fear as he dragged himself to cover amongst the shelves.

Carter was hit in the left arm, the bullet ripping through his tricep, sending a burning pain right through him.

With what wits he retained he managed to get off two rounds from the 9mm.

The first parted empty air. The second caught Burton in the chest. It punctured one rotting lung before erupting from his back, carrying with it gobbets of reeking tissue and a fountain of seething yellow pus which flowed from veins and muscles like polluted blood.

Billy Stripes fired once more and ducked back into the seventh aisle as Massey and Kelly opened fire with their shotguns. The massive discharges blasted holes in the shelving and Billy was forced to crawl through the dust to avoid the thunderous eruptions which ripped through the air above him. He rolled over, trying to get to his feet, to find cover.

Burton dashed across the entrance to the aisle firing as he ran.

Carter hissed in pain as another bullet nicked the lobe of his ear, spattering his face with blood.

In the blinding brilliance of the muzzle flashes he fired three times.

The first bullet missed Burton and ploughed into the

crucified body of Adam Giles, jerking the corpse as the heavy grain shell struck it.

The second blasted part of Burton's right hand away and, as he yelled his pain, the third caught him in the throat. It shattered his larynx and Carter saw more of the pus-like fluid spout from the wound as Burton collapsed in an untidy heap.

Duggan was moaning as he dragged himself along the floor, one hand clapped to the savage wound in his thigh. He could feel blood gushing powerfully against his palm as he tried to staunch the crimson flow. Sickness swept over him and he thought he was going to pass out. Carter scrambled along behind him, moving on his knees, teeth gritted against the pain, pistol pointed at the entrance to the aisle in case Ross should decide to open up.

In aisle seven Billy Stripes raised himself on to his haunches and prepared to run for the main doors. He knew that the only chance he and his companions had was to get outside. Back to the car if possible. He swallowed hard, glanced behind him and ran, his footsteps muffled by the thick dust.

He reached the end of the aisle and hurtled towards the check-out barrier, vaulting it, skidding in the dust and falling.

The thunderous blast of a shotgun filled the supermarket as Kelly fired once. Twice.

The first staggering discharge blasted part of the barrier away.

The second hit Billy in the stomach.

The concentrated buckshot tore through his belly and intestines, several lengths of which burst from his abdomen. Bile from his ruptured gall bladder mingled with the blood which poured from the hideous wound and Kelly ran towards his downed foe, the shotgun still levelled.

Billy lay back, his hand still gripping the .357.

Kelly reached him and stood over him, pressing the shotgun to his shoulder, preparing to finish the job.

In the split second before he could fire, Billy tightened his finger around the trigger of the pistol.

The bullet hit Kelly beneath the chin and exploded from the top of his head carrying most of the top of his skull with it. Brain and reeking fluid rose like a spray, forced upwards by the passage of the bullet, and bone shattered easily under the impact. Kelly was lifted several feet into the air, jerked upward on invisible strings. The shotgun fell from his grasp as he hit the ground once more.

Billy got to his feet, trying to hold his entrails in place with one blood-drenched hand. But as he swayed uncertainly by the main doors Massey fired with his own shotgun and the aim was as lethal as it was unerring.

The twin discharges hit Billy almost simultaneously, shredding his upper torso, lifting him off his feet.

The horrendous impact sent him flying backwards towards the glass doors. As if punched by some invisible fist he hurtled through the air, trailing blood behind him, only to crash through the glass. His body, already a bloody ruin, was catapulted through the window, coming to rest half in and half out of the supermarket. Blood spurted out around him, quickly forming a pool.

Massey remained at the end of the aisle, knowing that Carter and Duggan would have to pass him in order to escape.

He worked the pump action of the shotgun to chamber another round, and he waited.

Carter had heard the roar of the shotgun, had heard Billy's scream of pain. Now he realized that there were two of the enemy left.

All square.

'Right, you fuckers,' he whispered, getting slowly to his feet.

Duggan was lying a few yards from him, moaning incoherently, blood still jetting from the bullet hole in his leg. Carter realized that his companion would be dead from blood-loss in less than five minutes. Already he had left a slimy trail of blood behind him as he had crawled through the dust. Now he lay helplessly, the gun still clutched in his hand, his other hand gripping the ragged edges of the wound in a vain attempt to stem the gushing flow of his life fluid.

Carter looked behind him, towards the three crucified bodies, then ahead, towards the shattered main doors and the body of Billy Stripes. He strained his ears, listening for any movement from the aisles on either side of him. All he heard was the low burbling of Duggan whose ramblings were becoming softer by the second.

'Joe,' Carter hissed.

Duggan didn't answer.

'He's going to die.'

The voice echoed around the inside of the building, amplified by the cavernous size of the supermarket.

'You're both going to die. And so is your boss.'

'Fuck you,' Carter shouted back.

His yell of defiance was greeted by a chuckle which caused the hackles on the back of his neck to rise.

Then, suddenly, he was dodging a stream of bullets which ripped through the shelving to his left as Ross raked the Ingram back and forth, spattering the lethal rounds in two horizontal lines in an effort to down Carter.

The shelving was blasted to shreds by the furious explosion of automatic fire and Carter shouted aloud as his ears were filled by the roar.

A bullet caught him in the back of the leg. He went down in a heap, hugging the ground as another furious eruption of fire tore over his head, missing him by inches.

He began to crawl, hearing that vile chuckle once more.

As he reached Duggan he realized his colleague was no longer burbling. He lay still, what remained of his head in the centre of a spreading pool of blood.

A stray bullet had removed virtually all of the top part of his cranium. A sticky flux of brain and blood stuck to Carter's hands as he crawled past, glancing only briefly at Duggan, more concerned now with the searing pain which was devouring his own leg. It twisted uselessly behind him, bent into a ridiculous shape by the bullet which had shattered it.

Using his elbows to propel himself, Carter crawled on. Dust clogged his nostrils and, all the time, that infernal stench seemed to fill his head but he dare not cough, dare not give away his position.

The silence was unbroken, the dust acting like a carpet, deadening further the footfalls of his two adversaries. He lay still for a second, ears and eyes alert for the slightest sound or movement.

Nothing.

He crawled a few more feet, every inch causing him fresh agony. But he gritted his teeth, blood from his torn ear now running down his face and dripping from his chin.

Again he listened.

To his left he heard something.

A soft, sibilant mucoid breathing.

Carter raised himself up using his good leg, crouching on that one knee, steadying the Smith and Wesson automatic, aiming at the point from which the breathing seemed to be coming. The point where he guessed Massey was standing.

From such close range he knew the bullets would penetrate the shelving. He had to hope that his shots were accurate.

The breathing continued.

Massey waited.

Carter steadied himself.

And fired.

Once, twice, three, four times.

The pistol slammed back against the heel of his hand, the repeated thunderous retorts deafening him, the muzzle flashes blinding him.

The mucoid breathing was transformed into a series of deathly roars as Massey was hit in the chest, arm and face.

Five times.

The shot gun fell from his grasp.

Six times.

Carter's shout of pain became one of rage and triumph.

Then the hammer slammed down on an empty chamber.

He tore the magazine free and fumbled in his pocket for another, slamming it into the butt, working the slide, chambering a fresh round.

Then Ross appeared, the Ingram levelled. But Carter was waiting for him.

The supermarket, for the final time, was filled with the deafening roar of weapons.

Seventy

He drove with difficulty because of the wounds he bore.

Every now and then, in traffic, another driver would gaze across at him in bewilderment but he met that stare and drove on as best he could, teeth gritted against the pain.

Once he had difficulty controlling the car and ran through a red light but, as he checked the rear view mirror, he saw that no police were following.

The gun lay beside him on the passenger seat just in case. If he was stopped he would open fire. There was no way that the police or anyone else were going to prevent him completing his task now.

He had waited too long for the moment.

The moment when he could pull the trigger on the man he hated, see him fall lifeless to the ground.

He smiled through the pain, the thought sustaining him.

The clock on the dashboard glowed in the darkness.

10.08 p.m.

Another five minutes and he would be there.

The waiting was almost over.

Seventy-One

The banging on the door awoke Harrison.

He sat up quickly and groaned as he felt the pain inside his head. Beside him on the sofa the whisky bottle was empty and he knocked it aside irritably as he tried to rise.

Tina reached the door first and was about to unlock it when Harrison stumbled across in front of her. He pushed her to one side and reached for the lock himself, easing the door open cautiously.

Carter practically fell into the room.

Tina screamed.

Carter was spattered with blood, his face and upper body in particular stained with the crimson fluid. There were two or three holes in his jacket. One in his shoulder, another in the left side of his chest. Each time he inhaled there was a sound like escaping steam as the air hissed through the hole in his lung.

'Ray,' Tina whimpered, unable to control her emotion at the sight of her lover.

Harrison seemed to care nothing for the note of concern in her voice. His eyes were rivetted to Carter's bloodied frame.

'What happened?' he gasped, taking a step back.

Carter swayed uncertainly for a moment then slumped back against the wall, using it as support.

'Who did this?' the gang boss persisted, his face drained of colour.

'It's over, Harrison,' Carter croaked. 'They're dead. All of them.'

'Did you find Ross?' he asked, falteringly.

Carter nodded, a vague smile touching his lips. He licked them, tasting blood.

'Yeah,' he croaked. 'We found him.'

Tina had already crossed to the phone, was already dialling.

'What are you doing?' Carter wanted to know.

'Calling an ambulance,' she told him, tears welling up in her eyes as she looked at him.

'Don't bother,' he said, gritting his teeth as a spasm of pain tore through him.

'You'll die,' she sobbed.

And now Harrison *did* look at her. His eyes lost the look of concern for Carter and filled with anger.

'I said it was over, Frank,' Carter croaked, his voice slurred, his tone low and muted. 'And it is.'

He pulled the automatic from its shoulder holster and steadied himself, the pistol aimed at the gang leader.

Tina dropped the phone, the operator's voice fading away as the receiver swung back and forth on its cable.

'What the hell are you doing?' Harrison wanted to know, his eyes fixed on the pistol. He took a step back. 'Put the gun down.' There was fear in his voice now.

Carter smiled.

And fired.

Once, twice, three times.

Tina screamed but her exhortations were drowned by the thunderous retorts of the automatic.

The bullets hit Harrison in the chest, the face, the shoulder, their savage impacts catapulting him backwards over the sofa. Blood spurted madly from the gaping holes, staining his shirt and, as he lay twitching on the floor, Carter staggered across to look down at him.

Harrison was still alive, barely, his eyes already beginning to glaze over but, in his final seconds of life, he saw Carter lower the pistol at him.

Saw him smile.

Carter fired until the gun was empty, the six remaining shell cases flying into the air as each bullet exploded from the pistol and powered into Harrison's torn frame.

The stench of cordite mingled with overpowering odour of blood and excrement. And finally Carter dropped the empty pistol and stood swaying in the centre of the room.

Tina ran to him, catching him as he fell, falling with him, feeling his blood on her blouse. Tears were coursing down her cheeks.

'Don't die, Ray, please don't die,' she murmured, stroking his face, ignoring the blood which coated her hand. She ran her fingers over his cheeks and forehead then touched his lips, horrified when she felt how cold they were. Please God, don't let him be dying now. She turned towards the phone once more but he pulled her back, smiling weakly up at her as she cradled his head in her lap. 'Don't leave me,' she sobbed. 'I love you.' She brushed his cheek once more, moaning as she felt a flap of skin on his jaw come loose.

To her horror she found that two of her fingers were caught in a gash obviously opened by a bullet but, as she tried to ease them free, she felt more of his skin ripping.

It was coming free in her hand.

Her sobbing stopped, her eyes bulging wide now as she felt the skin lift, rising like some kind of fleshy mask.

She gripped the ragged flesh and pulled as if driven by some insane instinct.

The entire face seemed to come away in her hand and she felt her throat contract as she found that she was looking down into a face unlike any she'd ever seen before.

The rotting visage of Charles Ross grinned up at her.

Tina tried to stand, tried to back away, but her legs buckled beneath her and she fell across Ross, the lump of dripping skin which she'd been holding finally falling from her grasp.

The features had been expertly carved away by the rotting corpse beneath her.

The face which lay on the carpet before her was that of Ray Carter.

Outside the door there were shouts, banging.

Sirens wailed in the street.

But Tina heard none of it.

She gazed at Carter's face, the face which had covered Ross's putrescent features, and she screamed.